THE LAST DAYS
OF AUTUMN

Praise for Donna K. Ford

No Boundaries

"*No Boundaries* is an interesting tale that combines many elements of the traditional LesFic romance with the suspense of a traumatised past and the fear of an endangered future. The plot is well thought through, cleverly weaving characters mentioned in passing into the plot and maintaining the suspense. Ms Ford keeps us on tenterhooks about exactly what happened to Andi until the very last minute and cleverly replaces one waiting game for another."—*Lesbian Reading Room*

Tennessee Whiskey

"I liked the relationships Dane develops with Emma and Curtis. She seems to come into their lives and fit like a missing puzzle piece. It isn't lost on the reader that they become something that Dane needs as well. All of their interactions were well paced and feelings grew naturally."—*Bookvark*

"I was pretty much sucked into this small town mystery from the get-go. I found it gripping and intriguing. I enjoyed this book and I highly recommend it."—*Lee Staes, bookseller (Truthseeker Books)*

"Ms. Ford's descriptions of the place and the people in this area of Appalachia are spot on...There is quite a bit of angst in the novel, from the beginning until the end, but this is also a heartwarming tale that I think you will enjoy."—*Rainbow Reflections*

Love's Redemption

"[O]ne of those books that will stick with me for a long time… Ms. Ford…writes about hard to discuss issues, and makes you really respect Rhea as a reader…This book really pulls at your heartstrings and makes you want that happy ending."
—*Amanda's Reviews*

"[A] solid romance with thriller elements, and I'm certainly looking forward for what she'll write in the future."—*Critical Writ*

"A great new novel from Donna K Ford, with all the usual elements of a traditional romance, a strong dose of suspense and her own unique twist."—*Lesbian Reading Room*

Unbroken

"I always enjoy Donna K Ford's writing style and the balance she achieves between romance and the more serious issues she tackles, making them feel real for the characters rather than a bolt on for effect. Definitely on my recommended list, this is a slow burn and thoughtful read that also has some seriously hot encounters."—*Lesbian Reading Room*

Captive

"This is definitely an unusual romance, another distinctive tale from Donna K Ford…Well written, exciting and absorbing, this captivated my attention and I couldn't put it down."
—Lesbian Reading Room

By the Author

Healing Hearts

No Boundaries

Love's Redemption

Unbroken

Captive

Tennessee Whiskey

The Last Days of Autumn

Visit us at www.boldstrokesbooks.com

THE LAST DAYS
OF AUTUMN

by
Donna K. Ford

2020

THE LAST DAYS OF AUTUMN

ISBN 13: 978-1-63555-672-8

This Trade Paperback Original Is Published By
Bold Strokes Books, Inc.
P.O. Box 249
Valley Falls, NY 12185

First Edition: June 2020

CREDITS
EDITOR: RUTH STERNGLANTZ
PRODUCTION DESIGN: STACIA SEAMAN
COVER DESIGN BY TAMMY SEIDICK

Acknowledgments

Very few things in the world have as much power as the word *cancer*. Although the characters in *The Last Days of Autumn* are my own creation, the journey through cancer described in this book is the very real story of my dear friends Kim and Kim. I am very grateful to have them in my life and to be able to say their happily ever after continues today. I am grateful to have witnessed their courage, determination, and unwavering love.

For everyone out there who chooses to read this story, I hope it brings you hope and joy and solidifies the conviction that love is worth fighting for. Thank you for being willing to tackle the hard stuff with me and trusting me to deliver a happily ever after.

To Kim Bailey for never giving up the fight against cancer.
And Kim Massengale for never giving up
the fight for the woman she loves.
Enjoy your happily ever after.

CHAPTER ONE

The parking lot at the University of Tennessee Hospital was a nightmare as Autumn circled the rows of cars. She hated going to doctors, but today had her nerves on high alert. The series of tests and the recent biopsy were pointing in a bad direction. At forty-five, she hadn't expected to be staring her mortality in the face, but here she was. Despite several open spaces, she circled the lot again, not ready to commit to going inside. Her palms were sweaty, and she had started picking at the skin at the corner of her thumb. After her third trip around the lot, she finally parked, but it took another five minutes for her to get up the courage to get out of the Jeep.

"This can't be happening." She sighed. "Well, sitting here won't change the outcome. I might as well face my demons. Maybe it's nothing." Autumn pulled her coat around herself and went inside. The oncology office was much like any other doctor's office, with rows of chairs, small tables with piles of gossip magazines, and art tastefully hung on the walls.

"Good morning," a young nurse said as Autumn approached the counter to sign in.

"Good morning. I'm Autumn Landers here to see Dr. Mathis. I have an appointment."

The nurse smiled warmly up at Autumn. "I have you right here. If you'd like to have a seat, we will call you in a few minutes."

Autumn nervously looked around the room before taking the seat closest to the door. She briefly considered making a run for it. She rubbed her hands on her slacks and nervously picked at the skin of her thumb. She repeatedly reminded herself to breathe. Whatever it was, she would get through it. She set her mind to that resolve and felt some of her worry lessen.

"Autumn Landers," a nurse said as she looked down at a file in her hand before scanning the waiting room.

Autumn stood, brushing her hands nervously against her jeans before reaching for her coat. She followed the nurse into the inner sanctum where she went through the usual ritual of being weighed and having her temperature and blood pressure taken. The nurse explained that her test results were in and the doctor would be in shortly to review the findings. Autumn felt a lump form in her throat. The nurse was pleasant and smiled at Autumn as she worked, but she never fully met Autumn's gaze.

Sweat dotted Autumn's forehead and she felt a trickle run down her spine. She told herself this was just routine, that the nurse was probably tired or maybe she was nervous because Autumn was a lesbian.

A few minutes after the nurse left there was a faint knock at the door before it swung open and Dr. Mathis entered. As usual Mary's curly blond hair stuck out wildly at the sides as strands escaped the tie she used to try to tame it. Her glasses hung from a lanyard around her neck, and her white lab coat was clean and crisp.

"Hello, Autumn. How are you today?"

Autumn smiled anxiously. Dr. Mary Mathis was a longtime friend Autumn had met years ago at a charity event. She had a wicked sense of humor and a big heart. If not for the circumstances, she would have been happy to see her.

"Nervous as hell, to be honest."

Dr. Mathis gave her a knowing smile and took a seat on the familiar chrome and black leather stool that seemed to be in every doctor's office Autumn had ever visited.

"I've talked with Dr. Benning and reviewed your file. I know this is hard. I'm afraid I don't have good news."

Autumn gripped the side of the table, preparing for the words she didn't want to hear.

"The biopsy shows the tumor is malignant. We will need to do surgery to remove the tumor, and you'll need to start treatment right away."

"Surgery?"

Dr. Mathis placed her hand over Autumn's. "The section of colon will need to be removed."

Autumn swallowed. She nodded. "How bad?"

"Stage three-B," Dr. Mathis said, her gaze never wavering as she spoke.

Autumn closed her eyes. She had been afraid of something like this, but the reality was so much worse than anything she'd imagined. "When?"

"I would like to get you in next week."

Autumn flinched. "What? I thought there was always a long wait for surgery."

The doctor's mouth pressed into a thin line, but she never looked away from Autumn's questioning gaze. "We can't wait."

"Oh." Autumn felt tears sting her eyes. "One week is insane. I can't possibly get things in order."

Dr. Mathis squeezed Autumn's hand. "Okay. I'll schedule you for two weeks from now, but I am not comfortable waiting any longer than that. We have to move quickly." She patted Autumn's hand gently. "I've known you a long time, Autumn. I'm going to do everything I can."

Autumn nodded. Her chest was tight, and she felt like an elephant had just climbed onto her shoulders.

"Is your mother with you?" Dr. Mathis asked, her tone neutral.

Autumn shook her head. "No. I didn't want to worry her. You know how she gets."

Dr. Mathis nodded. "You should tell her. You're going to need help. The surgery will be hard, and the treatments are tough. You can't do this on your own."

Autumn thought about everything she'd heard. Was this really happening? She listened carefully as Mary explained everything about the surgery and the chemo. What was she going to do about work? How would she keep the business going if she was out for weeks or maybe even months?

"Yeah, I'll think of something." She peered into Mary's eyes. "You won't tell her, will you?"

Mary patted her hand again, her lips pressed into that thin line. She shook her head. "Of course not. But you should. I know she's a handful sometimes, but she loves you."

Autumn bit her lip. She would tell her mother, just not now. "Thank you for everything, Mary."

Dr. Mathis stood and placed her hand gently on Autumn's shoulder. "I'll schedule the surgery. If you need anything, please call." She lifted her hand to Autumn's cheek. "Can I call someone to take you home?"

"No. I think I need some time alone. You've given me a lot to think about."

Dr. Mathis smiled, understanding shrouding her eyes. "Okay. I'll see you in two weeks."

Autumn stared at her hands as if they belonged to someone else. She had so many questions but didn't know what to ask. That bright future she had worked so hard for suddenly seemed out of reach. Everything was uncertain. What was she going to do? How was she ever going to get through this?

❖

Autumn stood in the makeshift office in a utility trailer she used for site work. She studied her schedule, trying to figure out how on earth she was going to juggle everything that needed to be done. The sound of rapping on her door drew her attention, and she looked up to find her project manager leaning on the doorframe. Despite her muscular build, Kate Miller always looked relaxed in a way that made her look as if she didn't have a care in the world.

"Hey, Kate. Come on in."

Kate dropped into a padded folding chair in front of the card table Autumn was using as her temporary desk at this site. "What's up, boss?"

Autumn frowned. "What do you mean?"

Kate raised one eyebrow and cut Autumn a knowing look. "This project is wrapping up in the next two days. We're ahead of schedule. The only thing that would bring you out here is a complaint by the customer, or they want something changed last minute."

Autumn smiled. "Relax. Everything's fine. No changes. No complaints."

Kate grinned. "So you're just here to tell me what a great job I'm doing and give me a big fat raise?"

Autumn shook her head. "Don't get too carried away there, slugger. I have something I need to talk to you about, and it can't wait."

Kate sat up at the seriousness in Autumn's tone. "Okay, shoot."

"I need you to run the McDougal project and the Wallace build. I'm going to be out of pocket for a few weeks, and even after that I won't be at full speed."

Kate frowned. "What do you mean out of pocket? You never leave in the middle of a project. What's up?"

Autumn nodded to her Jeep. "Let's step into my real office and talk."

Kate shut the Jeep door, then turned in her seat to face Autumn head-on. "Spill it."

Autumn loved Kate's no-nonsense approach to everything. That was one of the things that made her so good at her job, and such a good friend.

"I'm having surgery in two weeks, and I'm not sure how long the recovery will be."

"What kind of surgery?" Kate asked, her voice tight and serious.

Autumn gripped the steering wheel and tried to force down her fear and worry. "I have a malignant mass on my colon. They need to take it out."

"Malignant, meaning cancer?"

Autumn nodded, her throat suddenly too tight to speak.

"Oh fuck. I'm so sorry," Kate said, shaking her head. "When did you find out?"

"Yesterday."

"Christ," Kate said, her hands slowly curling into fists. "I had no idea you were sick."

Autumn shook her head. "Me, either. I had some bleeding a few months ago. I thought it was a hemorrhoid or something. I didn't have any pain, except one day when my back gave me some trouble. Again, I just thought I was sore from the job. My gynecologist thought it was a hemorrhoid too but referred me to a gastroenterologist just in case. He did a colonoscopy." She cringed at the memory. "The tumor is pretty big. He was ninety-nine percent sure it was cancer, so he sent me to an oncologist. I've known Dr. Mathis for years. I trust her. She seemed pretty worried."

Kate swallowed. "I don't know what to say. That's so crazy. How can you be that sick and not know it?"

Autumn shrugged. "Evidently cancer itself doesn't hurt. The tumor just isn't in an area where it presses on other things that would cause pain. There was just no way to know."

Kate took and held Autumn's hand.

Autumn wrapped her fingers around Kate's, needing the connection. "I know it's a lot to ask, but I know you can handle things—"

"Of course I'll do it," Kate cut in. "Whatever you need. Anything."

Autumn glanced at Kate. "Thanks."

"So, what happens after the surgery?"

"I start chemotherapy," Autumn said with a sigh. "That part will take months. I won't be up to my usual tasks, but I intend to keep working."

Kate frowned. "Let's just take it one thing at a time."

"I wish I could." Autumn pointed at her schedule. "Unfortunately, I can't afford to do that. I can barely keep up as it is."

"Leave the business end to me. I'll watch the shop until you're better. I'll pass all the big stuff by you first and keep up with orders and the crew as usual. Come on, it's how you started out. I may not be as good as you are, but I did learn from the best."

Autumn smiled. "Thank you, Kate. I don't know what I would

do without you. But it's going to be tough with the baby coming. You're going to have your hands full with Lisa, the job, and a new baby."

Kate waved the thought away. "No problem. Multitasking is my middle name." Then her gaze grew serious again. "What about after the surgery and during your treatments? Are you going to stay with your mother?"

Autumn grimaced. "I haven't told her yet."

Kate's eyebrows rose into her hairline. "When do you think that will happen?"

Autumn leaned her head on the steering wheel. "I keep trying to figure out a way around it." She leaned back against the seat and closed her eyes. "Isn't it bad enough I have cancer? The idea of being trapped at my mother's mercy again is unbearable." Guilt hit her like a sting, and she turned to look at Kate. "Don't get me wrong, I love my mother, we're just so, so—different."

There was no judgment in Kate's eyes. Her gaze was serious but tender. "You could come stay with Lisa and me."

Autumn grinned. "I love you too much to do that to you. But I may need rescuing from time to time."

Kate laughed. "That's a plea for Lisa's cooking if I ever heard one. You know she loves to feed you."

Autumn felt tears sting her eyes again, and this time didn't have the strength to stanch them.

Kate leaned over and wrapped her arms around Autumn. "Hey, don't you worry. We're going to take care of you. It will be all right."

Autumn leaned into Kate, allowing the warmth of Kate's touch to soothe some of the loneliness that had crept into her heart.

Once she had calmed, Kate let her go. Kate tilted her head to the side the way she always did when she had an idea.

"What?" Autumn prompted. "I can almost hear the wheels turning in your head."

"Maybe you should think of hiring a live-in."

Autumn was shocked by the suggestion. "How desperate do you think I am?"

Kate laughed. "Not that kind of live-in, silly. Someone to take you to appointments, clean the house, cook, do your laundry, stuff like that. It would be a hell of a lot cheaper than home health care."

Autumn thought about the idea. "You think people really want a job like that?"

"Hell, yeah. When I was a college student, I would have done it for nothing if you gave me a free place to live and food."

"Hmm, you may be on to something. If I have someone taking care of me, I won't have to live with Mother."

Kate smiled. "Exactly."

Autumn felt her first ray of hope since leaving the doctor's office the day before. Maybe this could work. "Do you think there's time?"

Kate shrugged. "Post it online tonight, and I bet you'll have takers by the weekend."

Autumn nodded. "This is a good idea. This just might work."

Caroline Cross leaned back into the tattered old recliner in her father's den, feeling her body being drawn into the supple leather like an embrace. Her father had had the thing for years, and she swore the leather bore the permanent imprint of Jack Cross's body.

"It's been a while this time," her father said as he popped the top on a beer. "Are you planning to stick around this time?"

Caroline had worked on and off for her father over the past year in his construction company. He had been patient with her bad moods and supportive of her need to get away, sometimes for a month at a time. She knew he was worried about her, but he hadn't pushed for details.

"I don't know," Caroline admitted. "I'm getting tired of being on the road all the time. Maybe it's time I face reality and get this over with."

Her father scratched the stubble on his chin, his eyes narrowing. "So you're done? You're going ahead with the divorce?"

"She's fucking someone else, Dad. What else am I supposed to do?" Caroline looked away when his gaze fell to his hands. He was a sensitive man, and she knew he was only looking out for her. "I'm sorry, Dad." Caroline didn't mean to take things out on him. He was the one person in the world she knew she could count on.

"Are you sure? There could have been some mistake."

Caroline had told her dad the basics of why she had left Jane eleven months earlier, but she had avoided the details. Her dad liked Jane, loved her, and he couldn't accept things were over.

"I saw it with my own eyes, Dad. I came home a day early from a work trip and found her in bed with Stephanie."

"Steph? Your best friend?"

Caroline sighed. "That's the one."

"Damn, that's messed up." He went to the fridge and grabbed two more beers. He handed one to her as he passed to the sofa. "Why didn't you just tell me? Everything makes sense now."

Caroline stared at the bottle in her hand. "I don't know. I just wanted to get out of there, and I just couldn't talk about it. Jane didn't even know I knew until she came home and found I'd moved all my stuff."

He stared at her as if he couldn't believe what she was saying. His shoulders slumped as the reality set in. "I'm really sorry, sweetheart."

Caroline blinked away the sudden sting of tears. She refused to cry. Jane didn't deserve her tears. "I've done a lot of thinking over these last few months. I can't go back. I won't ever be able to get that image out of my mind. But I need to get my shit back together, start over, all the usual crap I thought I'd never have to go through again."

"You can stay here." Her father's voice was soft. "I know the place has gone down-at-the-heels a bit since your mother passed, but it's still home."

Caroline was tempted to fall into the safety of her childhood home, but she wasn't a child anymore. She needed to do this her way. "Thanks, Dad. I'll think of something."

He rubbed his hands down his thighs, his rough palms scratching against his jeans. "You know I could always use a hand on the job site. Things will be picking up as soon as the weather breaks."

She sipped her beer. "Yeah, maybe."

He stood, stretching his back. "I'm going to turn in. I've got an early day tomorrow. Make yourself at home. You know where everything is."

"Don't worry, Dad. I'll be okay."

He leaned down and kissed the top of her head. "I know how tough you are, but you're still my little girl, and I love you. I just want you to be happy."

She smiled up at him. "I love you too, Dad."

Caroline settled back into the recliner nursing her beer. A year ago, she would have said she was happy, that she had a good life with the woman she loved. Now everything had changed. That perfect life had been a lie. Everything she had held dear now meant nothing. Everything had been for Jane. She closed her eyes against the memory of Jane in Stephanie's arms. She was done. Her feelings for Jane were gone. It was time to move on.

❖

Caroline ignored her phone. Jane had called three times in the last hour. She'd listened to the voice mails but couldn't bring herself to talk to Jane, who sounded genuinely upset after receiving the divorce papers. Jane was relentless when she wanted something. She wasn't sure why it came as a surprise that Jane was fighting this. Jane hated to lose. It hadn't helped that Caroline had refused to even see Jane since the night she found her in bed with her best friend almost one year earlier. There had been a time when they wouldn't have gone a day without talking, but right now, she didn't want to hear Jane's excuses. She didn't want to hear her voice at all.

She turned her phone off. She'd call Jane later, before she did something desperate. She looked up at the sound of her father's footsteps on the old wooden floor, then heard a gentle knock at the door.

"You awake?"

"Yeah, come on in."

He sat on the edge of the bed, studying her. "Jane called." He held up his hand when she sat up. "I didn't say anything except that I talked to you and that you were fine."

Caroline leaned back against the headboard. "Thanks."

"You can't avoid her forever, you know."

"Why not?"

He sighed. "Because adulting is hard. You're no coward. And that woman needs to face what she did to you. She needs to see what she threw away."

Caroline frowned. "I'm not sure I agree with that."

He patted her knee like he did when she was a kid. "She seems to think she can talk you out of this. You need to face this so you can start putting it behind you. Are you sure you don't want to work things out?"

"No," Caroline said. "I can't live with someone I can't trust."

He nodded. "Very well then. But you're going to have to tell her it's over."

She hated it when her dad was right. "You would think the divorce papers would have said that for me." She sighed. "I just feel so stupid. I thought we were happy. I've been racking my brain trying to recognize some clue about what was going on. But I can't see it. I should have been able to see it."

"Maybe there wasn't anything to see until that night."

Caroline frowned again. "Maybe. I hope not. I can't stand the thought of her doing that behind my back and acting as if nothing was wrong."

Her father drew in a deep breath and sighed. "Give it some time. But don't think for one minute that you can make any sense out of any of this. There's no excuse for what she did. You are not to blame. Now you have to make a choice you can live with and go with that."

Caroline took a deep breath. "I'll talk to her."

He tapped his finger against the laptop she had put aside on the bed. "What are you looking for?"

"I don't know really. Inspiration." Caroline shrugged. "Anything to take my mind off Jane. I thought I'd look for one of those jobs people advertise sometimes—you know, where you go work on some ranch all summer or rebuild a community after a natural disaster. It might be good to step out of my life for a while until I can figure out what to do next."

His brows knitted together in a frown. She knew that look. That was his disapproving look. "Sounds like running away to me. You've already done enough of that."

Caroline smiled. "I promise I won't run away. At least not too far away."

"Well," he said, with a slight shake of his head, "did you find anything?"

"Maybe. I don't know." Caroline pointed to the ad she'd been studying when he came in. "This lady needs someone to help out around her house while she goes through cancer treatment. Free room and board. It gets me out of the city and out of your hair."

"You are not in my hair." He looked at the ad. "That's a tough gig. Do you think you want to take care of someone like that? You've got a lot going on."

Caroline knew he was thinking about her mother. She covered his hand with hers. "I don't know. Maybe. It might be nice to think of someone else's needs for a change and stop feeling sorry for myself."

He smiled. "Be careful, sweet pea."

Caroline smiled at the use of her childhood nickname.

"That's a big commitment to make to someone when your life is upside down." He took her hand and rubbed his calloused fingers across the top of her hand. "Just be careful. I don't want to see you hurt any more than you already are."

Caroline wrapped her arms around her father's shoulders, feeling his strong arms close around her. "I love you, Dad."

He kissed her cheek. "I love you too, sweet pea."

CHAPTER TWO

Autumn closed the door behind the fifth person she had interviewed that morning. When did college students start looking like twelve-year-old kids playing dress-up and acting about the same? She pinched the bridge of her nose in frustration. She was running out of time. She had one week left before her surgery, and not one single applicant had shown up that she would trust to clean an empty fishbowl.

She had one last appointment scheduled in ten minutes. Her last hope.

She heard a car door shut and then the chime of the doorbell. Autumn glanced through the window before opening the door. She was met with a warm smile and gentle gray-blue eyes.

"Hello. I'm Caroline Cross. I'm here to see Ms. Landers. We spoke on the phone."

Autumn was stunned. Caroline Cross was gorgeous, and not what she expected after the hours she'd spent interviewing hopefuls. "Yes, hello," Autumn stammered. "Please come in."

Caroline stepped inside clutching a file folder in her hands. She looked around the room appraisingly.

Autumn cleared her throat. Caroline was older than expected, possibly in her late thirties. Her blond hair was cut short at the neck and around her ears, but the top fell in playful strands draping across her forehead. Her skin reminded Autumn of buttercream. She wore a crisp white shirt tucked in at the waist of simple gray slacks that tapered down her long lean legs. "Can I get you something to drink?" Autumn asked, trying to sound relaxed.

Caroline smiled. "No. I'm fine, thank you."

Autumn liked Caroline's smile. It was warm and genuine, and she felt some of her tension ease.

She led the way to the living room and gestured for Caroline to take a seat before settling onto the sofa across from her.

Caroline shifted nervously. "Will Ms. Landers be joining us?"

Autumn smiled. "I am Ms. Landers."

"Oh." Caroline frowned. "I'm sorry. I guess I expected—"

Autumn grinned. "You expected me to be older."

Caroline shrugged. "Yes. I suppose I did."

"Well, I hope that won't change your mind about the position," Autumn said in a playful tone.

"No," Caroline said with a smile. "I guess that will teach me not to make assumptions about people."

"It's okay. It surprises me too." Autumn leaned back in her seat. "Tell me, Caroline, what makes you interested in this job?"

Something flashed in Caroline's eyes before she looked away—sadness, pain perhaps. "I guess I'm not what you were expecting, either."

"No," Autumn said honestly. "You're older than anyone else I've interviewed, and you don't strike me as someone who needs a roommate to get by."

Caroline drew in a deep breath, then let it out slowly. "I've had some personal changes this year. A divorce. I thought this would give me time and space to figure out where my life goes from here."

Autumn felt a tinge of disappointment. "I'm sorry. How long were you married?"

"Two years together and one year separated. Not long, I know," Caroline said dismissively.

Autumn frowned. Caroline obviously didn't want to talk about her marriage, but the pain was still evident. "It doesn't matter. Endings are never easy."

Caroline's face reddened, and Autumn instantly regretted her statement. "I'm sorry. I don't mean to sound morose. I just want to

THE LAST DAYS OF AUTUMN

get to know you. If I'm going to do this, I need someone I can trust not to leave when I need them most."

Caroline nodded. The statement hit much closer to home than Autumn could know. She was all too familiar with people leaving. She had needed the same thing from her wife. Trust. "I know what a commitment this would be."

Autumn's eyes glistened as Caroline met her gaze. She handed Autumn the folder she'd brought with her. "I brought in my vita. I thought you might want to see that I'm not a slacker here to take advantage of you. I have references there too, but I left my job as a marketing consultant last year. I've been working in my father's construction business on and off, and traveling mostly. I guess I needed a total reboot."

Autumn sifted through the file.

Caroline's gaze was drawn to Autumn's hands as she placed the file back on the table between them. Her hands were strong with long lean fingers. Caroline watched as Autumn lifted one hand and brushed a strand of dark hair behind her ear. Her tanned skin was smooth, with a tiny mole nestled in the small space between her ear and her jawbone. When Autumn looked up from the file, her sharp liquid blue eyes seemed to brighten, fixing on Caroline with obvious appraisal. Caroline got the feeling that not much got by Autumn Landers.

"To be honest, Ms. Cross, I don't really know what I will need from you in the next few months. The first few weeks after my surgery are going to be the hardest for me. After that, we'll have to learn together."

Caroline met Autumn's gaze, recognizing the fear and uncertainty she'd seen so often with her mother. She instantly liked Autumn. "My mother died of cancer five years ago. I'm aware of how bad it can get."

"Oh. I'm sorry." Autumn met Caroline's gaze with genuine sympathy.

"Breast cancer," Caroline said, before Autumn could ask.

Autumn looked like she might faint. The color had drained from her face, and she seemed to be struggling for air. Caroline moved next to Autumn and placed her hand on Autumn's wrist. "Are you all right?"

Autumn nodded. She glanced nervously at Caroline. "I haven't really gotten used to it yet. Sometimes it sweeps over me like a suffocating heat."

"Can I get you anything?" Caroline asked, hoping there was something she could do to put Autumn at ease.

Autumn smiled at Caroline as if she was the one needing reassurance. "No. I'm fine. I hope I'm not scaring you off."

Caroline returned the smile. "Not at all."

Autumn straightened, taking a deep breath. "Can I show you around the house, then? If we agree on this, you'll have your own room down the hall from mine, but there's also a living space in the basement for you to get away and have as much privacy as you need."

Caroline followed Autumn through the house, noticing the warm colors filling each room. The furnishings were soft and plush, but understated. The walls were tastefully decorated with paintings Autumn said were by local artists. Long sheer curtains hung to the floor by huge windows that filled the rooms with natural light.

"You have a beautiful home," Caroline said as they stepped onto the back deck looking out over a glowing in-ground pool. "Wow. This stonework is amazing," Caroline said as she studied the patio and outdoor kitchen.

"Thank you. I take a lot of pride in my work."

She turned to Autumn, surprised. "You built this?"

"Yes. I own a landscaping company and I specialize in rock structures."

Caroline studied Autumn, reassessing the woman before her, looking beyond the reason she was here. She realized she wanted to know her. Autumn was strong, beautiful, talented, and in need of help. How could she be sick? The thought pained her.

"What?" Autumn asked.

Caroline held her gaze. "I know you need time to check my references and to think things over, but I'd like to help you."

"Why?" Autumn asked.

Caroline shrugged. "I need to focus on something other than myself. From what I've seen, I like you. I think maybe we could help each other."

Autumn nodded. "Can I call you tomorrow? That gives us both a little time to think things over."

"That works for me." Caroline touched Autumn's arm as she turned to go. Autumn smiled at her, her eyes shimmering with a storm of emotion. "This doesn't have to be an ending for you. You don't strike me as someone afraid to fight. Whatever you decide, you can do this."

Autumn drew in a deep breath. She dipped her head in a slight nod. "Thank you."

Caroline heard the door click shut behind her. She breathed deeply, drawing the chill night air into herself. Was she up for this? She really liked Autumn. Maybe if she had someone to take care of, a place to channel her focus, she wouldn't have to think of her own loss.

❖

Autumn leaned back into the lounge chair and sipped her wine, ignoring the biting chill. She looked up at the clear night sky and marveled at the stars. There was so much she didn't know. So much she hadn't done. She knew she'd have to talk to her mother, but she wasn't ready for the storm that would follow. She briefly entertained the idea of not telling her mother. Perhaps she could get through everything without her knowing. She smiled at the thought. Wouldn't that be something.

She took another sip of the wine. Was she being selfish? How would she explain things to her mother if the treatment didn't go well? Time. How long would it take? How long did she have? Her mother was impossible, that was true, but she wouldn't cheat her mother out of that time. Even if it drove her crazy.

Autumn pulled herself up and went inside. The warmth of

the house surrounded her like an embrace, warming her skin. She shivered to shake off the last tendrils of cold. She sat on the sofa, her eyes drawn to the file Caroline had left her.

Caroline had been kind. Autumn had seen pain dull Caroline's eyes when she spoke of her divorce. She tried to imagine Caroline with someone. What was her wife like? What had driven them apart? She imagined Caroline's grief. In its own way, wasn't losing love like experiencing a death? The loss of a promise, a love, a dream. Each loss leaving a person changed.

Autumn shut the file. She'd make the necessary calls in the morning. She already knew she would offer Caroline the job. Caroline's words kept running through her mind. Maybe they *could* help each other. The thought warmed Autumn. She wouldn't feel like such a burden if she thought she had something to offer Caroline in return.

She knew Kate and Lisa would step in to do whatever they could, but she didn't like the idea of her illness disturbing everyone's lives. She didn't want them to see her so weak. The thought surprised her. These were friends, her family, the people she loved most in the world, but she couldn't imagine exposing her uttermost vulnerabilities to them. It would put things out of balance somehow. Wasn't that just like her, to prefer the care and comfort of a stranger rather than face the intimacy of those close to her.

Autumn tossed the file onto the table and took a sip of her wine. She had to get out of her head. She had to stop feeling sorry for herself and meet this thing head-on. Caroline was right. She was a fighter. Whatever was ahead of her, she would give it her best shot.

She reached for her cell phone. She took a deep breath and dialed. "Hello, Mother."

❖

Autumn barely had the door open before her mother pushed into the room with a flourish. Meredith Landers was a force of will like no other. "I made reservations at the Orangery for noon. Mary said she would meet us there."

Autumn closed the door. "Hello, Mother, it's good to see you too." She leaned down and kissed her mother's cheek. "I think it would be a good idea for you to see Mary without me. I'm sure she can explain everything much better than I can."

Her mother turned quickly, piercing Autumn with her glare. "Don't be silly. You need to eat. I'll have Markus come by later for your things."

"What things?"

"Anything you want to take with you to the house, of course."

Autumn planted her feet as if bracing herself for a fight. "I'm not going anywhere, Mother. This is my home. I'm staying right here."

Her mother waved her hand in the air as if swatting a gnat. "Don't be ridiculous, Autumn. You can't possibly stay here after the surgery. You'll need care. I'll arrange for a nurse, of course."

"No," Autumn said sternly. "I've already made my own arrangements. I will be staying here."

Her mother blinked, as if she didn't know what to make of her obstinance. Autumn braced herself for the storm she saw brewing in her mother's eyes. If she pushed much harder, her mother would snap.

"I appreciate you trying to help, Mother. But I have everything covered. There's no need for any more change than necessary. This is my home, and I'm staying."

Her mother's lower right eyelid twitched. Autumn recognized the sign her mother was losing her patience, and something was about to break.

"I'll go to lunch with you and Mary, but I'm not budging on this, Mother."

"I suppose you think those *friends* of yours are going to take better care of you than your own mother."

Autumn raised an eyebrow. *Going straight to the guilt, I see.* "No. I've hired someone to live here with me during my recovery and treatment. She will see to my care and take me to all my appointments. If more nursing care becomes necessary, I'll make those arrangements as well. You can come by as often as you like.

But as long as I am fit enough, I will continue to work and go on with my life."

"Let's talk about this over lunch," her mother said in a conciliatory tone. She seemed to see there was no compromise and was trying a different tack. "Mary will explain everything."

Autumn knew her mother planned to enlist Dr. Mathis to persuade her to move to the big house, as Autumn liked to call it, a sprawling three thousand square feet of impersonal space designed to show off her mother's money. But Autumn trusted Mary to take a professional stand and support her plan as long as her needs were covered. Mary was well aware of her mother's need for control, especially over her only daughter. Mary had served on countless boards and fundraisers with her mother at the Catholic church. Her mother was big into charity work, but Autumn knew her mother's heart wasn't really in the cause—she was there to be seen. Mary had seen her mother in action and knew exactly how to handle her.

"I agree." Autumn escorted her mother to the passenger side of the car, settling into the driver's seat after closing her mother's door for her. Her mother always had Autumn drive whenever they were together. Autumn wasn't really sure why, but she didn't complain. "I don't want you to worry, Mother. Everything is going to be fine."

"Of course it is," her mother said with finality, although she clenched her hands together in her lap as if she didn't know what to do with them.

Autumn felt sorry for her mother. She had to be just as terrified as she was. They had never been close. Not emotionally close, anyway. After her parents' divorce when she was fourteen, her mother had become even more obsessed with her. Her mother had pushed her to excel at everything. She'd expected Autumn to be the perfect student, the perfect athlete, and did her best to push her toward the perfect husband. Autumn had worked hard to please her mother in every way except the last. She suspected her mother had always been controlling, and her father had intervened as much as he could. But after he moved out, Autumn had been left to fend for herself.

Mary sat in the sunroom of the Orangery at a table next to a window. Sunshine illuminated the room, surrounding Mary in an ethereal glow. Wisps of wild hair seemed to dance about her face, making her look younger and somewhat frazzled. Mary stood and greeted her mother with a stiff hug before taking Autumn's hand and giving it a gentle pat.

"Thank you for meeting us, Mary," Autumn said apologetically.

"I'm happy to do it. It isn't often these days that I get such a treat."

"How is Justin?" her mother asked, spreading her napkin on her lap and waving down a waiter.

"He's playing golf today, so I suspect the answer to that question depends on his score."

Her mother laughed. "I know what you mean. I haven't played in ages. It's still a bit cold for my blood, but a few more weeks and there will be nothing like the greens."

Autumn took a mental note to use that against her mother in her defense of staying out of the way and not letting her illness interfere with her mother's life.

"So, Mary, tell me what's going on with my daughter."

Autumn stiffened. She hadn't expected her mother to tackle the issue until midway through her Cobb salad.

Mary looked from Autumn to her mother.

"I told her about the cancer and the surgery," Autumn said to ease Mary's squeeze between a rock and a hard place. "I think Mother will feel better hearing the specifics from you."

Mary nodded. A waiter delivered their drinks and took their food orders. As he stepped away Mary continued, explaining how Autumn had been referred to her care. She paused as the waiter returned and refilled their water glasses. "I've scheduled Autumn for surgery Thursday. After that she will begin intensive chemo-therapy."

Autumn's phone buzzed and she glanced at the screen. Kate. "I'm sorry. I need to take this. Go ahead, Mary."

She was relieved to have an excuse to escape the blow by blow of the nightmare she was living. She stepped into the lobby as she answered the call. "Hi, Kate. What's up?"

A few minutes later she returned to the table, unable to prolong her absence any further.

"She should come home," her mother insisted, as Autumn pulled out her chair. "How else am I supposed to be certain she's getting the proper care?"

Autumn met Mary's worried eyes. "I've explained to Mother that I have hired someone to stay with me at my house and take care of things while I heal and while I go through treatment. As I understand what you've explained to me, that should be adequate, but if not, I'm prepared to hire in-home nursing staff as I need it."

Mary nodded. "That sounds like a sound plan. Being in your own home with as little disruption to your routine as possible will reduce your stress and likely support better immune health."

Autumn could have kissed Mary. Relief flooded her as Mary continued to explain the benefits of Autumn remaining at home.

Her mother's disappointment was obvious. "She plans to keep working. How is that supposed to lower her stress?"

Mary shrugged and leaned back in her chair. "I can't say how Autumn will respond to chemo, but if she's feeling well enough, I see no reason why she can't handle the business as long as she doesn't do the heavy lifting herself." She sighed. "I know you're worried, Meredith, but Autumn is the only one who can decide how she feels and what she needs. Within reason, we need to respect that."

Autumn caught the *within reason* clause. She knew Mary would pull the plug on her bid for independence if she overstepped and pushed herself too much. She dipped her head toward Mary, nodding her understanding.

"Well, I can see there's no reasoning with either of you," her mother grumbled, folding her napkin and placing it on the table.

Autumn looked away when a movement to her left caught her eye. She looked over to see Caroline Cross being seated at a small table at the end of the room. She was surprised to see Caroline. What were the chances she would run into her so soon after their meeting, especially since their paths had never crossed before?

She glanced around the room, searching to see if Caroline was meeting someone. Her wife, perhaps. "Excuse me. I need to say hello to someone. I'll be right back." She glanced around once more before making her way to Caroline's table. Caroline was dressed in jeans with an almond cable-knit sweater. Her hair was swept casually across her forehead, and she wore small rimless glasses. She looked up as Autumn reached the table.

"Hello," Autumn said, smiling at Caroline.

Caroline returned the smile. "Hello," she said, moving to stand.

Autumn waved her away. "Don't get up. I just saw you come in and thought I'd say hello."

Caroline gestured to the seat across from her. "Have a seat. It's a surprise to see you."

"Yes, same."

"How are you?" Caroline asked.

Autumn pulled out the chair and sat. "For the most part, good. Unfortunately, I'm having lunch with my mother and my oncologist. The goal of the afternoon is to retain both my freedom and my sanity."

Caroline laughed gently. "Sounds tenuous. Is there any way I can help?"

Autumn smiled. "As a matter of fact, there is."

"I'm listening."

Autumn leaned forward, bringing her hands together in front of her, only the tips of her fingers touching. "I'd like to offer you the job."

Caroline smiled. "I've been giving it a lot of thought myself. I'd like to help you."

Autumn reached out her hand to Caroline. "Then we have a deal?"

"Deal," Caroline said, shaking Autumn's hand. "When do I start?"

"You can move in as soon as tomorrow. I'd like a few days for us to get to know each other before things get too personal."

"Personal?"

"You know, all the things I'll need after the surgery. I'll have a nurse helping part of the time for a couple of days, but for the most part it's going to be you and me."

Caroline nodded. "My schedule is open. Tomorrow is good. I'm sure my father will be happy to have his house to himself before his big weekend."

"That will be perfect." Autumn glanced back to her table. She could feel her mother's gaze boring into her back. "Would you like to meet the enemy, otherwise known as my mother?"

"Would you like me to?" Caroline said with a laugh.

Autumn thought about it. "No. I'll protect you as long as I can."

Caroline laughed again. She had a warm comforting laugh. "Is it really that bad?"

"I'm having lunch with my oncologist so my mother can try to strong-arm me into moving to her house. She's not happy things are not going her way."

"Ah. In that case, I'll trust your judgment."

Autumn stood, smiling down at Caroline. "I'll see you tomorrow. How does six sound?"

"Six o'clock it is."

Autumn returned to her mother just in time to pick up the check. Not only did her mother not drive when she was with Autumn, she apparently didn't pay for anything when they were together either.

Mary and her mother did their usual stiff hug good-bye. Mary squeezed Autumn's hand and gave her a wink.

"Thank you," Autumn said as she kissed Mary's cheek.

"Who was that woman you were talking to?" her mother asked as Autumn put the car in drive.

Autumn grinned. "She's the woman I've hired to stay with me." She stifled a laugh when her mother's mouth fell open.

"Are you serious? Why didn't you introduce us?"

Autumn cut her eyes at her mother. "Because I like her, and I need her. I didn't want you to scare her away."

Her mother's eyes grew stormy. "What are you saying?"

"You heard me."

Her mother huffed and sat back in her seat with her arms crossed obstinately across her chest, as if offended.

"Are you dating her?" her mother said accusingly.

It was Autumn's turn to gape. "What? No."

"Well, she looks a bit…sporty, don't you think?"

Autumn laughed. "I would say beautiful, but yes."

Her mother glared at her. "Is that what this is about? Are you planning to seduce her?"

Autumn laughed until her sides hurt.

"It's not funny, answer my question," her mother demanded.

"Mother, I just met her. I needed someone to help me. She's in a place in her life where she can. We get along, and so far, she makes me feel at ease. I don't know what's going to happen next week or what kind of shit storm my life will become. This is what I need right now, and you aren't going to take it away from me."

CHAPTER THREE

Autumn held the door as Caroline carried in the last of her things. Now that Caroline was here, Autumn wasn't quite sure what to do. Should she make dinner? Would Caroline want time to get used to the new surroundings? How did all this work?

"So, what now?" Caroline asked, hanging the last of her clothes in the closet.

Autumn shrugged. "I don't know, really. Can I get us some wine? Maybe we should just talk. Get to know each other."

"Sounds good."

Autumn had a fire going, so they chose seats on the floor close to the fire. Caroline fidgeted. "This is nice." She smiled at Autumn. "And kind of strange."

"I know what you mean. How do you suppose we get past the awkwardness?"

"Ask me a question," Caroline said.

"What?"

"You know, those little get-to-know-you questions people ask when they're forced into a blind date."

Autumn was amused, and she had to admit she liked the idea of this being a date and not what it really was. "Okay. Where did you grow up?"

"Ah. That's an easy one. My parents were from Oak Ridge. They knew each other since grade school and became high school sweethearts. They married right out of high school and started a family. I had a fairy-tale life until my mother became ill. My dad is essentially my best friend. I worked with him for years in his construction company before venturing into marketing. I think he secretly wanted me to take over the business. Who knows, maybe someday I will."

Autumn smiled. "How does he feel about you doing this?"

Caroline shrugged. "He worries about me. If he could protect me from ever getting hurt or feeling sad, he would."

"So he thinks you're going to get hurt?" Autumn asked, understanding why he would be concerned.

Caroline took a sip of her wine and stared into the fire. "My mother's illness was hard on him. Hard on us. He knows me."

Autumn followed Caroline's gaze to the fire. "Was your mother scared?" she asked, letting the question slip from her lips like a secret.

Caroline frowned. She didn't answer for several long moments, her expression thoughtful. "I think she was. I don't think she was as afraid of dying as she was of not being there to take care of us. There was so much she never got to do."

Autumn was quiet for a long time. She was trying to work through her own feelings about what was happening to her. When she pulled herself out of her thoughts, she found Caroline watching her.

"Sorry," Autumn whispered.

Caroline shook her head. "Don't be." She drew her knees up and wrapped her arms around her legs. "Are you scared?"

Autumn smiled a half smile. "Terrified is more like it."

"What are you afraid of?" Caroline asked, her eyes gentle as she watched Autumn.

"Everything. I'm afraid of what I don't know. I'm afraid of losing everything I've worked for. I'm afraid of losing control and having to depend on my mother. I'm afraid of waking up one day and realizing I got it all wrong. Mostly I'm afraid of what everyone is afraid of—running out of time."

"Time for what?"

"Hmm." Autumn frowned. "Good question. Time for all the things I put off, I guess. Travel, dating, a family."

"Your bucket list?" Caroline asked.

"Yeah, something like that. But mostly just the everyday stuff. Things like having dinner with friends, the challenge of a new project, learning something new, or seeing something beautiful for the first time. The little things." She was thoughtful for a moment. "I have always wanted to travel to Thailand. It just seems so pure to me in some ways, and yet it has everything."

"Sounds like a good start. Have you made a list?" Caroline asked.

Autumn laughed. "No."

"Why is that funny?"

"Because I am the queen of lists. I schedule everything. You would think I would have this planned out in detail like everything else in my life."

"I don't know," Caroline said thoughtfully. "It's okay not to know all the answers. It leaves room for spontaneity."

Autumn picked up her wine. "I can't remember the last time I did something spontaneous."

Caroline tilted her head with a faint frown furrowing her brow. "How about this? Does this count? I can't imagine you planned to be sitting here like this with me."

"No." Autumn smiled. "A week ago, I wouldn't have been able to imagine sharing a cup of coffee with someone I just met, let alone having them move into my house."

Caroline grinned. "So, there you go. I'm already good for you."

Autumn laughed. "Indeed."

"Tell me about your mother?" Caroline said as she poured more wine.

A guttural growl vibrated from Autumn's throat. "Ask me anything else. I really don't want to talk about my mother tonight."

"Okay. Tell me why you live alone. You mentioned time for dating and a family. Is there someone special in your life?"

"No," Autumn said, averting her eyes. "I have a few close friends, and I work a lot, but I haven't dated much in the last couple of years."

"Why not?"

"It was too exhausting. My mother doesn't say so outright anymore, but she doesn't approve of my life and always finds fault with the women I date. I got tired of being split down the middle."

"So you work," Caroline said.

"So I work." Autumn asked the question that had been needling her. "Why didn't things work out with your wife?"

Caroline's eyes went cold. It was as if someone had turned out a light from the inside. A muscle bunched in her jaw. "I'd rather not talk about that."

Autumn regretted the question. "I understand. Too personal. I'm sorry." Autumn wished she could take it back. She saw the pain in Caroline's eyes, and it hurt her to think she had been the one to put it there. "I can't imagine what it's like to love someone that much."

Caroline's frown deepened. "What do you mean?"

"I've never met anyone I wanted to spend my life with. I don't know what happened to you, but I suppose it wouldn't hurt you so much if you didn't love her."

Caroline nodded. "Yes. I love—loved her. But right now, it feels like I would have been better off never loving her at all."

Autumn heard the hurt in the words. She wondered if Caroline really believed them. "Well, let me tell you, the not loving someone thing gets pretty lonely sometimes."

"What do you do about it?" Caroline asked, changing the focus back to Autumn.

Autumn smiled. "Getting a bit personal, aren't we?"

Caroline laughed. "That's not what I meant."

Autumn gave Caroline's arm a playful shove. "I know what you meant. I spend time with my friends. I live through them."

Caroline seemed to think about the answer. "What do we do next?"

Autumn sighed. "Normally, I would have dinner with Kate and Lisa on Friday night. I would spend the weekend in the mountains or working on a project or whatever event my mother would drag me to. But I don't see that happening anytime in the future. These next few days I would like to spend time with you and try to get settled. But I don't expect you to be with me all the time."

Caroline took a sip of her wine and studied Autumn. "What do you want me to know?"

Autumn grinned. "No dirty little secrets or anything fun like that," she teased. "I want to go over my schedule with you. I've put together a list of contacts and other things you might need. But honestly, I just don't know."

"Okay. In that case, do you mind if I turn in? I'm a bit tired."

"Of course," Autumn said. "I'm just down the hall if you need anything."

"Thank you." Caroline stood. "I'll see you in the morning."

"Good night." Autumn watched Caroline go. "Caroline," she said before Caroline was out of sight.

"Yes?"

"Thank you for being here."

Caroline smiled. "Good night, Autumn."

❖

Caroline paced the patio. Her hands shook as she gripped the phone. "There's nothing left to talk about, Jane. It's over. Why can't you just let me go?" They had been through this a thousand times. She was tired of having the same conversation over and over again.

"You can't just throw everything away like this," Jane argued.

"I'm not the one who threw it away—you are."

She heard the heavy sigh through the phone and imagined Jane pinching the bridge of her nose, trying to hold her temper in check.

"I made a mistake. It's doesn't change how I feel about you, about us. We can work through this if you will just give us a chance. You can't just turn those feelings off."

"No," Caroline answered. "I can't turn them off. But I can't be that person who comes crawling back, pretending to trust you. If you were truly happy with me, this never would have happened. I love you enough to let you go find what does make you happy."

"Does this make you happy?" Jane's voice was softer now, almost a whisper.

"No," Caroline admitted. "But you can't, either. Not anymore."

"Just meet with me," Jane begged. "We can get together and talk. I don't even know where you are. Don't you understand how hard that is for me? I can't stand this."

Caroline shoved her hand through her hair in frustration. "I don't want to see you, Jane. Every time I think of you, I see you with her."

"Dammit, Care, please don't do this. I wish I could take that night back. I'm sorry."

Caroline blew out a deep breath. "I know. I believe you. But you can't take it back, and I can't unsee it. I need time to put myself back together."

"How much time? It's been a year."

"Don't push me on this. That's not what I meant."

"Okay." Jane sighed. "I'll give you time. But I'm not giving up."

Caroline closed her eyes. Part of her missed Jane so much she couldn't breathe. But in the past year she had learned that what she missed most was the idea of who they were together. The truth had turned out to be something entirely different. Caroline thought she was finally beginning to be honest with herself about the relationship. She was afraid if she saw Jane, if she allowed Jane into her space, Jane would place some spell on her, and she'd betray her own soul. She'd been captivated by Jane from the moment she saw her four years earlier standing outside a restaurant waiting for her blind date. That night Jane had effortlessly taken control of her heart.

"I love you, Care."

Jane's voice ripped Caroline from her thoughts, bringing her abruptly back to the present. Caroline closed her eyes. "Sign the papers, Jane," Caroline said and ended the call.

❖

"Are you all right?" Autumn asked as Caroline passed the den.

Caroline came to the door and leaned on the frame. "I'm sorry—I didn't realize you were home."

"I got in a few minutes ago. Have you had dinner?"

Caroline shrugged. "Not really. I can cook you something if you like."

Autumn smiled. "That's not necessary. How about we order something in? Do you like Asian food? I know the perfect place. They have the best hot and sour soup."

Caroline smiled. "That sounds nice, actually."

"Good. Any requests?" Autumn asked, picking up her phone.

Caroline lifted one shoulder in a shrug. "Surprise me."

Autumn laughed. "You could regret that."

Caroline's laughter filled the hall as she walked away.

"Give it thirty minutes," Autumn called after her.

She was glad Caroline had said yes. She'd seen her outside on the phone and could tell the conversation wasn't pleasant. The ex, she guessed. Caroline tried to be upbeat for the most part, but Autumn could see the hurt weighing on her. Caroline didn't go out except when it had to do with Autumn. She spent a lot of time alone in her room or downstairs reading.

Caroline met Autumn in the kitchen half an hour later. Her eyes were red rimmed, and her skin was paler than usual. Autumn placed the take-out containers on the table and handed Caroline the plates. She placed a bottle of sake on the table in a warmer.

Caroline picked up a small ceramic glass and poured them both drinks. "Is this the surprise part?"

Autumn grinned. "Maybe."

Caroline shook her head. "How are you feeling today?"

"Nervous," Autumn answered with a shiver. "I feel like today is my last day of freedom and this is my last meal. I'm not looking forward to the prep for surgery. I feel like I'm sliding on ice and I'm about to hit a wall."

Caroline handed Autumn a glass of sake. "You won't. I won't let you fall."

Autumn smiled. "I'll hold on to you if you hold on to me."

Caroline looked away.

Autumn sipped her drink "I'm guessing you've had a hard day."

"You could say that," Caroline said, taking a sip of the hot grassy drink. "My soon to be ex-wife, Jane, called. She won't sign the papers. She's pushing me to see her."

"What do you want to do?"

"I can't," Caroline said shaking her head. "She keeps trying to convince me this is something we can work through."

"But you don't think so."

"I know I can't work through this. I've spent the last year learning how to live my life without Jane. I need to start over. I question everything. Things I like, what I feel, what I want to eat. I'm having to learn *me* all over again without always wondering what Jane would think, what Jane would want."

Autumn tilted her head as if contemplating the idea. "What have you learned so far?"

Caroline grinned. "That I like sake."

"That's a start," Autumn said with a laugh.

Caroline changed the subject. "What can I do to help you get ready for the surgery?"

"The pre-surgery bowel prep will be unpleasant. I don't think there's really much for you to do until after the surgery. I think I'll just want to be quiet and get my head ready along with my body."

"How do you do that?"

Autumn held up her glass. "This helps," she said with a smile. "You know, I don't usually let people help me. Maybe it's because we don't really know each other, but having you here has been a big step."

Caroline sipped her sake. "So you're basically saying this is a good excuse to lie around the house all day and watch movies."

Autumn laughed. "That sounds good, actually."

"Do you want me to be there for the surgery?" Caroline asked.

"Do you want to be there?"

Caroline frowned. "I don't want to make your family and friends uncomfortable."

"You won't," Autumn said, then grimaced. "Although you would have to endure my mother."

Caroline picked up a bite of broccoli with her chopsticks. "What about your father?"

Autumn looked away. "He hasn't said yet. I'm not expecting him. It doesn't make sense for him to fly all the away out here. He's really busy at work, and he has a family there that needs him. I can call him once I'm out of recovery."

Caroline pushed her food around on her plate. She couldn't imagine going through anything like this without her father by her side. Autumn was good at rationalizing the distance in her relationships, but Caroline couldn't help but feel lonely for her. What would that be like, to hold everyone at such a distance that you didn't know how to need anyone? "You're very strong. I don't think I would be so calm if I were in your shoes."

Autumn finished off the last of her soup and poured another round of sake. "Oh, that's an old trick I learned when I was younger. I never knew what kind of mood my mother would be in, so I learned to keep my emotions close to the vest. The outside may look cool and calm, but there's a storm on the inside. I really am terrified. I don't want to deal with my mother, and part of me is mad as hell. But what can I do? I have to fight through this."

"Do you ever just let it all out?" Caroline thought of her own relationships. She and her dad had always talked through things. Growing up, he'd always been the one to come to her when something bad happened. He had taught her that talking made things easier to feel.

"Sometimes." Autumn sighed. "Kate and Lisa are the ones I'm most open with. Kate started working for me a year or two after I started my business. She's very no-nonsense and can see right through my crap. Lisa is a little more subtle in her approach. She has the nurturing thing down. She's going to be a great mom."

Caroline was surprised. "Is she expecting?"

"Yes. She's due in September with their first."

"Wow." Caroline wondered what it would have been like for her and Jane to have had children but quickly pushed the thought out of her head. Part of her was glad they hadn't, considering the way things had turned out. But the question still needled her. Did she want kids? Would she be a good parent?

As if reading her thoughts, Autumn asked, "What about you? Any kids?"

Caroline shook her head. "No. I've never really thought about it. I was thirty-five when Jane and I met. Jane is pretty career focused, and I never really thought of myself as the mother type. I was always a little reckless. It never came up." She sighed. "And you? Is that one of the things you put on that list you're working on?"

Autumn shook her head. "I don't think children are in the cards for me. I can't even find time to date. I think I'll be happy playing the doting aunt."

Caroline laughed. "Maybe all that will change."

"Some things, maybe. But I'm forty-five years old. I can't see it." Autumn considered the road ahead of them, wondering how much of her life she should open up to Caroline. Should she take her to meet Kate and Lisa? Should she take her to the office? And what about her mother? Autumn mentally shrugged. Caroline would meet everyone at some point anyway. Most of them would likely be at the hospital the day of surgery. Besides, Caroline was someone she could see fitting into her circle of friends easily under normal circumstances. She smiled at the thought. Yeah, Caroline was definitely someone she could see being a friend.

"I would like you to meet Kate and Lisa. They'll be around a lot after, so I figure it's only fair to introduce you before—well, you know."

Caroline smiled. "Sure, I'd like that."

"I can take you to the office tomorrow and show you around there too if you like. I do a lot of the office stuff here at home, so there's not much going on at the actual office, but you're welcome to ride along with me as I check on projects too."

"Sounds like we have a busy day tomorrow."

Autumn nodded. "I think it will make me feel better. I don't expect you to do my work, but if something comes up and I need you to run something by the office, I'd like you to know where things are and meet everyone."

Caroline reached out and took Autumn's hand. "We can do whatever you need. And it will get me out of the house."

Autumn nodded again.

Caroline stood and gathered their plates. "How about that movie?"

"A movie sounds perfect."

❖

Landers Landscaping was not what Caroline expected. It was a small bungalow that had been converted to office space. The grounds in the back of the property had giant stalls of stone, gravel, and various types of mulch and topsoil. There was a greenhouse to the right in the back of the house where Autumn grew some of her own plants and stored the plants she needed for ongoing projects.

Two young women worked outside moving large stones with small excavation equipment, while a third worked inside the office answering phones and scheduling deliveries.

Autumn explained how everything worked. "The rest of the crew is off-site today. They just started a new project for one of my biggest clients, and we have another one scheduled to start next week. Talk about a bad time for me to skip out on them."

"I would hardly call this skipping out," Caroline said, hearing the note of worry in Autumn's voice. "You'll still be able to make decisions and guide them where they need to be. It's not like you're going on vacation."

Autumn nodded as she climbed inside the Jeep. "Let's hope that's good enough. I know I shouldn't worry. Kate could probably take over this place tomorrow and not miss a beat."

"But…?"

Autumn sighed. "Clients are particular. They hired me to do a job. Sometimes not seeing my face for a day or two is enough to shake their confidence in a project."

"Have you let your clients know what's going on with you? Maybe just knowing the truth can ease some of the tension."

"Yeah, I've been up-front about it."

Caroline watched a tall dark-haired woman in a navy-blue polo shirt over a long-sleeved black T-shirt and khaki work pants jog toward the Jeep as Autumn settled some paperwork.

"There's Kate now," Autumn said with a grin, climbing out of the Jeep.

Caroline followed Autumn and rounded the Jeep as Autumn embraced Kate in a genuine hug.

"I might have known you'd show up," Kate said with a big smile that lit up her eyes.

"Last-minute details." Autumn turned to Caroline. "Kate, this is Caroline Cross. She's going to be helping me out for the next few months. Caroline, this is my friend, Kate Miller."

Caroline extended her hand to Kate. "It's good to meet you."

"Likewise," Kate said, taking Caroline's hand. "I'm glad to see someone is going to be looking after her. I don't know if she's told you, but she can be a bit stubborn."

Caroline smiled. "I can't imagine."

Kate's smile was warm and contagious. Caroline liked her immediately.

Autumn bumped Kate's shoulder with her own. "Don't start," she said, smiling. "I thought it would be good for Caroline to meet you and see how things work. She'll be my eyes and ears for a while, so be nice."

Kate shook her head. "Like I have anything to worry about. You wouldn't know what to do without me."

"This is true," Autumn said with a smile.

Kate waved them on as she started back toward the work site. "Come on, let me show you what's going on."

Caroline looked over the plans and then out over the site. She was surprised by the size of the project. She had worked with landscapers on projects around construction sites, but nothing like this. Autumn was the real deal.

"Did you do the design?" Caroline asked Autumn.

"Yes. We're just finishing excavation and drainage on this one. I planned to oversee the stonework myself, but I don't think I'll be on my feet in time."

Caroline nodded. "I'm impressed. Are all your projects this huge?"

Autumn shook her head, but Kate cut in before Autumn could answer. "Thankfully, no, although Momma Bear there wouldn't mind. One or two big projects like this a year is plenty. I'll be happy when I get to put in a simple patio for a pool. I could do those in my sleep."

Caroline smiled.

Autumn gripped Kate's shoulder. "I'm really sorry about this, Kate."

"Don't even," Kate warned. "You know that's not what I meant. Nothing is more important than you getting better."

Autumn patted Kate's back and walked away. Caroline had seen the mist of tears coat her eyes. She couldn't imagine everything that Autumn must be feeling.

"Damn," Kate mumbled. "I didn't mean to upset her."

"Don't worry about it," Caroline said, her tone gentle. "She's just having a hard time not knowing what to expect."

"Yeah. This is so fucked up. Autumn is the last person anyone would expect to get sick. It's just not right."

Caroline watched Autumn stop at the top of a hill, her hand raised to shield her eyes. "No. It never is."

Kate looked to Caroline. "I'm glad you're going to help. She won't let us do it. She's too damn proud. She likes to swoop in and save the day for everyone else, but she won't let anyone help her when it counts."

"Why is that?"

Kate raised an eyebrow. "Have you met her mother yet?"

Caroline shook her head. "She doesn't want me to meet her mother until the surgery. She's afraid her mother will scare me off."

Kate laughed. "She's got a point there."

"Is she really that bad?"

Kate sighed. "Her mother is not a bad person. She loves Autumn. She just has…issues."

It was Caroline's turn to raise an eyebrow. "What does that mean?"

"Meredith is so wrapped up in herself that I'm surprised she didn't forbid Autumn from having cancer because it interfered with Meredith's social calendar. She's never been the nurturing, caring type. Autumn has spent her life trying to please her mother, even when it cost her her own happiness. I think that's the reason she can't let anyone help her. She thinks it's her job to do everything for everyone else. And I don't think Meredith was ever there for Autumn when it counted, not in the way Autumn needed, anyway."

"Oh."

Kate turned to face Caroline. She studied her with such intensity that it made Caroline uncomfortable.

"What?"

"I can see why she likes you." Kate frowned. "Do you plan to see this through?"

Caroline looked up to find Autumn making her way back to them. "I plan to do my best. That's all I know right now."

Kate nodded, seemingly satisfied. "I hope you stay. She's going to need you. And the fact that she admits that is everything."

Caroline didn't know what to say. She could see the pain and worry on Kate's face as she watched her friend. This was going to be a lot harder than she thought. Autumn wasn't the only one who needed help getting through Autumn's illness.

CHAPTER FOUR

Autumn had been up most of the night staring into the fire, the bowel prep keeping her awake. She had risen early and showered. Caroline leaned against the doorframe, watching her pack. She could feel Caroline's gaze on her as she moved.

"Looks like you're all set," Caroline said, her tone light. "What can I do?"

"Tell me there's been some terrible mistake, and this isn't happening." Autumn turned and sat on the bed, her head bowed, her hands clasped in her lap.

Caroline stepped into the room and pushed the overnight bag aside, taking a seat on the bed next to Autumn. "I wish that were true. Everyone's going to be there. You'll have an army of love surrounding you. Take that strength with you and kick some cancer ass today."

Autumn sighed. "It's going to be a crazy day. Are you sure you want to go with me? I mean, you can just stay here and enjoy the alone time. In a few days you won't be getting much of that."

Caroline shrugged. "I'm good." She took Autumn's hand and squeezed. "I'd rather be with you today."

Autumn tightened her fingers around Caroline's. "Thank you," she said, her voice small and frightened, betraying her need for comfort, a need she could not articulate directly.

Caroline stood, still clasping Autumn's hand. She looked down at Autumn with a determined look in her eyes. "Come on. Let's do this."

Autumn nodded. She drew in a deep steadying breath. "Let's do this."

The drive to the hospital was unbearable. Autumn stared out the window, seeing but not seeing. She wanted to memorize everything about the day, but she couldn't quite focus on anything. Dark clouds tumbled across the sky as a thunderstorm blanketed the city. Rain pelted the windshield in waves as the wind picked up. Autumn closed her eyes, shutting out the storm that reflected the turmoil boiling within her mind.

Warm fingers covered her hand, drawing her from her thoughts. She didn't look at Caroline but was thankful for the connection. She laced her fingers through Caroline's. She wasn't alone. Her friends would be there. Her mother. She would get through this. She had too much to do to let this get her down.

Caroline pulled up to the hospital entrance and let Autumn out. "I'll see you inside as soon as I get parked."

Autumn swallowed the sudden knot of fear that had developed in her throat at the thought of walking in alone. She nodded.

While Caroline parked, Autumn made her way through the maze of corridors, registered, and was taken back to a room to begin her prep. Everything felt so surreal. She had difficulty accepting what was happening.

She heard a knock at the door as it was gently pushed open. "Is it all right if I come in?" Caroline asked, peeking her head inside.

"It's fine," Autumn answered, instantly relieved now that Caroline was with her.

Caroline kept her expression neutral as she stepped inside. Autumn was in a hospital bed. She wore a light blue hospital gown. And she looked vulnerable and frightened.

"Nice outfit," Caroline joked.

Autumn smiled down at the horrible gown. "I'm thinking of starting a new fashion trend."

"If anyone could, it would be you." Caroline glanced around the room. "Kate called to check on you. She seemed to think the surgery was scheduled for ten."

Autumn felt her face heat and knew it had turned a telling shade of pink. "I didn't want them sitting around here all day."

"Ah, I see. Is that why your mother isn't here?"

Autumn grinned. "Maybe."

Caroline laughed. "You're terrible."

"Just wait till she gets here. You'll thank me for sparing you those hours."

There was a knock at the door and she and Caroline both turned as Mary pushed into the room. She extended her hand to Caroline. "Hello, I'm Dr. Mathis."

"Hi. I'm Caroline Cross. I'm glad to meet you."

Dr. Mathis nodded, then turned to Autumn. "Good morning, Autumn. How are you feeling?"

"Terrified," Autumn said honestly.

Dr. Mathis smiled. "There's no need. I'm going to take good care of you." She gestured to Caroline. "I see you brought reinforcements." She smiled at Caroline. "I expect a lengthy surgery. In this case, the longer the better. We want to make sure we get all the affected tissue and do a clean resection. Best case scenario we get everything without having to do an ileostomy. But that is a very real possibility. We won't know until we are inside and see how the transection goes. If all goes as planned, you can expect this to be at least a four- or five-hour procedure."

Autumn nodded. "Fingers crossed. No ileostomy. Got it."

Dr. Mathis gave Autumn a questioning look. "Where's Meredith? I expected her to be here taking charge."

Autumn averted her eyes. "I might have given her the wrong time. She'll be here later."

Dr. Mathis smiled. "I see." She leaned closer to Autumn. "You know she's going to make you pay for that."

Autumn shrugged. "I know. I just couldn't handle her right now."

Dr. Mathis nodded and patted the back of Autumn's hand. "I understand." She straightened. "Are you ready?"

"I'm ready," Autumn said with a heavy sigh.

"I'll see you in there." Dr. Mathis nodded to Caroline on her way out. "Once we take her back, you can go to the waiting area. I'll let you know something as soon as I can."

Caroline smiled. "Thank you."

A nurse bustled into the room moments after Dr. Mathis left, followed by two orderlies. "We're ready to take you down to surgery." She pushed a lever with her foot that released a brake on the bed, and they turned Autumn toward the door. The nurse looked to Caroline. "You can watch updates on the screens in the lobby. We'll call down and let you know how things are going, and the doctor will speak to you once the surgery is complete."

Caroline nodded.

Autumn reached out to Caroline. "See you in a few hours."

Caroline smiled, but it didn't reach her eyes. Their normally vibrant blue was dark and stormy, clouded by the fear she was trying to hide.

"No worries, remember. I'm going to go kick some cancer ass."

"You do that. I'll be right here cheering you on the whole time. And I'll be here when you get back."

Autumn nodded. "I'm glad you're here."

Autumn let Caroline's fingers slip from her hand as she was wheeled away. She closed her eyes and set her mind to the task ahead of her. She wouldn't let cancer win. Not today. Not ever.

Caroline stood as Kate clamored through the door, looking like she'd missed the bus on the first day of school. A beautiful brunette shuffled in behind Kate, her hand gently resting against her slightly swollen pregnant belly. This must be Lisa, she guessed.

"Where is she? Are we too late?" Kate asked, rushing up to Caroline.

"They took her back two hours ago."

Kate's shoulders fell. "Dammit. Two hours? How did I get the time wrong? I thought I was doing good leaving the house as early as we did. I can't believe we missed her. How was she?"

Caroline rested her hand on Kate's forearm. "She was fine.

I think she was a little scared to face everyone this morning. She actually told you the wrong time on purpose."

Kate rolled her eyes and crossed her arms over her chest. "Figures she would pull something like that."

"Something like what?" Lisa said, stepping up to Kate and wrapping her arm around her waist.

Kate slid her arm around Lisa's shoulder. "Autumn gave us the wrong time on purpose, so she didn't have to face anyone before she went in."

Lisa smiled. "Sounds like something she would do."

Caroline stuck out her hand. "You must be Lisa. Autumn has told me a lot about you. I'm Caroline Cross."

Lisa smiled. "It's nice to meet you, Caroline. Thank you for looking after Autumn."

Caroline nodded. "It's going to be a long wait. We should have a seat." She pointed to the large television screens mounted around the room. "Updates will come up on the screen throughout the surgery. We may even get a call to let us know the progress. As I understand it, they think this will take up to four or five hours."

"Geez," Kate muttered.

"Yeah," Caroline said in agreement. "It's a long time to be in there, but they said the longer it takes, the better. That means they are able to get in and get to the problem."

Lisa looked around the room, frowning. "Have you heard from Meredith, Autumn's mother?"

Caroline drew in a deep breath and sighed. "No. Just before she went in, Autumn admitted she told her mother to be here at two."

Lisa's eyes widened. "Two?"

Kate laughed. "Hey, at least she told her about it. I half expected her to wait until her treatments were finished before she told her mother. I'm giving Autumn points on this one."

Caroline smiled. "I haven't met her yet. Autumn has been adamant about us not meeting until after the surgery."

"More points for Autumn," Kate said. "She was afraid her mother would sabotage this for her. She wanted to make sure she has a chance to stay at home after this. Going to her mother's would be the worst thing that could happen to Autumn."

Lisa shifted in her seat, then stood. "I have to pee. I'll be right back."

Kate watched Lisa make her way across the room, then turned back to Caroline. "Meredith is a really hard one to describe. You'll just have to see for yourself. When I first met her, she seemed perfectly normal—I liked her. But after being around her for a while, she started saying little things that pissed me off. At first, I had trouble placing what was bugging me, but then her digs became more apparent, and she started saying things that put Autumn down. There were lots of little disparaging remarks that became more hurtful if Autumn wasn't doing what Meredith wanted her to do."

Caroline couldn't imagine. Surely, she wasn't that bad.

"Well," Kate continued, "I hope she behaves herself today. I wouldn't put it past Autumn to have her mother barred from her room." Kate stood. "I'm going to go check on Lisa. Can I get you anything?"

Caroline shook her head. "No. I'm fine. Thanks." She watched Kate walk away. If Autumn's mother was everything Kate had described, this was going to be a very long day, and a lot harder than she'd thought. She checked her watch, then the screen. If they were sticking to the timeline, Autumn was only halfway through the surgery.

Caroline jumped when her cell rang. She'd meant to put the ringer on silent. She grabbed the phone, answering without checking caller ID.

"Hello."

"Hey. It's me."

Caroline closed her eyes and sank into her chair at the sound of Jane's voice.

"Care? Are you there?"

"I'm here."

Jane cleared her throat. "You don't sound so good. Are you okay?"

Caroline pinched the bridge of her nose. "I'm fine. What did you need, Jane?"

"I'm having a bit of a bad day. I just wanted to hear your voice. I miss you."

"Jane, don't do this. I can't talk right now."

"Please, Caroline. Just talk to me for a while. If I can't see you, please just talk to me."

Caroline considered hanging up the phone, but her conscience got the better of her. Jane sounded sad. Caroline knew these moods. She knew what Jane needed, but she wasn't the one to give that to her anymore. "What's wrong?"

She heard Jane's sharp intake of breath. "Thank you."

Caroline sighed. "Tell me what's wrong."

"I had a panic attack this morning. I had a presentation at eight. I had everything ready. I knew everything by heart. But when it came time, I couldn't move. I just lost it."

Caroline swallowed. She knew how bad the anxiety got sometimes. On the outside Jane looked like she was a force ready to take on the world. But inside she could be a boiling mess of self-doubt and debilitating fear.

Jane sniffed. Was she crying? Caroline's gut twisted.

"Are you okay?"

Jane launched into a recount of the episode. "Robert managed to step in before anyone caught on that I had freaked out. I was able to play off him and get through the presentation, but I thought I was going to die right there in the boardroom."

"It sounds like you made a good recovery. Are you still taking the medicine?"

"Not lately." Jane hesitated before continuing. "I—I just…I don't think about it."

Caroline shook her head. "Take them."

"I know. My head has just been so screwed up since you left. I can't think straight. Why can't you just come home so we can work this out? You're my wife. You should be here with me."

Tears born of anger pricked at Caroline's eyes, and she pressed harder on the bridge of her nose to push them away. "I just can't, Jane. I'm sorry you had a bad day, but I can't fix it for you. I don't even know how to fix things for myself right now."

"Just talk to me," Jane pleaded. "We always talk through things together."

Caroline saw Kate and Lisa ambling toward her. "Not this time. I've gotta go, Jane."

"Wait," Jane said hurriedly. "Can I call you tomorrow?"

"I'm busy tomorrow." Caroline hesitated. "Maybe sometime next week," she conceded just to get Jane off the phone.

"Okay." Jane's voice seemed small on the line. "Thanks for listening."

Caroline was dying. "I have to go, Jane. I'll talk to you later." She ended the call, looking up and smiling at Kate and Lisa. She pointed to the screen.

"Looks like things are going as planned, and she's stable. It's not much, but it's better than sitting here not knowing anything."

Kate stared at the screen as if willing it to tell her more. Lisa took Kate's hand and squeezed. Kate glanced at Lisa and a faint smiled flickered at the corners of her mouth. Caroline missed that. She used to have that with Jane. At least, she thought she did. She wasn't certain about any of it anymore.

Caroline followed the nurse to Autumn's recovery room. The hairs on her arm rose as she entered the room. She was suddenly overcome with the memory of visiting her mother in the hospital during one of her last hospitalizations before her death. Caroline slowed her breathing and moved quietly into the room.

Autumn lay asleep on the bed, her hair pulled back from her face in disarray. IV tubes snaked from her arms, and a light blanket hugged her body.

Caroline studied the machines, knowing too well how to read the lines and numbers recording Autumn's heartbeat, her blood pressure, and her oxygen levels. She was overcome with tenderness for Autumn. For all of Autumn's strength and independence, she lay vulnerable and exposed. Autumn was trusting her to take care of her at her most weakened state. Caroline was deeply humbled. She sat next to the bed, watching Autumn's face for any sign that she might wake. Tentatively, Caroline reached out and took Autumn's hand. To her surprise, Autumn's fingers closed around hers. Caroline held her breath, waiting. Autumn didn't stir.

Caroline had been with Autumn close to an hour when Autumn's eyes fluttered and opened.

"Hey there," Caroline said, smiling down at Autumn. "Welcome back."

Autumn frowned and grimaced in pain.

Caroline gripped Autumn's hand and leaned closer. "What do you need? What can I do?"

Autumn settled down as the pain apparently subsided. "Thirsty."

Caroline reached for the pitcher a nurse had left by the bed. "It will have to be ice chips for now."

"Okay. Good," Autumn muttered.

Caroline spooned small bits of ice into Autumn's mouth. Autumn's lips were dry, and her tongue snaked across the rough skin, as if trying to soothe the dry discomfort.

"Here." Caroline took a larger piece of ice between her fingers and held it to Autumn's lips, letting the cold liquid melt against the tender flesh. Autumn closed her mouth around the ice, her lips brushing against Caroline's fingers. Caroline's fingers tingled at the delicate touch.

Caroline chose another piece of ice. She traced the line of Autumn's lips with the ice, mesmerized by the curve of Autumn's lips and how the color pinked as the ice cooled her flesh. Autumn's usually tanned bronze skin was pale. Caroline brushed a strand of hair from Autumn's face, untangling it from the ties of the gown at her neck.

Autumn groaned.

"Hey," Caroline soothed. "You're okay."

Autumn's eyes opened and she looked wildly around the room. Caroline gently took Autumn's hand. "No one's here. It's just me for now."

Autumn turned her gaze to Caroline. The wild fear faded from her eyes and she settled back against her pillow. Autumn tried to brush her hair back from her face but cringed.

Caroline's heart ached at Autumn's pain. She took Autumn's hand, stopping her from hurting herself. "Let me." She took a brush from the bag Autumn had packed and gently brushed her hair, then wet a small towel and tenderly washed Autumn's face. "There. Is that better?"

Autumn looked into Caroline's eyes with wonder and gratitude. "Thank you."

Caroline smiled.

Autumn closed her eyes and swallowed. "Could you give me more ice?" Her voice was hoarse and weak.

Caroline spooned ice chips into Autumn's mouth. Autumn stared up at her as if holding to a lifeline.

"What is it?"

Autumn's eyes became pleading and worried. "Mother will be difficult. Please don't let her upset you. I don't want you to leave."

Caroline smiled again. "I made a promise to you, and I intend to keep it. I'm not going anywhere."

Autumn nodded. "Kate and Lisa?" she asked.

"Yes. They're waiting in the lobby."

Autumn smiled. "I want to see them so they can go home. Lisa doesn't need this."

Caroline shook her head. "I think she very much needs this. They love you."

Autumn nodded.

"Okay," Caroline stood. "I'll send them in."

Autumn closed her eyes as Caroline's hand slipped from hers. Her hand was warm and comforting. Caroline had been unexpectedly tender as she cared for her. Autumn was grateful for that. She was scared, and Caroline made her feel safe.

When she opened her eyes again Kate and Lisa stood by her bed. She must have fallen asleep. Lisa gently brushed her fingers along Autumn's cheek and Kate gripped the bed rail as if she was trying to strangle it.

Autumn smiled up at them. "What? You'd think you'd never seen someone sleeping before."

Lisa leaned down and kissed her cheek. "We're so glad you're okay. Do you need anything, sweetie?"

Autumn shook her head. "Just sleepy. Thanks for being here. You know you guys don't have to stay. I'll be okay."

Lisa rubbed her baby bump. "We just wanted to be here when you woke up. We'll let you rest and come back tomorrow."

Kate hadn't moved.

Autumn raised her hand and pointed at Kate. "Do I need to get you a chair? You don't look so good."

Kate sighed and loosened her grip on the bed rail. "I'm good."

Autumn reached out her hand and Kate took it. "I'm fine. Stop worrying."

Kate nodded.

"Take little Momma here home and get some rest. I'm counting on you."

Kate nodded again.

Lisa rested her hand on Kate's shoulder and looked at Autumn. "Don't worry. I'll take care of her. She's just not used to seeing her superhero like this."

Autumn let out a weak laugh and rolled her eyes. "Get out of here. I'll see you later." Autumn pulled her hand away, but instead of leaving, Kate leaned down and placed a kiss to her forehead. Autumn felt the sting of tears at the tenderness. She grinned up at Kate. "I'll be okay. I promise."

Kate smiled. "You better be." She glanced at Lisa's growing belly. "This kid is going to need you. We all do." She squeezed Autumn's hand. "I'll see you tomorrow."

Autumn closed her eyes at the sound of the door closing. She was so tired. Would this day ever be over? She needed to rest. She was so tired.

❖

Autumn opened her eyes as the dream she was having slipped away. Bright lights intruded on her peace, hurting her eyes. She was in a different room than before. When had she been moved? What was happening? "Caroline?"

There was a rustling sound of paper across the room and feet scuffing the floor.

"Hey," Caroline said in a whispered voice.

"What happened?"

"They moved you into a regular room. I'm glad you're awake. The doctor should be in soon."

"My mother?"

"She hasn't been in yet. But it should be anytime now."

There was a sharp knock at the door, and Dr. Mathis stepped into the room.

"I was hoping to catch you awake," Dr. Mathis said as she pressed a stethoscope to Autumn's chest, then moved down her abdomen.

Dr. Mathis took Autumn's hand and looked down at her with gentle eyes. "Things went better than we could have hoped. We were able to keep the entire surgery laparoscopic. We removed the tumor and one foot of your colon along with fifteen lymph nodes. We managed it all without having to put in an ileostomy."

"Perfect," Autumn whispered.

Dr. Mathis smiled. "It was pretty darn close to perfect in my book, yes." She looked to Caroline and back to Autumn. "As soon as we get you healed up a bit and see how your bowels are going to respond, I want to start chemotherapy. We'll discuss putting in a port to administer the meds a little further down the road. Rest up. I'll check back on you later." Dr. Mathis looked around the room, her brows furrowed in question. "Where's Meredith?"

Autumn frowned and closed her eyes.

Caroline spoke up. "She hasn't made it in yet. We are expecting her anytime now."

Dr. Mathis raised one scolding eyebrow and looked down at Autumn. "You're playing with fire, Autumn. I'll do what I can to head her off, but you know she's not going to be happy about this."

Autumn nodded. "I know. It was what I needed."

"All right then." Dr. Mathis patted Autumn's hand. "I'll see you shortly."

"Where is my daughter?" a voice audible from the nurses' station demanded, though the speaker was still invisible.

Dr. Mathis sighed. "Right on cue." She grinned at Autumn. "I'll speak with her."

"Thank you," Autumn said, smiling apologetically.

Autumn looked to Caroline as Dr. Mathis left the room. "Are you ready for this?"

Caroline nodded. "Don't worry about me. Do you want me to give you some time alone with your mother?"

Autumn frowned. "Let's see how it goes." She looked at a water pitcher sitting on the table by the bed. "Can I have some ice?"

Caroline reached for the cup and filled it with ice. "Do you think you can do it?"

Autumn reached for the cup and spoon. "Let me try."

Caroline was leaning over Autumn when the door opened, and Dr. Mathis escorted a clearly ruffled Mrs. Landers into the room. She wasn't at all what Caroline had expected. She was a small woman, only about five feet tall in heels. She had jet black hair that wasn't at all natural, and she couldn't weigh one hundred pounds soaking wet. Her black eyes were a fierce contrast to Autumn's warm blue. Caroline struggled to see a resemblance between Autumn and her mother. Clearly Autumn took after her father.

Autumn's hand closed around Caroline's as she gripped the cup, her hand squeezing tighter than needed. The monitor next to the bed began to beep faster, and Autumn's oxygen dropped.

Dr. Mathis silenced the machine and straightened the IV tube. "I've just explained everything to your mother, Autumn. You can visit for a few minutes, but I really want you to rest for the remainder of the day. You'll need your strength. I want you up walking tomorrow."

As Dr. Mathis ran interference between Autumn and her mother, Caroline stood by watching. "Hello, Mrs. Landers. I'm Caroline Cross, it's a pleasure to meet you." Caroline extended her hand.

Mrs. Landers glared at Caroline. "I was told to be here at two. Perhaps you would like to explain to me why my daughter has already been through surgery and I was not contacted."

Caroline didn't allow herself to flinch despite the urge to take a step back from the rage emanating from Autumn's mother. "That was Autumn's request. She was concerned about you having to sit through the long wait and decided it best that you be here for her recovery. She's been expecting you."

This news did nothing to mollify Meredith Landers. She turned to Autumn. "I should be angry with you. Why must you always upset me so? Don't you know how much I worry about you?"

Autumn took a series of controlled breaths, likely so the damn machine would stop wailing while her mother's annoyance filled the room. "It was my choice, Mother. I thought it would be best for us both. It's done. I don't have the strength or patience to fight with you about it. As you can see, I'm doing fine."

"I'm your mother. I am responsible for you. I just want what's best for you."

Autumn narrowed her gaze at her mother. "Then we agree—there is no problem. Why don't you have a seat and tell me about your day."

Dr. Mathis placed a hand on Meredith's shoulder on her way out. "She needs to rest. Visit with her a few minutes. Tomorrow she'll be stronger." She looked around the room making eye contact with each of them. "If I hear of anything upsetting Autumn, I will bar visitors from this room for the rest of the evening." She met Meredith's gaze. "That includes you, Meredith."

Caroline resisted the urge to smile. Dr. Mathis was all right in her book. Caroline cleared her throat. "I think I'll step out for a moment. Would you like some coffee, Mrs. Landers?"

Meredith glanced at Caroline and straightened. "Yes, thank you. Coffee would be fine."

Caroline looked to Autumn. "Do you mind? I'll only be a minute."

Autumn nodded. "Okay."

Caroline smiled. "Is there anything else I can get you, Mrs. Landers?"

"No," Mrs. Landers said bitterly. "I would like to talk to my daughter."

Caroline thought she saw a sheen of tears in the older woman's eyes. Despite all her bravado, she was scared and hurt. Caroline stopped next to Mrs. Landers as she passed. "Autumn didn't want to worry you any more than was necessary. She didn't mean to upset you."

Mrs. Landers cleared her throat. "Yes, well, Autumn has always been difficult."

Caroline caught her breath. The bait had been cast, but she wasn't about to take it.

"I'm sure we all want what's best for Autumn." Before Mrs. Landers could comment, Caroline stepped away, following Dr. Mathis out of the room.

CHAPTER FIVE

Autumn stared out the window of her room at the mountains hovering beyond the city like beacons calling her outside. She was enjoying some rare time alone. She had been in the hospital for eight days due to her gut having trouble waking up from the surgery, and being trapped inside was taking its toll. She was walking more and more each day, but she couldn't eat, and despite the feeding tube, she was losing weight. Caroline was spending a lot of time at the hospital, and Kate and Lisa had been by every day as well. She and her mother had come to a temporary truce, though, making things much less stressful. She tried not to worry. She knew things could be so much worse. Dr. Mathis had explained that the bowel sensitivity was normal, and that it could take two or more weeks for her digestive system to respond. But she was frustrated about not being able to go home, and she was sick of the NG tube. Popsicles were great, but she desperately wanted to be able to eat on her own.

Autumn turned away from the window at the sound of a knock at the door. Her spirits lifted as Caroline stuck her head into the room.

"Hey, are you up for company?"

"Yes, please. I'd love some." Caroline had been a godsend. She was the one person with whom Autumn felt she didn't have to pretend to be strong. She didn't have to protect Caroline's feelings. As it turned out, Caroline had been intuitively understanding of Autumn's needs. There were even times when Autumn could turn the attention to Caroline and escape her own fear-filled drama for a while.

Caroline pushed through the door with a bag of fresh games and books to pass the time.

Autumn laughed. "Planning a party?"

Caroline smiled. "Yep. First, I thought we would take a stroll around the nurses' block, followed by your favorite banana Popsicles. Then we can sit up in the chair for a couple of hours and play some games. Then, if you're really good, I can see about getting you a real shower."

"Oh, goodie," Autumn said sarcastically.

"How has it been today? Any news?"

Autumn shrugged. "I thought I heard some more gurgling a little while ago, but I'm not sure."

Caroline's eyes widened. "Wow, that would be a step in the right direction. Do you want me to get a nurse to listen?"

Autumn grimaced. "No. The bloating is awful. At least there's no more fever. I'm sure someone will be coming through here any minute to poke and prod me for one reason or another. At this point I feel like a pincushion."

"Sounds like someone's getting grumpy."

Autumn scowled. "Wouldn't you be?"

"Yes," Caroline said quickly. "I'd be unbearable in your situation. I'm a terrible patient."

Autumn reached for Caroline's hand. "I want to hear more about this." With Caroline's help she slowly slid off the edge of the bed, letting her socked feet rest on the floor. A moment later she gingerly stood, resting her hands against Caroline's shoulders. Caroline was strong, her arms and shoulders firm, and the muscles bunched beneath Autumn's hands as Caroline took part of Autumn's weight.

Caroline steadied Autumn, then guided her slowly across the room. "I'm insufferable when I'm sick. I hate it. No one can bear being near me."

Autumn laughed, shuffling her feet with each miniscule step.

"I can't imagine you that way. You seem so comfortable taking care of me."

Caroline smiled. "There's a big difference in being cared for and caring for someone else."

"True." Autumn realized that was how she had always been too. This was the first time in her life she had ever really allowed anyone to care for her. "How did that come about?"

Caroline sighed, her arm tightening around Autumn's waist. "I loved taking care of my mother. I would sit for hours on our sunporch just brushing her hair. When she no longer had hair, I painted her nails, we made flower arrangements together, and I read to her. I would cling to her and those moments together. But if I got sick, I couldn't be around her like that. She had to be careful with infections. So being sick was like a punishment for me. A simple cold was the worst thing ever."

Autumn stopped halfway across the room. She held tightly to Caroline's hand. She met Caroline's gaze, regretting taking Caroline back to that memory. "I'm sorry."

Caroline's eyes sparkled when she looked at Autumn. "It's okay. I don't mind talking about her with you." Caroline was quiet for a moment. "That's really strange. I never talk about her to anyone."

"I'm glad you share her with me." Autumn took another step and shifted to make the turn. Caroline's arm was a comfort around her shoulder, her hand an anchor steadying her. "It makes me feel... normal. I like it that you aren't afraid to talk about cancer with me. It makes it feel less formidable."

Caroline frowned. "How so?"

Autumn bit her lip as a stabbing pain ripped through her abdomen. She sucked in a sharp breath, pausing to let the pain pass. Caroline's grip tightened around her. Her expression grew intense, focused, and penetrating.

"I'm okay," Autumn reassured. "It will pass."

A moment later, Autumn resumed her shuffle around the room until she was confident she could make it around the unit. As they walked arm in arm, Autumn tried to explain. "I feel like I have to put on this brave front for everyone. I can see the fear and sadness on their faces when I talk about the cancer or treatment, or any of it. I see the sympathy in their eyes, and I recoil. I don't want them to see me as weak."

Caroline shook her head. "No one sees you as weak. Quite the opposite. Everyone is scared, of course. Someone they love has this terrible thing, threatening to take you from them, and there's nothing they can do."

Autumn nodded. "I know. But when we talk, I feel like I can really look at cancer as the enemy. I don't have to pretend anything. Looking it in the face makes me feel stronger, braver, more determined. Tiptoeing around it just feels like everyone has already given up."

"Okay," Caroline continued, shifting her weight to allow Autumn to make a turn without getting tangled up in her assortment of tubes and IV pole. "Maybe if you talk about it, your friends can get more comfortable too. They haven't been through this before. Tell them what you need."

Autumn thought about the answer as they made the long journey back to her room.

Caroline placed her hand over Autumn's holding to the IV pole. She brushed her thumb across the back of Autumn's hand. "So, on the stronger, braver front. How are you today, really?"

Autumn grimaced. "I think I'll go mad if I don't get out of here soon."

Caroline smiled. "I thought so. Let's get the nurse to come listen to your tummy. Who knows, today might be your lucky day. If we can lose that NG tube, you'll be one more step closer to home."

❖

Caroline leaned against the wall and took in the nurses busily moving about from room to room, the never-ending sound of beeping machines, the smell of antiseptic, and the strained faces of family members visiting loved ones. It was an all too familiar scene. Had it really been five years since she had stood in a similar place grasping the last moments of her mother's life, trying to accept the finality, the devastating loneliness of loss? Her mother had been so frail in the end.

Seeing Autumn with the NG tube and the IVs running from her arms brought home the reality of what was happening. Caring for Autumn through her surgery was harder than she'd imagined. She had known Autumn's illness would bring up things about her mother, but she hadn't expected the memories to be so vivid or so painful after so many years. Her time with Autumn was forcing her to look at things she'd pushed aside back then. Talking to Autumn about her mother made her realize how much she missed her. She had found it easier to busy herself with life than to dwell on death, but in doing so she hadn't allowed herself to nurture her memories of her mother.

The first year after her mother's death, she hadn't recognized herself. She barely remembered that year at all. She had been so angry at the unfairness of having her mother ravaged by such a cruel disease and then ripped from her life. She became reckless. She put herself in situations she never should have been in, daring death. She hadn't cared about her own life. Then she had met Jane.

Caroline frowned at the memory. At the time, Jane had seemed like a godsend, the breath of fresh air she needed to live again. But looking back, she realized Jane had been a substitute she had used to fill the emptiness in her heart. Jane had been full of life, in control, and not afraid to go for whatever she wanted, and she had swept Caroline off her feet and settled her down. Being with Jane had been intoxicating. She'd lost herself in her. She had pushed aside all her pain and had immersed herself in the whirlwind Jane brought to her life. Was that what she was doing with Autumn? Was she using Autumn's illness to hide from her own failure? She hadn't been able to save her mother. She hadn't been enough for Jane, either. What did she hope to accomplish here?

Dr. Mathis and a nurse exited Autumn's room. Caroline straightened and prepared herself. She knew Autumn's NG tube had been removed, and she was slowly trying to introduce liquids and bland food orally. It hadn't been going well, but Autumn never complained. Caroline headed into Autumn's room. She wasn't sure what all of this meant in the jumbled-up mess that had become her life, but she would do what Autumn needed her to do. She wouldn't make the mistake of getting lost in Autumn's illness to fill her own needs. Not this time. Autumn trusted her. Autumn deserved better than that.

Autumn looked up with a smile as Caroline pushed through the door.

Caroline grinned. "How did it go?"

Autumn held up both hands, thumbs extended upward. "All good. Dr. Mathis is going to let me go home today."

"Fantastic."

Autumn's eyes sparkled with excitement. "I can't wait to get out of this room and sleep in my own bed."

Caroline laughed. "You'll definitely rest better without the nurses coming in and out at all hours. But I could do that for you at home if you like that kind of attention."

"You're cute," Autumn teased back. "But no thanks."

Caroline plopped down in the chair next to the bed. "Has your mother been in today?"

Autumn nodded. "Yeah, she was pretty insistent that I come to her house, but I think at this point she's getting more mileage out of playing the dejected parent. And to be honest, I just don't have the energy to placate her." Autumn narrowed her eyes at Caroline. "I've noticed you've been suspiciously absent when she's been here. How is that?"

Caroline laughed. "I caught on to her schedule. I figured it was easier on you if I let her have that time with you. On the days I was here, she seemed more combative and challenging."

Autumn grinned. "Very perceptive, Ms. Cross. And very well played."

Caroline bowed. "I do what I can." She looked around the room. "I guess we need to get you ready. I can gather your things and take them to the car. Do you want me to help you dress, or do I need to get a nurse?"

Autumn considered the question. "Do you mind? I just have sweats. Most of it I can do myself."

Caroline gathered Autumn's bag from the closet and pulled out the clothes, holding up the black track pants. "I don't know. I think I'm going to miss that hospital gown. There's something to be said for those little ties in the back."

Autumn threw a piece of ice at Caroline. "You weren't supposed to be looking at my butt. You were supposed to cover my ass, remember?"

Caroline shrugged. "Was that what we agreed on? I'm not sure I remember."

Autumn narrowed her eyes. "I see how it is." She grasped the pants Caroline held out to her. "I'd have a witty comeback for that, but unfortunately I still need help getting these on." She grinned mischievously. "But I'll get you back when you least expect it."

Caroline slipped the pants over Autumn's feet and gently slid the fabric up her legs. She helped Autumn to her feet and held her as Autumn pulled the pants up. She wrapped her arms around Autumn's waist and tugged at the strings of the hospital gown. She hesitated before sliding the gown off Autumn's shoulders.

"Can you do this part?"

Autumn met her gaze and nodded. "Yeah, just let me sit." She gently settled back onto the edge of the bed. "No bra, though. I don't think I can stand that. Just hand me the T-shirt."

Caroline handed over the T-shirt and turned her back to give Autumn some privacy.

"All done," Autumn said managing to tug the T-shirt down over her breasts.

Caroline turned and studied her. She reached out and grasped the hem of the shirt, straightening it where it snagged a bandage covering Autumn's abdomen. She met Autumn's gaze. "There you go." She brushed the hair away from Autumn's face. "Now let's do something with this wild mane you have going here."

Autumn closed her eyes, lost in the feel of Caroline's hands in her hair as she pulled the brush through the tangled mess. A thread of pain shot through her with each tug of the brush, but she didn't mind. Caroline's touch was gentle and reminded her that she was alive and that she had so much more to look forward to.

"What's the first thing you want to do when you get home?" Caroline asked as she stroked Autumn's hair.

Caroline's breath was warm against Autumn's ear when she spoke, making the skin on Autumn's arms rise as if she had been caressed. Autumn cleared her throat, not wanting Caroline to hear the intimacy in her voice when she spoke. "I don't know. Maybe sit by the fire or look out over the backyard. I don't care, really. I just want to be in my own home."

"I picked up some things I thought you might like to eat," Caroline said as her fingers grazed the delicate skin at Autumn's neck. "I know that's a bit touchy right now, but we need to find something you can get down."

Autumn's spirits lifted at the thought of real food. "Hot wings sound good or a greasy hamburger."

Caroline smiled. "Do you think you can handle that?"

Autumn frowned. "Not really. How about plain mashed potatoes? I might manage that. Anything but Jell-O or chicken broth."

"You've got it. Anything you want."

Autumn reached up, stilling Caroline's hand. "Thank you. I know I've said it before, but it makes all the difference having you here."

Caroline squeezed Autumn's hand. "We're a good team. You're going to get through this."

Autumn was quiet as Caroline continued to brush her hair. She hoped Caroline was right, but this was only the first step. The battle was just getting started.

"Are you ready for this?" Autumn said with more than a little uncertainty in her voice.

"I'm ready. The sooner you get home, the faster you will heal."

Autumn swallowed the knot of worry that had formed in her throat. "Dr. Mathis says the treatments will last at least six months. That's a long time, don't you think?"

"I don't know. It will just be fall by then. You'll have all summer by the pool and may even be able to get out and enjoy the changing of the season when the leaves turn. By the last days of autumn, you'll be getting your strength back and starting on that bucket list."

Autumn swallowed. "What about you? I know this hasn't been easy for you."

Caroline smoothed Autumn's hair, then put aside the brush and came around the bed to face Autumn. "We have a deal, remember? I plan to be here enjoying that pool too. And I happen to love fall. I don't want you to worry about anything but getting better."

Autumn caught and held Caroline's gaze. "I'm afraid I'm asking too much."

Caroline brushed her thumb along Autumn's jaw. "No need. I admit I'm facing some things about my mother's illness that I had pushed aside for too long. But I think that's a good thing. I promise to take care of myself." Caroline sighed. "But if it makes you feel better, let's just agree to take it one day at a time. Who knows, you may get sick of me and decide you want your house back."

Autumn smiled. "I doubt that will happen, but okay. One day at a time sounds good to me. As long as you promise to talk to me if things get too hard or this isn't working out for you."

"I promise. Now, let's get you out of here."

Autumn laughed. "I'm all yours." She felt the heat creep into her face the instant the words were out of her mouth. But she had to admit, it was a nice thought.

❖

"No, Kate. Everything's fine. I'm on my way home now. Caroline is driving me," Autumn reassured her.

"So you're going to take it easy, right? I mean, you aren't going to be your usual self and push too hard to get back to work?"

Kate sounded worried. Autumn was immediately on alert. "Is there something you haven't told me? What's happened?"

Kate laughed. "There's nothing. Really. I just know you. I'll come by the house every week and we can go over the projects. You won't have anything to worry about but getting better."

Autumn rolled her eyes. "Easy for you to say. I've been going stir-crazy already. I can't wait to be home, but I don't want to be a prisoner there. Once I'm back on my feet, I plan to be back at work at least part-time."

"What about treatment?" Kate asked.

Autumn shifted the seat belt so it wasn't pressing against her incision, and tried to find a more comfortable position.

Caroline kept her gaze on the road as if steeling her focus forward gave Autumn some privacy as she talked.

"I'll deal with that as it comes. Everyone reacts different to chemo, but I plan to work when I can. I can't just sit by and let you do everything."

"I'm really glad you're going home. Lisa and I will stop by later this week if that's okay. Give you a little time to settle in." Kate cleared her throat. "Of course, if you need anything—"

"I know," Autumn interrupted so Kate didn't have to say it. "I'll call you tomorrow. Give Lisa a hug for me."

Autumn ended the call and looked to Caroline. "One down, one to go."

Caroline glanced at Autumn. "Meredith?"

Autumn nodded. "I have to call before she shows up at the hospital and finds I've left without telling her. That would be bad. She still hasn't forgiven me for not letting her be there for the surgery."

"Do what you have to do," Caroline said with a grin.

Autumn cued the phone, took a deep breath, and pressed *call*. "Hello, Mother."

Caroline steered the car into the drive, half listening to Autumn talk to her mother. She couldn't get used to the tenuous nature of their relationship. Her own mother had been attentive and engaged and wanted nothing more than Caroline's happiness. Caroline smiled at the memory of her mother putting bandages on banged-up knees, kissing her good night, holding her hand as she cried after her first heartbreak. Her mother hadn't been perfect, she knew that, but they had been as close as Caroline could imagine. She had been her best friend. Hearing Autumn struggle to have a simple conversation with her mother was almost like listening to a hostage negotiator or a kindergarten teacher trying to talk sense into a volatile child or crazed bomber.

Caroline parked the car and gathered the bag from the back before coming around to help Autumn from the car.

"I have to go, Mother—we're at the house now," Autumn said as she slid her legs around to the edge of the seat. "I'm already beat. I'll probably lie down and rest for the night. I'll call you tomorrow."

Autumn reached up her hand to Caroline. "Thank goodness that's over. I have a twenty-four-hour reprieve."

Caroline grasped Autumn's hand, gently pulling her up to stand. "It might have been nice if everyone could have been here to welcome you home."

Autumn shook her head. "I don't want to be a bother." As Autumn shifted, she caught sight of the flower bed by the mailbox. "Oh," she gasped. Autumn turned to look around the yard.

Caroline watched Autumn intently, enjoying the moment of surprise and joy on her face. She and Kate had freshly weeded, mulched, and filled the flower beds with blooming flowers. Cheddar pinks, sweet potato vine, and blue asters filled the beds with color.

Autumn was smiling when she met Caroline's gaze.

"Kate and I thought you might like them." She shrugged. "And Kate was afraid you'd get out and do it yourself if she didn't."

The hint of tears glistened in Autumn's eyes. "They're beautiful. Thank you."

"Come on," Caroline urged. "Let's get you inside so you can rest. I'll make a nice place for you next to the window so you can look out over the garden and the pool, or wherever you want."

Autumn closed her eyes and drew in a deep breath, grateful for her friends. She nodded, letting Caroline lead her to the house. She was finally home. She had pulled it off. She was really home, and her mother hadn't managed to step in and take control of her life.

Autumn stumbled over the threshold of the door. She hadn't realized how many stairs there were in her home until she felt each one rip at her insides as she climbed. She loved her house, but if she ever moved, she would insist on a rancher. If she was going to age in place, there wouldn't be a single step or stairway to her house. Everything would be one level. She groaned as a stab of pain sliced through her abdomen.

"I'm sorry," Caroline said, tightening her hold around Autumn's waist. "I didn't think this part through."

Autumn shook her head. "It can't be helped. There's no way into the house that doesn't require steps. Once I'm inside, I don't think I'll be coming back out for a while, though."

"Where are we headed? Sofa or bed?" Caroline asked.

"Sofa for now. I don't want to lie down just yet. I can recline back for a while and catch my breath."

A sheen of sweat broke out on Autumn's cheeks and neck as Caroline eased her down on the sofa. She was relieved to feel the soft plush fabric beneath her as she settled onto the couch.

"Can I get you something?"

Autumn licked her lips, her erratic breathing a testament to her discomfort. But she didn't complain. "Water."

Caroline got the water and pulled the prescription pain meds from the bag. "Here." She handed Autumn the glass and shook the pill bottle. "Maybe it's a good idea to have one of these."

Autumn shook her head. "Not yet. I think I can make it without those. Just give me a minute." She looked up at Caroline, trying for a reassuring smile but failing miserably.

"Don't be a tough girl. If you need these, you should take them."

Autumn took the bottle and set it aside. "I'm okay. I already feel much better. I think I'll take a little nap for a while before we make the hike to my room."

Caroline nodded. "Okay." She pulled a blanket from the adjacent chair and covered Autumn. She pulled out the recliner, helping Autumn settle into a comfortable position, and then removed Autumn's shoes. "There, you're all set."

Autumn nodded, her eyes already half closed in exhaustion.

"Thank you. I don't know how I would have gotten through this without you." She sighed. "It's good to be home."

Caroline gathered up the book she'd been reading and settled into the chair across from Autumn. She knew she didn't have to hover, but she didn't want to leave Autumn alone. This was a big step for Autumn. She wanted to be there to assure her she would be okay if she needed her.

Caroline watched Autumn sleep. Images of her mother flooded her memory. The old recliner her father refused to give up had been the one spot in the house where her mother could rest. They had moved that chair from room to room, from one end of the house to the other, depending on what mood her mother had been in that day.

She often teased her dad about getting rid of it but understood why he didn't. She too was guilty of stealing moments of comfort in the worn leather. Sitting there was like being held in her mother's arms.

Caroline recognized Autumn's attempts at bravery, her innate desire to protect those around her. Her mother had been the same way. Caroline wondered now what her mother's journey had been like. What truths had not been spoken? What had it been like to face the end of her life? Caroline choked back tears. It had all been so unfair. Her mother had been so young. She still had so much life left to live. But what was fair? Nothing was fair. It wasn't fair that this young vibrant woman in front of her should have to endure this pain. It wasn't fair that she might never have her dreams.

The thought angered Caroline. She sighed, trying to shake the grief from her heart. Autumn still had a chance. Autumn's cancer was different than Caroline's mother's cancer. Dr. Mathis was certain they had gotten all the damaged tissue, but eight of the lymph nodes they had taken during Autumn's surgery had been positive for cancer. Caroline knew the statistics too.

What if the cancer came back? What if it moved to other parts of Autumn's body? Caroline cringed. She prayed that wouldn't happen. She wanted Autumn to be okay. She wanted her to have a chance to make that bucket list, crush it, and start a new one.

A stab of pain hit her as she suddenly thought of Jane. Her own ideas of happiness hadn't exactly worked out like she'd planned. She and Jane hadn't been planners. Jane liked spontaneity. She wouldn't even plan for a vacation, preferring instead to just wake up one morning and decide to take off wherever her mood led her. More than once they had ended up in some remote town with no place to stay. Caroline had learned to keep a tent and a sleeping bag in the car. But most of the time Jane would grab a last-minute flight and spend a weekend in Vegas, or Los Angeles. It had bothered her that Jane could just take off without notice, leaving her home, alone. At the time she'd played it off as part of Jane's quirky personality, that she needed those times to get away and clear her head. But looking back now, Caroline wondered if there was more to it. Had Stephanie really been the only other woman like Jane said, or had there been others?

Caroline pushed her hand through her hair, not liking where her thoughts had drifted. This wasn't about Jane. It was about choices. The truth was, she had been lying to herself about her relationship with Jane from the start. Jane might have delivered the crushing blow, but Caroline shared in the responsibility of the relationship not working. Jane wasn't a bad person. Caroline had loved her. She was starting to accept that was not only true, but it was okay. It was over now. It was time to move on. Time to figure out what she wanted. In the year since she left Jane, she had traveled to every place she had wanted to go during the relationship, every place Jane had convinced her wasn't practical or fun enough to spend their time going to. She had slept under the stars, ridden a train across the country, she had been white-water rafting and even learned to ride a motorcycle. Hadn't she been working her way down her own bucket list? But this year had been different than after her mother died. She hadn't wanted to tempt death. She hadn't been reckless. She was grateful to Jane for bringing that sanity to her life at least.

She looked back at Autumn, watching her chest rise and fall with each breath. Her hands lay limp in her lap. Her eyes fluttered beneath her closed lids. Caroline wondered what she was dreaming. Was it a good dream? Suddenly she imagined her and Autumn strolling along the streets of Taos, plundering through galleries, and drinking wine under the stars. She smiled. Where had that come from? It wasn't that hard to imagine, really. Autumn was easy to be with. They had a lot in common. If the circumstances were different, she knew they would have been good friends.

Autumn reminded her not to take things for granted. She had her own life to live, and it was time she got to it. There were too many things she had given up in the last five years, things that had once been important to her. She had some changes to make, and it thrilled her to have something to look forward to that was her own.

CHAPTER SIX

Caroline put down the magazine she had been pretending to read and made her way to the small table at the back of the waiting room. She poured a cup of coffee and tried not to watch the clock. Dr. Mathis had taken Autumn back almost two hours earlier to insert the port in her chest, giving access directly to the superior vena cava vein just above Autumn's heart. It was a necessary step, but it made Caroline uneasy. The port would allow the doctors to administer medications, especially the chemotherapy, without having to insert an IV line each time. But Autumn would need to be careful. They would need to watch for infection and clotting.

The door to the doctor's office opened and a nurse stepped out. "Caroline?"

"Yes."

The nurse smiled. "You can come back now. She's all done. We're just monitoring her for a while."

"Thank you."

Autumn lay back in a reclined position, her feet up. She smiled tentatively when she saw Caroline.

Caroline returned the smile. "They said you were just hanging out back here, but man, you're getting the royal treatment."

Autumn shook her head and rolled her eyes. "Good thing you missed the torture session."

"Was it that bad?" Caroline asked, taking a seat next to Autumn.

"Not really." Autumn pulled at the edge of the gown. "Want to see?"

"Sure." Caroline was glad her voice was steady, because her nerves were a jumbled mess. She kept her hands clasped in her lap to hide the shaking.

Autumn lifted the gown, pulling the fabric to the side. Small sutures marked the incision that had been made in Autumn's chest just below her collarbone. The skin was raised as if a balloon had been placed just under the skin.

"Wow," Caroline said. "That's a little freaky."

Autumn laughed. "Tell me about it. I feel a little bit like Frankenstein right now. But the wildest part was that I was awake the entire time."

Caroline's eyes widened. "Did you watch?"

Autumn grimaced. "I tried, but that just made me freak out more. Dr. Mathis did a great job of distracting me. I have learned one thing through all of this, though."

"Yeah, what's that?"

"I am not cut out for the medical field. I'll stick with rocks, dirt, and plants."

Caroline laughed. "Good to know you made the right career choice."

They both looked to the door as Dr. Mathis stepped into the room, Autumn's chart in hand. "Hello, Caroline. Good to see you again."

"Hello, Dr. Mathis."

"Well, Autumn, everything looks good. I want you to watch for any redness, streaking, swelling, or discomfort. Any problems, I want you back in here ASAP. Do I need to show Caroline how to flush and clean the port?"

"I'm familiar with the process, but I'd like the instructions anyway," Caroline said flatly.

Dr. Mathis nodded. "Okay, I'll have the nurse run through the process with you both, and then you're free to go. The other good news is that your carcinoembryonic androgen level—that's the tumor marker—has gone down since the surgery, and your white cell count is good. We're clear to start chemotherapy."

Autumn nodded. She had been preparing herself for chemo,

but the thought still made her stomach uneasy. "Thank you," she said, her voice breaking.

Dr. Mathis placed a hand on her shoulder. "Don't you worry. You're going to do fine. In addition to the chemo, I want you to take Neulasta injections every two weeks to help fight infections."

"Okay," Autumn said with a sigh. "Let's get started."

"That's my girl." Dr. Mathis patted Autumn's hand. "I'll see you next week."

The nurse came in only moments after Dr. Mathis left. She thoroughly went through the care instructions. "You can get dressed now. When you're ready, take this form to the window at the end of the hall. Don't hesitate to call if you have any questions."

Autumn blew out her breath as the nurse left the room. "I'm not sure I heard half of what she said."

Caroline handed Autumn her shirt. "That's okay. I can fill in the blanks for you."

Autumn took the shirt and smiled when Caroline turned away. This was getting to be a routine for them. She slipped into her clothes, once again thankful to have Caroline with her. "All done."

Caroline turned to face her. The corners of her mouth lifted in a crooked grin. "Pool time."

Autumn smiled. "You've got that right. I'm beat."

"All right then, let's blow this joint." Caroline reached out her hand to Autumn. "Shall we?"

❖

Autumn stared at her reflection in the mirror. She had lost weight, making the port stand out against her chest with more prominence. She ran her finger along the lines of the incisions, forever reminders of the monster that had invaded her body. She felt fine, but this invisible intruder had somehow slipped inside and threatened everything.

The room was quickly filling with steam as she turned and stepped into the shower. Autumn ran her hands across her body, inspecting her skin, the sensation of touch, the subtle changes to her body. How long had it been since she had been touched by a woman? Would she ever know that pleasure again? Was it too late? What would she do differently if given a second chance? She let the hot spray of the water burn away her melancholy. She set her mind to the future, believing that a second chance was hers to take. She pressed her hands against the wall and drew in a deep breath. She was determined not to let this cancer get the best of her. She had friends and family who needed and loved her. She had a business to run. She still had too much to do to let this slow her down.

The house was quiet as she made her way to the pool. Even though it was still too cool to swim, she found the gentle lap of the water and the soft glow of the lights soothing. Caroline had been gone most of the day, and Autumn found the solitude refreshing, although more than once she had almost called out to Caroline to ask some question that came into her mind. Caroline had so easily become a part of her life that it was hard to imagine her not there.

Caroline was beautiful, thoughtful, and caring, and she made Autumn laugh. She wondered how things might have been different between them if they had met under different circumstances. She imagined meeting Caroline at a dinner party or maybe on a jobsite. What might have happened if she did not have cancer and Caroline was not going through a divorce? She smiled. She knew she would have been wildly attracted to Caroline. She had to admit she had been drawn to Caroline in a way she couldn't remember feeling before. A twinge of sadness passed over her, but she quickly brushed it away. She was glad Caroline was in her life, even if there would never be anything more between them. She had grown to rely on Caroline's caring touch, her soothing voice, and even her cheesy movies. Caroline made her feel safe and loved. She warmed at that last thought. How ironic that it would take cancer for her to open herself up and allow someone in the way she had Caroline.

Autumn sat back against the lounge chair, wishing for a glass of wine. Listening to the night sounds and the water, she drifted off to sleep imagining Caroline's hands brushing through her hair, the tender caress of Caroline's fingers against her skin.

❖

Caroline hung her keys on the hook by the door, listening for sounds that would give her a clue if Autumn was still awake. She checked in the living room and kitchen, then glanced down the hall to Autumn's room. The door was open, meaning Autumn was up, but where was she? Caroline headed for the place Autumn loved most, the backyard. She stopped at the top of the steps on the porch and looked down at Autumn sleeping in a lounge chair by the pool. She stood mesmerized by Autumn's elegant beauty. Her dark hair cascaded onto her shoulders like strands of black silk. Her hands lay still across her lap, her long fingers entwined together. Caroline had the sudden urge to slip her hand into Autumn's, to feel the gentle touch of her strong slender fingers.

Caroline shivered. *Get a grip*, she chided herself.

Despite Caroline's attempts to be quiet, Autumn opened her eyes and met Caroline's gaze as if feeling Caroline watching her.

"Hey. How was your day?" Autumn asked, sitting up a little straighter.

Caroline ran her hand through her hair, still damp with sweat. "I had a good game." She smiled down at Autumn as she stepped closer to the pool. "I was a bit rusty, but it felt good to be back on the pitch."

"Tell me all about it." Autumn brushed her hair back from her face, pulling it to the side and tucking it behind her ear. Caroline imagined her fingers doing the same and shivered at the thought of the simple movement she had done so many times, but in this moment the meaning was much more intimate.

Caroline kicked off her shoes and dipped her foot into the water before sitting to let her legs dangle in the pool. She had to focus. "I didn't know anyone there, but everyone was very nice and welcomed me in right away. I filled in for a couple of games when regular players didn't show up. I think I'll go back. I'd like to play soccer a couple of times a week. Between that and the new gym down the street I should be able to get back in shape."

Autumn scanned Caroline's body, assessing her. Caroline could almost feel Autumn's gaze on her as if she had been touched.

"You seem in perfect condition to me."

Caroline's cheeks warmed. "Thanks. It just feels good to be moving again. I haven't been very disciplined in the past few months. The structure will do me good."

"I'm glad you're finding things that make you happy." Autumn's voice was low and silky smooth as she spoke, making Caroline's skin warm. What was going on with her?

"Me too," Caroline said. "I'm going to take a shower and fix something to eat. Can I make something for you?"

Autumn shook her head. "I ate earlier."

Caroline raised a knowing eyebrow. "Really? What did you eat?"

"Half a cheese sandwich."

"Half? Really?" Caroline stood. "That's an improvement."

Autumn rolled her eyes. "Okay, so maybe the squirrel got the crust of the bread."

Caroline laughed. "That's what I thought. Are you sure I can't get you anything?"

"No. I just want to sit here for a while."

"Okay. Let me know if you change your mind." Caroline jogged back up the stairs, needing to put some distance between them. Autumn trusted her to take care of her, not ogle her when she was sleeping. What was she thinking? It must be the adrenaline from the game. Yeah, that must be it. She was just keyed up and her body was misdirecting that energy. She'd feel more like herself after a shower.

Caroline towel dried her hair as she stepped into the hall. The light was on in Autumn's room and the door was ajar. She padded down the hall and stopped to knock on the door.

"Come in," Autumn said from inside.

Caroline pushed the door open. Autumn sat on the edge of the bed, a brush held loosely in her hand as she looked up at Caroline.

"Are you okay? I saw the light on and thought I'd check in."

"I'm okay," Autumn said, her voice tight.

Caroline stepped farther into the room, noticing the lines of worry creasing Autumn's brow, making her eyes look sad. Caroline sat on the bed next to Autumn. "Do you want to talk about it?"

Autumn sighed. "I don't know what to say."

Caroline knew Autumn was scared. Tomorrow was the first treatment. "Tomorrow is a big day."

"A really big day," Autumn agreed.

"If it were me, I would be terrified."

Autumn dropped her gaze and nodded again. "I have an idea what to expect, but I've heard the horror stories. It doesn't make sense. I have cancer that is trying to kill me, but I feel fine. So now I've signed up for six months of poison that will make me sick in order to save my life."

"It doesn't make sense," Caroline said, validating the madness Autumn had so perfectly described.

"Do you think I'll lose my hair?" Autumn asked, her voice barely a whisper.

"I don't know. Maybe. But if you do, it will grow back."

Autumn nodded. She looked down at the brush in her hand.

Oh, Autumn. "Here. Let me." Caroline reached for Autumn's hand, slowly pulling the brush from her fingers. She crawled onto the bed, sitting at Autumn's back. She gathered Autumn's hair into her left hand and began long gentle strokes with the brush. Normally, she would run from these feelings of pain that struck her each time she saw the flash of fear in Autumn's eyes. But this time, she had the overwhelming desire to be closer to Autumn. From the first day they had met, she had been taken by Autumn's willingness to face her vulnerability. Everything else Caroline had seen about Autumn said that she rarely let anyone see her need, her fear, or her pain. To have Autumn so openly allow her access to those most guarded emotions made Caroline even more determined to protect her.

Caroline stilled her breath as Autumn leaned her head back into Caroline's hands. Her fingers brushed the tender skin of Autumn's neck, sending pleasant tingles through her fingers. Caroline loved the way Autumn allowed her to comfort her. She loved the look of tranquility that passed across Autumn's face as Caroline's fingers ran through her hair. Caroline watched the tiny lines around Autumn's eyes lessen, her breathing slow, and the faint hint of a smile crease her lips. Caroline hoped that each stroke of her hand would chase away all thoughts of poison, cancer, and sickness.

Autumn sighed, making Caroline smile. She could feel the tension ease from Autumn's body. Autumn slowly leaned back until her back rested against Caroline's chest, and she rested her head on Caroline's shoulder. Caroline stilled. Her heart was racing, and she wondered if Autumn could feel it against her back, hear the thundering pulse against her ear. A moment passed, and then Caroline wrapped her arms around Autumn's waist. Caroline let out her breath and eased into the embrace.

Caroline leaned her head against Autumn's, drawing in the scent of her shampoo, reminding her of sunshine and a summer breeze. Autumn's hair had been like silk in her hands and like satin against her cheek as she buried her nose in her hair. She couldn't explain this closeness she felt with Autumn, but she knew she didn't want it to end. But she was certain if she kissed Autumn, it would ruin everything. Autumn was vulnerable, and Caroline was in no position to give her more than the care she had promised.

Caroline was still. She held Autumn in her arms until she felt her drift off to sleep. She gently guided Autumn onto the bed and pulled the covers over her. She sighed as she watched Autumn sleep, her heart heavy with fear and worry for the battle still ahead.

❖

Caroline sat next to the pool, her feet in the water, watching the swirling water echo the churning feelings warring within her. She tried not to think about what the next day would be like.

She could still feel the press of Autumn's body against hers as she'd held Autumn in her arms. She wasn't sure where the sudden need for Autumn had come from or the overwhelming urge to press her lips to Autumn's neck, but she had responded to Autumn. She had been so close to crossing a line. It was the first time she had wanted to touch another woman since Jane. Jane, who had betrayed her trust and her love. She did not want this. Her reaction to Autumn was wrong on so many levels. Autumn was sick, for Christ's sake. The last thing she needed was to have Caroline make a move on her. And the last thing Caroline needed was to fall for another woman who might leave her.

Caroline shook the thoughts from her mind, determined not to think about the heat of Autumn's neck, the silky-smooth strands of her hair slipping through her fingers, or Autumn's body pressed against her breasts.

She looked out beyond the glowing light cast by the pool and the patio lights that illuminated the backyard. She knew the gardens lay hidden in the darkness. She peered past the line of trees she knew lined the property and reached into the past. She hadn't been there for her mother's treatments. Her father had always insisted he be the one to take her. But Caroline clearly remembered the sickness, the debilitating fatigue, the nausea that stole her mother's ability to eat, and the sleepless nights that wouldn't allow her escape from her pain.

These feelings for Autumn were wrong for so many reasons.

CHAPTER SEVEN

The waiting room was smaller than Autumn expected. She noted the chairs lining the wall and placed in rows through the center of the room looked more comfortable than the usual standard waiting room furniture. The seats had plush padding and could be reclined slightly to offer more range of motion and body support. The walls were a calming warm blue, the carpet a darker, richer blue. Pictures of seascapes hung along one wall, while mountain scenes lined another. Gentle music floated through from hidden speakers, just audible enough to soothe without being intrusive.

A young woman who looked to be about thirty, with a petite build and a bouncy energetic stride that said cheerleader, crossed the room and disappeared with a waiting nurse as Autumn signed in. Caroline had taken Autumn's bag and chosen two seats under a watercolor painting of a lake at the edge of a forest with beams of light streaming through the trees illuminating the water.

Autumn took her seat next to Caroline, her body stiff with anxiety. As if sensing her unease, Caroline reached for Autumn's hand. Autumn hesitated. Then, accepting the warmth and comfort Caroline offered, she laced her fingers through Caroline's. The corner of Caroline's mouth lifted in a faint smile.

"You've got this," Caroline said. "I'm right here with you."

Autumn nodded. "Well, at least that's one good thing."

Caroline smiled. "Where else would we be if not here?"

"Oh, I can think of a million things we could be doing." Autumn felt the heat rise to her cheeks as she realized how that sounded.

"Do tell," Caroline said, her smile growing wider.

"That's not what I meant."

"I'm listening," Caroline prodded, rubbing her thumb across the back of Autumn's hand.

Autumn opened her mouth to respond but stopped as her name was called from across the room. She turned to the nurse standing in the open door with a chart held against her chest. Her breath caught as she recognized the tall, thin brunette. Autumn stood, letting her fingers slip from Caroline's. She felt the gaze burn through her as she approached the nurse.

"Hello, Nancy."

"Autumn?" Nancy whispered. "I saw the name on the chart, but I didn't want to believe it was you."

Autumn shrugged. "It's me."

Caroline caught up with them and stepped close. Autumn watched Nancy's eyes drift up and down Caroline's body appraisingly. She looked back at Autumn, her eyes questioning.

"Nancy, this is Caroline. Caroline is helping me through my treatments."

Nancy nodded. "I see." She shifted the file to her other hand and motioned Autumn to the treatment room. She led Autumn to a blue recliner with a table to the left and an IV station to the right.

Autumn settled into the chair as Caroline pulled up a second smaller chair. Autumn realized it was the same setup all around the room. Everywhere she looked, people sat in blue recliners with plastic tubes snaking into their arms or chest. Some wore headphones, others read books, while others played board games with companions.

Autumn spotted the young woman she playfully nicknamed the cheerleader. She talked rapidly to one of the nurses, her hands moving almost as fast as her mouth as she told a story that had something to do with a flat tire and a dog.

Nancy placed her hand on Autumn's arm, drawing her back to her own reality. "Are you okay?"

Autumn nodded. "Fine."

"I'm really sorry about this, Autumn. We're going to take good care of you."

Autumn swallowed. "How have you been, Nancy?"

Nancy shrugged. "Things are good. A lot has changed since—" She stopped. "It doesn't matter. Right now, we need to take care of you."

To her credit, Nancy didn't look away. Autumn wanted to apologize. She should have called. She should have at least tried to be friends. Nancy was a good woman, and she had stuck around longer than most before Autumn's mother had simply become too much to deal with. Autumn didn't blame Nancy for ending things. She would leave too if she could.

"We're going to start you on FOLFOX today, but before we get started, we need to give you something for nausea," Nancy said, forcing the reality of the situation to the front of Autumn's mind. "If we give it first it works better. We'll start with Compazine. If that isn't enough, there are other medicines we can add from here on out. Today will take about six hours."

Autumn nodded.

"You have a port already, right?"

"Yes." Autumn reached for the buttons on her shirt and slowly opened three buttons. A blush rose up Nancy's neck and colored her cheeks. Autumn stilled her fingers. "Uh…"

"That's fine," Nancy said, averting her gaze.

It wasn't like Nancy hadn't seen it before. Autumn turned to see Caroline watching the exchange, a knowing look in her eyes. Autumn felt heat flood her skin as she realized Caroline had figured out that she and Nancy had a personal history.

Autumn closed her eyes. Today was hard enough. She didn't need to bring her sex life into it. She never would have imagined Nancy would be here.

"How long have you been with UT Medical?" Autumn asked, trying to sound normal.

Nancy smiled as she reached for the leads to attach to the port in Autumn's chest. Her fingers brushed against the skin just above Autumn's breast. The touch was necessary in order for Nancy to know where to insert the needle to set up the medication, but Autumn still felt a little embarrassed.

"I made the move three months ago. I was ready for a change," Nancy said conversationally. "So far, I love it here." Nancy leaned back, creating more space between them. "There you go. I'll be by to check on you in a few minutes. I'll let you settle in."

Nancy glanced at Caroline. Autumn saw the question in Nancy's eyes, but she wasn't about to explain.

"Thank you. I admit this is a bit scary. I'm not sure what I should do."

Nancy placed her palm against Autumn's cheek. "There's nothing to worry about. Just relax and try to pass the time. Let me know if you feel sick or have pain. Oh, and don't drink or eat anything hot or cold, and no yogurt. The live bacteria is a big problem."

"Okay."

Autumn turned to Caroline as Nancy walked away. Caroline's eyebrows rose in question, a faint grin forming at the corners of her mouth.

"So, you two know each other?" Caroline said playfully.

"Don't start," Autumn warned, unable to hide her own smile.

"I thought you said you didn't date."

Autumn did smile this time. "I didn't say I never dated. I just said I hadn't dated in a while."

Caroline looked around the room, checking to see where Nancy was. "So what happened between you two?"

Autumn frowned. "Meredith."

"Ah. Momma drama got the best of her?"

Autumn shook her head. "No." She paused. "And yes. The closer we became, the more pressure my mother put on the relationship. Eventually Nancy wanted me to choose between them. I wasn't able to stand up to my mother. When Nancy left, I let her go. I thought it was best, considering. She's a great woman. She deserves to be happy. I didn't think that was possible with me."

"Why?" Caroline asked.

"It's difficult to explain. I guess it was easier to walk away than face my mother."

Caroline looked shocked, her frown furrowing deep lines in her forehead. "Did you love her?"

Autumn stared across the room where Nancy was busy helping another patient. "Yes, I loved her," she whispered, "but not enough."

❖

Six hours later, Caroline helped Autumn into the car, sliding her arm around Autumn's waist, guiding her down into the seat, then helping her lift her legs in. The skin at the corners of Autumn's eyes was creased with pain, her normally vibrant blue eyes dark and glazed. The day had been grueling, to say the least. Autumn had suffered unbearable nausea and more pain than she would admit. Autumn wouldn't say it, but she was exhausted.

The ride home was quiet. Caroline stole quick glances at Autumn as she drove. She wanted so much to ease Autumn's pain. Early on she had teased Autumn about Nancy, then questioned her about her likes and dislikes. They had played chess, and when Autumn grew tired, Autumn had settled for headphones and an audiobook. Caroline had brought her own book but mostly just watched Autumn.

By the time they pulled into the drive, Autumn had drifted off to sleep. Caroline hated to wake her, thinking of the pain that waited for her the moment she woke. Caroline had the unmistakable need to reach out and touch Autumn.

She climbed out of the car and went to Autumn's door, pulling it open and kneeling at Autumn's side. She brushed her fingers lightly against Autumn's cheek.

"Autumn, sweetheart, we're home."

Autumn stirred. Her eyes opened, quickly searching. When her eyes met Caroline's, her gaze burned through Caroline like fire.

"We're home. Come on." Caroline took Autumn's hand, guiding her out of the car, and she slid her arm around Autumn's waist as she got to her feet. "Are you okay?"

Autumn swallowed, nodded, and took a deep breath. "I'm okay. I just want to get inside so I can lie down."

Caroline kept her arm around Autumn as she walked. Each step seemed to take a tremendous amount of effort, and she could see Autumn's strength wavering. This was just the first day—she knew there would be worse days ahead as the treatment began to take its toll. Six months seemed like an eternity.

Caroline held tight to Autumn's hand, but Autumn pushed onward on her own. She never complained. Even when the nausea had become unbearable, Autumn had been reassuring, insisting she was okay. Caroline felt her old anger bubble to the surface. Cancer was such a cruel disease. It was a thief, sneaking into a person without them knowing and robbing them of strength, destroying hope, and vandalizing the body. Cancer destroyed dreams and left pain and despair in its wake. She chewed the inside of her jaw, pushing aside memories of her mother's suffering. She would give almost anything to spare Autumn from that pain.

Autumn squeezed Caroline's hand, pausing at the door to her room. "Are you okay?"

Caroline was surprised by the question, but then Autumn always seemed to know when Caroline was struggling. "I'm fine. I just want to get you settled so you can rest. You've had a tough day."

Autumn wrapped her arms around Caroline's neck and hugged her. "We both had a tough day. But look at us. We made it. One down."

Caroline smiled. "One down."

Autumn hesitated, holding Caroline longer than she knew she should. Caroline's arms were warm and strong around her waist, and she desperately needed that strength right now. The day had been hard, not only because of the toll it had taken on her body, but the emotional price she had paid as well. Her fear had been almost paralyzing, and then there had been Nancy. Regret coated her throat the moment she had seen Nancy. But no matter how she played out the scenario, the ending was always the same. She never could have been everything Nancy needed her to be.

As a teenager, she had foolishly thought that once she graduated and moved far away, she could get on with her own life away from her mother, that she would actually escape the toxic emotional destruction her mother created. But she couldn't have been more wrong. Every time she thought she had captured happiness or attempted an autonomous move that did not include her mother, her mother had managed to draw her back in and basically destroy everything. Five months after leaving home, her mother followed her, showing up at her apartment one evening to take Autumn to dinner. Autumn was surprised she had managed to graduate college. More than once she had left school in the middle of finals when her mother called in a panic, some medical emergency or other equally alarming crisis involving the men her mother dated. After college Autumn had moved to Tennessee and started her own business. For a few years, things had been mostly good. But her mother had eventually followed her here too. Autumn had considered moving again, but she didn't want to give up her friends and her business. Besides, she knew her mother would always find a way to insert herself back into Autumn's life. The situation with Nancy was the most recent in which her mother had managed to drive a wedge between her and someone she was dating. Autumn just hadn't had it in her to try anymore.

This illness, the cancer, had been the first time in her life she had truly put her foot down and put herself first. She'd fought for that independence for the first time as if her life depended on it. She frowned, realizing that very well might be true. Her life did depend on it.

Caroline pulled her arm from Autumn's waist. Autumn missed the touch the instant Caroline withdrew. She steadied herself against the wall as Caroline opened the door.

"Just a few more steps," Caroline soothed.

Autumn allowed Caroline to help her into the bedroom. Caroline leaned down to take off Autumn's shoes. "Do you need help undressing?"

"No. I can do this," Autumn insisted. "I'm just tired, but I can do it."

"Of course." Caroline stood. "Is there anything else I can do?"

Autumn shook her head, biting back the moan stuck at the back of her throat at the thought of Caroline undressing her. Deep down all she wanted was for Caroline to hold her. After the day she'd had, she needed Caroline's touch to remind her that there was still hope, that there was promise in tomorrow.

Caroline pulled away, shoving her hands into her pockets. She looked back as Autumn slid the shirt off her shoulder.

"Can I get you anything?" Caroline asked. "Some water, maybe?"

Autumn looked up and their eyes met. Autumn melted inside, wanting so much to ask Caroline to stay with her.

"No. I'll be okay now. I just need to sleep for a while."

Caroline nodded and left the room, closing the door behind her. Autumn listened for Caroline's footsteps, but there was only silence as if Caroline had stopped just outside the door. She considered calling Caroline back. She could feel her heart beat loud against her ears as if it too wanted to call out to Caroline. A moment later she heard the faint sound of footsteps as Caroline moved away, the steps fading as the distance between them grew. Autumn sighed. She fell back onto the bed, pulling the covers over her. She was just tired. She needed to get a grip. She had already asked too much of Caroline. She would feel better after a little rest.

❖

Caroline went to the kitchen and drew out a beer. She turned on the television, looking through the channels until she found an action film, hoping the senseless, unrealistic violence would distract her from the feelings stirring in her body and the thoughts raging in her mind.

It was hard to leave Autumn, but she knew Autumn needed to rest. She sipped her beer, frustrated by a situation she could not change, and feelings for a woman who was not hers. She sighed. She had too many demons of her own to exorcise. She had no right to these feelings for Autumn. She was no knight in shining armor.

She didn't have the power to do anything about what was happening to Autumn.

She thought of Autumn and Nancy together. She had seen the caring, gentle way Nancy looked at Autumn. And she had seen the pain of regret etched in Autumn's face when they talked. Autumn had denied herself the chance at happiness. She had allowed love to slip through her fingers as if she didn't believe it was something she deserved. If Autumn could deny herself that most basic need, how was she ever going to believe she deserved to win this battle for her life?

Caroline shuddered at the thought. She refused to believe that. Autumn was a fighter. She would do whatever it took to beat this. Caroline thought of what Autumn said about Nancy, how she hadn't been able to choose Nancy over her mother. She couldn't imagine such a thing was even necessary. She clenched her jaw. She would just have to remind Autumn how deserving, how important, and how strong she really was. If Caroline had anything to do with it, nothing and no one would get in the way of Autumn's recovery.

❖

Autumn woke. The room was dark. The faint glow of the streetlight outside filtered through the curtains, dimly illuminating the room. She looked at the clock on the bedside table. It was three in the morning. Had she really slept that long?

She wanted to slide back under the covers and go back to sleep, but the urge to go to the bathroom was persistent and strong. Autumn pulled back the covers and slid out of bed. The wood floor was cool beneath her feet. She didn't bother turning on the lamp, choosing instead to move by the faint light filtering in from the outside. As she made her way back to bed, she thought she heard voices coming from the living room. That was odd. Who could it be at this hour?

Autumn crept down the hall, pausing first at Caroline's door. The door was open, and the light was off. Autumn continued to the living room where she found Caroline asleep on the sofa, a documentary on war machines playing on the television.

Autumn watched Caroline sleep. Her normally watchful blue-gray eyes were closed, making her look younger, peaceful. A month ago, Caroline had been a stranger to her, albeit a beautiful stranger. But in those short weeks, something had been growing between them. Autumn didn't understand it, and she was afraid to speak of it out loud for fear of losing Caroline, but it was there. Caroline had managed to get closer to her in five weeks than anyone had in years. Autumn stared at the sleeping woman, her heart aching with a loneliness she hadn't known she had until Caroline had come into her life. She frowned. Was she just projecting her feelings onto Caroline? She didn't know. All she knew was that Caroline gave her hope.

Autumn turned off the television. She reached out a hand and tenderly brushed her fingers against Caroline's cheek. Caroline stirred.

"Caroline. Caroline. Wake up, sleepyhead," Autumn whispered.

Caroline took hold of Autumn's hand, grasping her fingers, pulling her closer.

The reaction was somehow intimate, and Autumn's breath hitched. She hesitated, enjoying the feel of Caroline a moment longer. She was beautiful.

"Caroline, it's Autumn."

Caroline's eyes shot open with a start. "Oh my God. Are you all right? Is something wrong?"

"No, sweetie, I'm fine," Autumn soothed. She placed her hand on Caroline's chest to keep her still. "Hey, it's okay. I'm okay. I just didn't want you sleeping out here all night. You'll have your neck out."

Caroline peered into Autumn's eyes, searching her face for any sign something was amiss. She brushed her hand across her face. "Oh, thank God," she said, suddenly wrapping her arms around Autumn's neck and drawing her into a hug. "You scared me. I thought you needed me and I didn't hear you."

Autumn pulled back from the hug, but Caroline's arms lingered around her neck. "I'm sorry. I didn't mean to scare you. What are you doing out here anyway?"

Caroline glanced around the room before meeting Autumn's eyes. "I was afraid I would sleep too soundly if I went to bed. I was afraid I wouldn't hear you call for me."

"So you thought you'd stay up all night watching old movies?"

Caroline shrugged. "Something like that. You were so tired when we got back, and you slept for a really long time. I kept checking on you, but you seemed to be resting."

"I was," Autumn agreed. "You don't have to worry so much. I'm feeling better already." Autumn shifted her weight to get a better seat next to Caroline. When she moved, her hand brushed Caroline's breast. Warmth rushed through Caroline like air had ignited smoldering embers to a hot glow.

"I'm sorry," Autumn said, moving to stand.

Caroline grabbed Autumn's hand before she could move away. "Wait," she said, trying to stall. She didn't want Autumn to pull away. "What were you doing out here anyway? Did you need something?"

Autumn shook her head. "I just woke up to go to the bathroom and thought I heard voices out here. I came to investigate."

Caroline rubbed her stiff neck. "I'm glad you did. If I'd stayed here much longer, I wouldn't be able to move my head tomorrow."

"Come on, sleepyhead. Let's get you to bed."

When Autumn didn't move, Caroline realized she still held on to Autumn's hand. "Sorry," she said, letting go. "I guess I'm still a little fuzzy."

Autumn smiled. "It's cute, actually." She stood and held out her hand to Caroline again. "Shall we?"

Caroline took Autumn's hand and followed her down the hall, stopping just outside her door. She tightened her fingers around Autumn's, pulling her closer to her.

"You promise to wake me if you need anything?"

Autumn smiled. "I promise," she said, placing a light kiss on Caroline's cheek. "Good night, Caroline."

"Good night, Autumn," Caroline said, watching Autumn step into her room and gently close the door.

Oh my God. What just happened? Caroline couldn't believe she hadn't heard Autumn get up. She brushed her fingers against her cheek where Autumn's lips had touched her. It was a friendly gesture, she knew, but her body had responded as if Autumn had really kissed her. Caroline rolled her eyes. She had really blown it when Autumn had accidently brushed against her breast. She hadn't been able to control the instant tightening of her nipple and the swift surge of arousal. *What is happening to me? Has it really been so long that I can't control myself?* She didn't want Autumn to think she was coming on to her. That would put an end to everything. And as hard as it was to see Autumn go through the surgery and then the treatment today, it would be even harder to walk away when Autumn still needed her. She would not let that happen. She had to pull it together.

Autumn woke the next morning feeling surprisingly good—not great, but she wasn't sick, and she had been able to rest. She decided to make use of the time while she had it. As she made her way down the hall, she heard the shower running. She decided to make coffee before heading into her study. It was the least she could do. Caroline had been taking care of her for days, and this small thing would at least be something she could offer.

The phone rang, its insistent chirp drawing her to the living room. She checked the caller ID and sighed. She had put her mother off too long, she knew. If she didn't face her soon, there was no telling what stunt her mother might pull.

"Hello, Mother," Autumn said, answering the phone.

"It's about time. I didn't hear from you at all yesterday," her mother said petulantly.

"I had my first chemotherapy treatment yesterday. By the time I got home, I was tired and went to bed early. I didn't really have it in me to do much more than that."

Her mother huffed. "Well, how long do those treatments take, anyway. I can't imagine you couldn't make time to make a simple telephone call since you won't even let me help you."

Autumn gritted her teeth. She knew deep down her mother cared for her, but it would be nice to hear some concern in her voice. She refused to allow her mother to guilt her on this. "Obviously, caring for me isn't on your priority list. I'm sorry me having cancer is such an inconvenience for you," Autumn said sharply.

Her mother gasped. "What's gotten into you, Autumn? Don't be silly. I only want what's best for you."

"Really?" Autumn said, steadying her voice. "Because I just told you that I was tired. I had spent six hours being pumped full of poison, which, by the way, made me sick. If you want to ask me how I'm feeling, ask me how things went, and then we can talk, but I don't have the patience to deal with being guilted because I didn't call you."

"I'm heading downtown this morning." Meredith's voice softened, as if she realized this was not a fight she was going to win. "I thought we could go to breakfast or coffee at least."

Autumn considered going just to keep her mother appeased. She knew she had pushed her and was surprised when her mother had changed the subject.

"I'm pulling into the drive now. I'll see you in a minute," her mother said, ending the call before Autumn could answer.

Autumn turned as Caroline entered the room carrying a steaming cup of coffee. Her hair was still damp from the shower and her skin glowed from the heat of the hot water.

"Everything okay?" Caroline asked, bringing the mug to her lips and blowing across the rim before taking a sip.

"My mother is here," Autumn said, holding up her hands in a frustrated gesture.

Caroline opened her mouth to say something but stopped as the doorbell rang. She reached out, placing a sympathetic hand on Autumn's shoulder. "I'll get it."

Her mother barely waited for Caroline to open the door. She pushed past her as if she wasn't even standing there.

"Good morning, Mrs. Landers," Caroline said as she passed.

Autumn braced herself against the counter, trying to prepare herself for her mother's force of will. "Good morning, Mother. Would you like some coffee?"

"Autumn, you're not even dressed." Meredith looked at her watch. "We need to be going if we're going to get a table. I want to go by the gallery before we meet with Sandra about the opening."

"I'm not going." Autumn held out the fresh cup to her mother.

"What do you mean? Surely you aren't working today?"

"No." Autumn decided she couldn't stomach the coffee and reached in the fridge for a bottle of water. "I don't feel like going out."

"You can't just sit here in your house for the next six months, Autumn. You can at least come to breakfast. Sandra would love to see you."

"I don't feel like going out, Mother." Autumn held her mother's gaze. She uncapped the water and took a sip. Instantly her throat closed. Autumn choked. The bottle hit the floor, spraying water across the room.

Caroline stepped into the kitchen just as Autumn took a drink of water and choked. Autumn grabbed her throat and clutched the counter, gripping the granite so hard her knuckles were white. Caroline grabbed Autumn, rubbing her back, brushing the hair back from her face, peering into her terrified eyes.

"Autumn," her mother screamed.

"Can you breathe?" Caroline asked, holding Autumn's gaze.

Just as quickly at the sensation had come, the tightening grip on Autumn's throat eased. She quickly drew in a deep breath and gasped. She took a couple of breaths and nodded. "Better. Sorry."

"What happened?" Caroline asked, cupping Autumn's cheek in her hand.

Autumn pointed to the water bottle. "Cold water. I forgot they told me not to drink anything hot or cold. I had no idea. It was like someone was choking me."

Caroline stroked her thumb along Autumn's cheek. She smiled. "Good thing it wasn't the coffee."

Autumn let out a tremulous laugh. "My God, that would've been awful."

"Come sit down," Caroline said motioning to the living room. Autumn pulled away from Caroline, straightening and taking a deep breath. She turned to see her mother staring at her, her mouth slightly agape. Autumn almost laughed. If the ordeal hadn't been so uncomfortable, she would have been grateful for the reality check her mother had just witnessed.

"What was that?" her mother asked.

"It's a side effect of the chemo. They warned me about drinking hot or cold things, but I didn't expect that. I wasn't thinking. I guess I have a lot to learn about how this is going to affect me." Autumn walked to the living room and settled on the sofa, followed closely by Caroline and hesitantly by her mother, who looked shell-shocked.

"I'm sorry, Mother. I really can't go with you today."

Her mother seemed to snap back to the present. Her eyes flashed. "Yes, well, I'm sure Sandra will understand." She took an exaggerated sip of her coffee. "I need to go." She carried the cup to the kitchen. When she returned, she kissed Autumn lightly on the cheek. "I'll call to let you know about the plans for the opening."

Autumn nodded. "Tell Sandra I said hello."

Her mother ran her hands nervously down her slacks, then across her blouse as if smoothing invisible wrinkles. She looked as if she couldn't leave fast enough.

"I'll walk you out." Caroline rose.

"No," she snapped. "I can see myself out." She turned her gaze back to Autumn. "I'll expect you for Sunday brunch, Autumn. Don't be late."

Autumn's jaw dropped. The minute the door snapped closed, she turned to Caroline.

Caroline shook her head and shrugged. "I'll add brunch to your calendar."

Autumn laughed. "I guess I should be glad to have the rest of the week to prepare." She frowned. "Remind me not to drink anything else cold. That was awful."

CHAPTER EIGHT

Caroline sat in her car, watching the street—her street, her house. This was the first time she'd returned since the day she gathered her things and left. Everything seemed the same, but somehow everything was different.

Jane had been calling almost daily, insisting that they had to meet before she would sign the divorce papers. Caroline knew Jane thought she could change Caroline's mind if they were alone together in person. There had been a time that would have been true, but not anymore. Caroline knew this part of her life was over. She had spent months driving herself mad remembering the images of Jane and Stephanie together. She had raged against them both. First Jane, then Stephanie. Stephanie had been her best friend, the one person she would normally go to when she needed to talk. That betrayal hurt as much as knowing her wife was cheating on her, lying to her about everything.

Caroline straightened as the garage door opened and a petite blonde in a dark pantsuit stepped out, followed by Jane. Caroline's jaw clenched as she watched the woman take Jane's face in her hand as she kissed her. The blonde walked to her car, lifting her hand in a wave before getting in and driving away.

Jane climbed into her BMW and backed out of the drive. Caroline narrowed her eyes, her resolve solidifying with each second that passed. She didn't feel jealousy at another woman touching Jane. She no longer felt the loss of their love. Coming here had been exactly what she needed. She hadn't been rash in her decision to leave. She hadn't been unfair in her insistence on the separation. She had been right to demand a divorce. She was ready to face Jane. She had moved on. She had known it for months, but Jane's insistence had made her question herself, the way Jane always did when they were on opposite sides of an issue. Not again. Never again would she deny her own feelings, her own needs, her own desires, to placate another. There had been a time when she believed her happiness came from making Jane happy. Now she understood that she wanted more. She wanted a woman who shared her desires too.

Caroline dialed the phone and waited as Jane's voice mail message played. Then she left a message.

❖

Two hours later Jane stepped onto the patio of the coffee shop outside her office. Caroline had insisted they meet in a public place.

Jane smiled brightly and hurriedly crossed the patio. She wrapped her arms around Caroline and kissed her on the lips. Caroline stiffened. Jane pulled away before she could protest, settling her bag beneath her chair and ordering a coffee as the waiter passed.

"I'm so glad you finally agreed to see me. I've missed you so much," Jane said placing her hand over Caroline's. She rubbed her thumb over Caroline's ring finger and frowned at the absence of her wedding band. Jane took a deep breath as if refocusing. "It's so good to see you, but I'm not sure how I should act."

Caroline watched Jane struggle to gain control of the situation. She looked at Jane's face, studied her eyes, searched for a hint of the woman she had loved so deeply. She felt a bit like the curtain had been pulled back to reveal that the wizard was nothing more than an old man twisting dials, manipulating her life. Somehow, she knew that was partly true. She had seen what she had wanted to see in Jane, and part of her loss had been realizing she had been dishonest with herself about their relationship.

"You look well," Caroline said.

Jane propped her elbows on the table and leaned toward

Caroline. "Thank you. You look beautiful. Nice tan. And you cut your hair. I like it." Jane sat back, accepting the coffee from the waiter. She turned back to Caroline. "What have you been doing all this time?"

Caroline avoided the question. "It's time, Jane. I need you to sign the papers."

Jane put up a hand. "I don't want to talk about that yet. I want to talk about you—us."

"There is no us anymore," Caroline said flatly.

Jane closed her eyes and took a deep breath. Caroline imagined her mentally counting to ten. "I haven't seen you in almost a year. In all this time, you never let me explain."

"What is there to explain?" Caroline interrupted. "I saw you with my own eyes. I'm not stupid. I know what sex is, and I know what you look like when you are enjoying a woman."

Jane colored. "I made a mistake. I didn't plan for it to happen. I had closed a big deal that day and had a little too much wine. Stephanie came over to plan a party for your birthday and—"

"I really don't care to hear this," Caroline said, hoping to stop the play-by-play image forming in her mind. "It doesn't matter why it happened now, just that it did. There were obvious problems in our marriage long before that night."

"Okay," Jane acquiesced. "Let's say that's true. We should at least try to work through them. Maybe we could see a marriage counselor?"

Caroline gritted her teeth. "Have you thought about how we got to this place in our marriage? Has anything changed?"

Jane looked confused. "What do you mean?"

"Can you honestly say you want a monogamous relationship?" Caroline studied Jane's eyes, watching the pupils dilate, then recede to pinpricks. She waited for the answer, wondering if Jane had it in her to tell her the truth.

"Sweetheart, you are the only woman I love," Jane answered.

Caroline sat back in her chair. "That isn't what I asked. Tell me, how many other women have there been? I suspect Stephanie wasn't the first, and I know she wasn't the last."

Anger flashed in Jane's eyes before she quenched it. Jane wasn't used to losing.

"That was just sex. You are the one I love. There's a difference. Maybe I can help you understand that if you'll just give me a chance."

"I do understand," Caroline said softly. "And I do believe you love me, at least as much as you can. But we need different things. You need the rush of knowing you can claim a woman. I need to know I am enough. I won't share."

Jane's eyes flicked back and forth as she searched Caroline's until she seemed satisfied with what she saw there. She smirked, cocking her head to the side as if catching Caroline in a lie. "Who is she?"

"What?" Caroline asked, shocked by the question.

"Who is she? The woman who has you thinking you can live without me."

Caroline shook her head. "See, that's another difference between us. There hasn't been another woman in my life since you." The moment the words were out of her mouth, Caroline thought of Autumn.

Jane studied her with a knowing smile. She leaned closer to Caroline. "Keep telling yourself that. You may not have another woman in your bed—yet. But there is someone, even if you don't realize it."

"Don't try to put this on me. I'm not the one—" Caroline stopped herself. She wasn't going to take the bait. "We want different things, Jane. We can't be happy together anymore. I want you to sign the papers. I want this divorce."

Sadness filled Jane's eyes for the first time. "You're serious."

"Yes," Caroline said. "I can't go on like this. I need my life back."

Jane pulled a manila envelope from her bag, opened it, and pulled out the divorce papers Caroline had sent her weeks ago. "I still love you," she said, tears glinting in her eyes. "I know we could work things out. But this time, I want you to be happy more than I want to win." She flipped through the papers, initialing each page, then signing the last page. "You were more than fair with this. Why didn't you ask for more?"

Caroline shook her head. "I never wanted to take anything from you. I only wanted what was already mine."

Jane took a deep breath and sighed. "I guess that's it, then. You'll ride off into the sunset, and I'll never see you again."

"Something like that," Caroline said, not wanting to make any promises of keeping in touch.

Jane nodded. She gathered her bag and stood. "This woman, whoever she is, I hope she can live up to those expectations of yours." She smiled. "If not, you know where to find me."

Caroline watched Jane walk away. If she did give her heart to anyone ever again, she wanted it to be someone who wanted her above all others. Someone who would stand by her through the good and the bad days to come. Was that asking too much? If so, she was content being alone.

The house was dark except for the soft glow of candles. Music wafted through the air, a gentle lilting melody that lifted Caroline's spirt.

"Autumn?" Caroline called. Getting no answer, she made her way through the house, stopping in the kitchen for a beer. She made her way to the back patio, the music seeming to follow her, drifting from speakers strategically mounted throughout the house. Outside, the music continued. The notes seemed to hang in the air, filling the space with energy. Autumn lounged in a floating chair in the pool. Her eyes were closed, her face relaxed and serene.

Caroline opened the beer. The snick of the compressed air startled Autumn, making her jump. The lounger swayed back and forth on the water until she regained her balance.

Caroline laughed. "Looks like you're having a good day."

Autumn smiled and flicked a handful of water at Caroline. "You really shouldn't sneak up on people like that. I could have drowned."

"Whatever," Caroline said skimming her toes into the pool, kicking water back at Autumn. "If that's what you're worried about, maybe you shouldn't sleep in the pool."

"Hmm. Maybe."

Caroline took a drink of her beer. "How are you feeling today?" They had pretty much figured out a routine with the chemo. The first day and two days after that were the worst. The further Autumn got away from chemo day, the better she felt, and although the fatigue and cold sensitivity never went away, most days were tolerable. Caroline knew Autumn pushed herself more than she should, but she had to let Autumn set the pace. She still went into work at least three days every other week, even if she only worked half a day.

"It was a good day. I managed to eat some eggs this morning and macaroni and cheese for lunch. I even managed to mow the lawn."

Caroline choked on her beer. "You did what? Autumn, you should let me do that."

Autumn smiled and shrugged. "It's a small yard, really. It was no big deal. I enjoyed it."

Caroline shook her head. "You better be careful, or word might get out, and your mother will be over here expecting you to go shopping."

Autumn tossed another handful of water at Caroline. "Now you're just being mean."

Caroline laughed.

"What about you?" Autumn asked. "What have you been up to all day?"

Caroline's smile fell and she turned her gaze to something in the distance.

"I went to see Jane."

"Jane?" Autumn asked, sounding surprised.

"My wife," Caroline said in a low voice. "Well, my ex-wife," she corrected, although Autumn knew exactly who she was talking about.

"Oh. How did it go?"

"As good as I could expect, I guess."

Autumn pushed against the water until her float had settled at the edge of the pool next to Caroline. "You don't talk about her much. I didn't know you two were seeing each other."

Caroline looked up surprised. "We're not. I mean, this is the first time I've seen her in almost a year."

"Did something change?" Autumn asked, her voice neutral.

Caroline shrugged. "She's been pushing me to see her. She refused to sign the divorce papers until I did. I think she thought once we saw each other, all the problems would be forgotten, and we'd just go on pretending to have a happily ever after."

"A year is a long time. What made you want to see her now?"

Caroline turned the beer bottle in her hand repeatedly, trying to find the answer to that question. "I guess I was finally ready. I knew that no matter what happened today, I wouldn't be sucked back in. That, and I'm tired of being in limbo. It's time to move on with my life."

"How did it go?"

"Better than I expected," Caroline said with a grin. "I thought she'd put up a fight. But she didn't really."

Autumn rested her hand on Caroline's thigh. "She signed the papers?"

Caroline nodded. "She said my happiness was more important to her than winning."

"Hmm. That's telling."

Caroline laughed. "Isn't it?" She shrugged. "Anyway, it's done. I am no longer a married woman."

"Is that what you wanted?"

"Yes," Caroline answered quickly. "I mean, when I got married, I was all in. I wanted it to be forever. But as I learned the hard way, we wanted different things. This past year has been difficult for me. Even though I knew the relationship was over, I couldn't move on as long as we were still married. Now I'm free to finally do that."

"But?" Autumn asked, reaching down and lifting Caroline's legs from the water, draping them across her lap to steady the raft so she didn't have to keep holding on to the side.

Caroline settled her feet onto the raft with a heavy sigh. "But I feel like I just lost part of my identity. I'm no longer Caroline, Jane's wife. I'm just Caroline. It takes some getting used to."

"It's a big change. I can see now what you meant by needing time to figure out where your life goes from here." Autumn rested her hand on Caroline's leg and massaged her calf muscles. "Is it still what you want?"

Caroline smiled, enjoying the comfort of Autumn's touch and her willingness to listen. "Yes. I've learned a lot about myself and what I want. Next time, if there is a next time, I won't make the same mistakes. I know not to settle for anything less than a one hundred percent commitment. And I won't run from my feelings anymore."

"What does that mean?" Autumn asked.

"When I met Jane, I desperately wanted to escape the grief of my mother's death. I lost myself in the thrill of a new relationship because it was such a contrast to everything else I was feeling. I didn't take the time to heal. I jumped in headfirst. I told myself the red flags staring me in the face were nothing, and I could live with them as long as I had Jane. In the end I wasn't enough for her. She had needs, desires she fulfills with other women. I don't want to share. I want a love that fills me up. I want to be more than enough for someone—I want to be everything." Caroline looked away, embarrassed by her admission. "Not very realistic, huh?"

Autumn stared at Caroline, her gaze sympathetic and reassuring. "I think that's wonderful. Any woman would be lucky to have you. I can't imagine anyone needing anything more."

Caroline felt her skin burn as she blushed from the compliment. "Thank you for saying that."

"I mean it," Autumn whispered. "You deserve so much more. I guess we're both at a crossroads of sorts. We both need to figure out what is important to us and how to get there from here."

Caroline smiled. "We'll get there. It may take a little time, but we'll get there."

"I hope you're right."

Caroline contemplated Autumn for a moment. "What are you looking for in love?"

Autumn laughed. "Who said I was looking? Haven't we already had this conversation?"

"No, I mean it. What do you dream about?" Caroline coaxed.

"Right now, I'm just trying to live through the next few months," Autumn said breathlessly. "I can't imagine anything but that. Until then, what do I have to offer? You see me every day, and most of the time I'm doing good to get out of bed. I don't have the energy for much else. If I did meet someone, what am I supposed to say? Hello, my name is Autumn and I have cancer. Would you like to go to a chemotherapy treatment with me?"

"Autumn..." Caroline spoke in a whisper, pained by the despair in Autumn's voice.

"No. This is my reality right now." Autumn blew out her breath. "Don't get me wrong. I'm not complaining. I know this could be so much worse. Hell, most of the time I wonder what's wrong with me that I don't feel worse. I drag myself through work and don't have anything left. I rarely see my friends right now, and I adore them. I'm not even there to help them prepare for the birth of their child. Without you, I don't know how I would be getting through any of this."

"Maybe we should rethink this." Caroline set the bottle down and reached for Autumn's hands. "Let's change the schedule. You used to have dinner with Kate and Lisa every Friday night. We can still do that. If not every week, maybe every other week. You don't have to go out. We could cook here. It would do everyone good to relax at the end of the week, and Fridays are usually one of your good days."

Autumn peered at Caroline's hands holding hers. "You're right. We should do things differently. I miss them, and I don't want to get to the end of the six months and look back on the time I've missed and regret not living more. It isn't like my life is on pause—the clock is still ticking."

"Okay," Caroline said, smiling. "Let's do that."

Autumn's smile was radiant, as if the sun had burst free of a cloud. The warmth of it made Caroline's skin tingle and suffused her with energy. She laughed at herself. Maybe she needed this as much as or more than Autumn did.

❖

Autumn tossed and turned in her bed that night, unable to sleep. Caroline's question to her earlier reverberated in her head. What was she looking for in love? The question bothered her. She hadn't been a big dater, but she had been involved with a few women over the years, each one special to her in different ways, all ending the same.

She hadn't admitted her growing feelings for Caroline. She had been terrified when Caroline told her she had been to see her ex-wife. She had expected her to say they were reconciling, that she needed to give the relationship another chance. It had been easy to rationalize why she shouldn't have feelings for Caroline when she thought of her as a married woman, but now she was divorced, single. More than that, Caroline had admitted she wanted to move on, was looking for love. The timing sucked. Autumn had meant what she said about having cancer. Until she knew if her cancer would respond to treatment, she couldn't get involved with anyone. That wouldn't be fair. But she had been attracted to Caroline from the moment they met. She had told herself that the intimate moments they had shared were innocent, that the feeling she had for Caroline was misplaced gratitude. But as they had talked by the pool and she had held Caroline's legs in her lap, felt Caroline take her hand, she wanted it to be so much more.

Why am I torturing myself like this? Even if there was something between us, it isn't fair to do this to Caroline. She's already lost so much. Autumn closed her eyes against the pain of realizing this was one more dream she would have to let go.

Frustrated, she slipped out of bed. As she moved down the hall, she stopped at Caroline's door, listening for any sounds to suggest that she might be awake. Hearing nothing, she continued to the study. She flipped on the desk lamp and sat down, feeling the leather cradle her body. She loved this chair. She fished through the top drawer until she located a small black journal. She opened it, then thumbed through its pages as if plundering a treasure chest. She smiled at the sketches she had made of the pool and patio when she was renovating this place. Then there was the brochure about Hawaii she had saved from the travel agent client who'd tried to sell her on a trip. She smiled at the thought of trekking through rainforests, peering into volcanos, bathing in the spray of a waterfall, and surfing a big wave.

Autumn smiled, turning to a blank page. She picked up her favorite fountain pen and wrote at the top of the page: *Autumn's Bucket List.*

CHAPTER NINE

Caroline turned the burgers and added hot dogs to the grill. Autumn was seated comfortably by the pool, talking with Lisa about the baby, while Kate did a perimeter check of the grounds, taking notes of what needed to be done around the yard and in the gardens in the coming weeks.

"Hey," Kate said, as she slipped a beer from the cooler. "Need any help?"

Caroline looked up. "No, I've got it. Just relax."

Kate stepped closer to Caroline, keeping her voice low when she said, "How is she doing, really?"

Caroline smiled. "She's surprisingly good. She has her bad days, but I've been amazed at how strong she is."

Kate took a sip of her beer. "Did she really mow the yard again?"

"Yep. Despite my protests, she won't have it any other way." Caroline glanced around to make sure they weren't overheard. "Honestly, I think she needs it. I think it's important for her to feel like she isn't losing control."

"Yeah," Kate said, running her hand through her hair. "She's the same way at work. She doesn't actually get out there and pick up rocks or shovel dirt, but she's still on top of everything that's going on. I don't know how she does it. She can get more done in three days than I feel like I get done all week."

Caroline laughed. "I know what you mean. The night of her first treatment she came home beaten into the pavement. I was really worried about her. She went to bed to get some rest, and the next thing I know it's three in the morning and she's waking me up to go to bed myself. I didn't even hear her get up. But to be honest, she has some really bad days. The treatment weeks are pretty hard on her, and it seems that just when she starts feeling better, it's time for another treatment."

Kate looked over her shoulder to where Lisa and Autumn sat talking. Caroline understood her instinct to have her eyes on Lisa every few minutes. Add what Autumn was going through, and it seemed Kate was almost crazy with the need to hover.

"They're okay," Caroline said, sensing Kate's unease.

Kate smiled and took another sip of her beer. "I can't help it. Autumn is getting so thin." She sighed. "I can't imagine what a wreck I'll be once the baby gets here."

"You'll do great."

"Yeah, we'll see, won't we?" Kate said with a nervous laugh. "Thanks for setting this up, by the way. We've missed Autumn terribly but had no idea how to get her to let us in. This feels like old times."

"I'm glad I could help," Caroline said. "Hand me that platter, the dogs are ready."

Kate helped Caroline with the hot dogs and set things up for the burgers. Caroline had cooked enough for an army. "What's this?" Kate asked, lifting the lid on a Crock-Pot.

"Mac and cheese," Caroline answered. "It's for Autumn. It's about all she can eat right now. Most food has a bad taste to her. That's the one thing she can eat. Well, that and scrambled eggs."

"Huh." Kate shrugged and returned the lid. "Does that mean we can't have any?"

Caroline laughed again. "No. There's plenty for everyone. It's a good thing you like it. I bet you'll be having a lot of it once that little girl gets here and discovers cheese."

Kate laughed. "No doubt."

They gathered the rest of the food and set the table.

"All right, you two. Time to eat," Caroline called. She watched Autumn slowly rise from her chair. She knew this was going to push the limits of her energy, but Autumn had refused to cut back on her day. A stab of worry swept over her as Autumn stopped to steady herself against the lounger. Caroline wasn't fooled by Autumn's attempt to hide her discomfort by reaching out and offering her hand to Lisa. Lisa, as it turned out, was having even more trouble figuring out how to get out of the low-seated chair.

Caroline took a step toward the two but stopped just as Lisa took Autumn's hand and heaved herself up. Kate was a second too late for the job but slid her arm protectively around Lisa to keep her from toppling over. Caroline was even more relieved when Kate reached out a hand and placed it against Autumn's back. The gesture was subtle, but Caroline recognized the worry in Kate's eyes.

Autumn looked over to Caroline and caught her watching them. Autumn flashed Caroline one of her heart-stopping smiles. Caroline caught her breath, feeling a tingling sensation start in her chest and work its way down to more intimate places. She gasped as if she'd been touched. She returned the smile, happy to be a part of putting that smile on Autumn's face.

From the moment they met, Caroline knew Autumn would be important in her life. She felt drawn to her right away. She hadn't been wrong. Autumn was important. They had become friends, but Caroline knew what she was feeling for Autumn in that moment was much more than friendship.

"So, tell me about Caroline. How are things going, huh?" Lisa asked playfully as she and Autumn cleared away the last of the dishes.

"What do you mean?" Autumn asked, pretending not to know what Lisa was talking about.

"You know what I mean. She's gorgeous. Did you actually just put out an ad for her?"

Autumn shook her head. "Stop it. It wasn't like that, and you know it."

Lisa leaned her hip against the counter and watched Kate and

Caroline through the window. "Really, Autumn, tell me you've noticed how hot she is."

Autumn placed the last plate in the dishwasher and turned to face Lisa. Before she could answer, she saw Caroline through the window and was suddenly taken by how attractive she was. "Yes, I've noticed," she said softly. "But don't get any ideas. This is a job for her, remember. We're just friends."

"Friends with benefits?" Lisa teased, her eyebrows raised suggestively.

Autumn rolled her eyes. "As if. What are we, nineteen? Besides, it isn't like I could do anything about it anyway."

Lisa's gaze flashed to Autumn. "Is everything going okay? Are you having problems with the treatments?"

"No," Autumn said quickly. "Nothing like that. But I'm not exactly a catch. I mean, who wants to meet someone and fall in love if it might only be for a few months, or a couple of years."

"Oh, Autumn, honey. You can't think like that. Besides, if anyone deserves happiness, it's you."

"Thanks." Autumn put her arm around Lisa and squeezed. "I've missed you."

Lisa smiled. "I've missed you too. I hope we get back to doing this more often."

"Me too." Autumn looked back to the yard. "Should we go break up their bonding moment?"

Lisa cradled her hand beneath her stomach. "Yes. I hate to leave so early, but my feet are swelling, and I'm ready to get out of these clothes for the day. My underwear is cutting into me." Lisa grimaced. "Sorry if that's too much information."

"Not at all." Autumn laughed. She followed Lisa outside. She knew Lisa was bowing out because she could tell Autumn was tired, and she appreciated her not saying so.

"Next time I expect more details about tall, blond, and gorgeous," Lisa said, leaning close to Autumn's ear as they approached Kate and Caroline.

"So," Lisa said to Caroline. "What bad idea has my wife talked you into while we were away?"

Caroline laughed at the incredulous look on Kate's face.

"What makes you say that?" Kate fussed.

Lisa smiled and placed a kiss to Kate's lips. "I know you, sweetie. You're always up to something, and it's usually a bad idea."

Kate stuck out her bottom lip in an exaggerated pout.

"Don't mind them," Autumn said, stepping close to Caroline. "They pick at each other, but it's never serious. I think it's a game they play so they can have makeup sex."

Caroline laughed. "That's not a bad idea." The instant the words were out, Caroline felt heat rise to her cheeks. She hadn't meant to sound suggestive. She glanced at Autumn and caught the slight rise of her eyebrow as the corner of her mouth quirked in a faint smile.

Lisa bit Kate's lip. "Come on, love, take me home."

Kate looked to Autumn apologetically. "Thanks for having us over. Everything was great." Kate put her arm around Autumn, pulling her into a hug. As she pulled away, she looked as if she wanted to say something, but then the moment passed, and she just grinned. "I'll see you next week, boss."

"Sure thing." Autumn patted Kate's back.

Kate paused. "You have another treatment Monday, right?"

"Yeah, why?" Autumn answered, her brows knitting together in a frown.

Kate shook her head. "Just keeping up. I'm counting down the weeks."

Autumn had the feeling there was more to this story, but Kate was obviously worried about something and didn't want to talk about it. She would have to dig a little more once they were at the office. Was something going on with Lisa and the baby? Was there something they weren't telling her?

Lisa kissed Autumn on the cheek and squeezed her hand. "We love you. You know that, right?"

"I know." Autumn smiled. "I love you too."

As soon as the door closed, Caroline turned to Autumn. "How are you holding up?"

Autumn grimaced. "I feel like I've been run over by a bulldozer." She met Caroline's concerned eyes. "But I've had a good day. Thank you for this. Thank you for knowing what I needed, even when I didn't."

Caroline smiled, brushing her fingers lightly down Autumn's arm. "You're welcome. Now, what's going to help you relax and get some sleep? Foot rub, bedtime story?"

Autumn laughed. "Hardly. I think I'll just turn in." She turned to go but stopped and turned back to Caroline. "But I'll take a rain check on that foot rub."

"Anytime," Caroline said, smiling. "You just say when." Caroline's heart fluttered at the thought of her hands massaging Autumn, soothing her with her touch. She bit down on the inside of her lip, her heart beating rapidly. She took a deep breath to settle the surge of energy slowly infusing her body.

Caroline waited for the light to go out in Autumn's room before turning in herself. It had been good to see Autumn smile and laugh with her friends. She liked Kate and Lisa, and they clearly loved Autumn. Who wouldn't love Autumn? She was amazing. She was smart, funny, kind, hardworking, and stunningly beautiful. She just had that one little problem—cancer. Caroline sighed. But that was temporary. Autumn was a fighter and Caroline believed she was going to make it. She had to believe that. Because a world without Autumn in it was beyond her imagining.

Caroline closed her eyes, conjuring the brilliant smile Autumn had flashed her earlier. She wanted to fall asleep to that smile. She wanted to dream of that smile. *Autumn.*

❖

Autumn looked up from the book she was reading to see Caroline coming down the hall wearing soccer shorts and a T-shirt. Her gym bag hung from her left shoulder. Autumn trailed her eyes down the long lean muscles of Caroline's legs, which looked powerful and strong as they flexed.

"Ready for the game?" Autumn asked.

Caroline grinned, her eyes flashing with excitement. "I'm always ready for soccer."

Autumn watched as Caroline tied her shoes. "Can I come? I'd like to see you play." The words were out before Autumn could think about what she was saying. "Unless you'd like some time away from me. I mean, I don't want to intrude on your personal time."

Caroline looked up as she finished tying her laces. "I'd love for you to come," she said excitedly. "Are you sure you feel up to it?"

Autumn shrugged. "I need to get out. I'm going a bit stir-crazy."

"It's settled, then. Can I get you a jacket or a blanket?" Caroline asked. "It can get a little chilly being indoors with the air-conditioning."

"I'll get it. I'll meet you at the car." Autumn left the book on the coffee table, a sudden rush of excitement causing her heart to flutter. It had been weeks since she'd looked forward to doing something outside the house that wasn't about work. This felt like an adventure, not just an indoor soccer game. She was going to get to see Caroline play. She felt heat flush her cheeks, an image of Caroline sweat drenched and out of breath flashing in her mind. She shook herself. Since when did a game of soccer become sexy? She laughed. Anything Caroline did would be sexy.

Autumn climbed into the car a few minutes later, noticing Caroline had the heat on low. Autumn had been having trouble regulating her body temperature during her treatments and her hands and feet were always painfully cold. She reached out and brushed her fingers along Caroline's hand. "Thanks."

"For what?" Caroline said smiling.

"For letting me come with you, for…for everything."

Before Autumn could pull her hand away, Caroline clasped her fingers. "Let's go have some fun."

The sports complex was only a few miles from Autumn's house, but she had never been there. She observed the thin indoor-outdoor carpeting through the entryway, an indoor court to her right, and a room to the left with large mats on the floor where several young girls were practicing tumbling. There was a long row of batting cages at the rear of the building, the sharp crack of the bat hitting the ball bursting every couple of seconds as young men and women practiced their swings. They turned right, walked along the batting cages, and turned into one of the indoor courts. Several men and women were already warming up, dribbling and passing the ball, stretching, and chatting about the game.

Autumn took a seat on a low row of benches while Caroline changed her shoes, slipped on shin guards, and stored her bag.

"Are you okay?" Caroline asked, a hint of worry in her eyes.

"I'm fine. Go on. Don't worry about me—just have fun."

Caroline smiled before sprinting onto the field.

Autumn watched Caroline talk to several players before joining in on some simple passing drills with a couple of the women from her team. When the game started, everyone moved so fast it was hard for Autumn to keep up. Caroline stole the ball from another player in a fierce battle of feet and body shoves, but she broke free, running ahead a few feet before passing the ball, which her teammate quickly kicked toward the goal. The goalie launched herself into the air, her body almost vertical, her fingers grazing the ball, but unable to stop the goal. Score!

Autumn felt a surge of adrenaline as the ball sailed through the air and smacked the back of the net. There was hardly a moment of rest before the ball was back in play and the battle was on again.

"Hi," a young woman said, sliding onto the bench beside Autumn. "I haven't seen you here before."

Autumn turned, meeting deep brown eyes cloaked in thick dark eyelashes. Her skin was a rich copper, her hair glossy black. She looked at Autumn appraisingly.

"Hello," Autumn replied. "This is my first time."

"Lucky me," the woman said, dropping her gaze to Autumn's lips. "I'm Cora." She reached out a hand to Autumn.

"Autumn," she replied, taking the offered hand.

Cora tilted her head to the side, looking Autumn over. "Are you here to play or just watch?"

"I'm just watching."

"Ah, I see. Which of our beautiful jocks is yours?" Cora asked, never taking her eyes off Autumn.

Autumn laughed. "No one is mine. I came to see Caroline

play." Autumn pointed to the pitch where Caroline was chasing the ball alongside her opponent, fiercely battling for position.

"Hmm, yes, she is...very nice."

Autumn felt the sudden stab of jealousy as Cora watched Caroline.

"You two aren't together?" Cora asked. Her voice thick and suggestive.

"No. Friends," Autumn answered. She wanted to change the subject. She didn't want to have to think of Caroline or who they were or weren't to each other. "How about you? Do you play?"

"Oh yes, I'm in the next game. Would you like to stay and watch? We could...talk, after."

Autumn swallowed, realizing Cora was hitting on her. "I would love to, but I already have plans this evening."

Cora pursed her lips in an exaggerated pout. "Too bad. Maybe next time."

A chorus of shouts caught Autumn's attention, and she turned to see what was happening in the game. A player broke into a run with the ball, and his defender gave chase. Just as it looked like he would be overtaken, he kicked the ball forward, sending it sailing through the air to the other side of the pitch to the right of the goal. Caroline and another player jumped into the air simultaneously, throwing their heads into the ball's path. Caroline connected and sent the ball flying into the goal just as her head collided with the other player's. Both women hit the ground hard, and Caroline lay still, while the other woman writhed on the ground, holding her head in her hands.

The crowd cheered as Caroline scored the goal, and then fell into a collective moan as she hit the ground. Autumn was on her feet instantly. The referee stopped the game as several players went to their fallen teammates. Autumn hadn't seen Caroline move. She held her breath. *Oh no. She's not moving.* Autumn couldn't stand by and just watch. She bolted onto the field, running toward Caroline. She pushed a player aside. "Let me through." She kneeled on the ground beside Caroline as someone felt for her pulse and checked her neck for injury.

"Caroline, can you hear me?" Autumn spoke sharply, her voice pleading.

Caroline groaned and tried to open her eyes. Her head hurt like hell and her vision was blurred. She heard Autumn's voice.

"Caroline, can you look at me, sweetheart?"

Caroline blinked. What had happened? Was Autumn okay?

"Be still." Autumn's voice again. Gentle fingers brushed the side of her face. She groaned as a terrible pounding beat inside her skull. She lifted her hands to her head, trying to push the pain away. Despite the pain, her vision started to clear. She looked up into Autumn's fierce blue eyes.

Autumn smiled down at her, worry and relief clouding her face. Caroline realized where she was as the memory of what happened came into sharp focus.

"I'm okay," Caroline muttered, trying to keep her voice steady. "Just a little dazed is all." She forced her eyes to remain open.

"An ambulance is on the way," a deep voice said from behind.

"No," Caroline protested. She tried to sit up, but the pain in her head intensified and her stomach did a roll. *Please don't let me be sick in front of all these people. God, Autumn doesn't need to see this.* "Give me a minute. I'll be all right."

Caroline took a deep breath, then another, until she felt the nausea ease. But before she could manage to get up, the paramedics were there.

Autumn stepped back to let the paramedics work. A stocky brunette, her hair pulled back at the base of her neck, kneeled beside Caroline. She brushed the hair away from Caroline's forehead, revealing a goose egg that was already purple.

"Did you lose consciousness?" the medic asked.

"I don't think so," Caroline said, trying not to flinch when a bright light was shined into her eyes, making the already excruciating pain pierce through her brain like a lance.

"Yes, she did lose consciousness," Autumn said, leaning closer. "She was out for a few seconds at least."

The medic nodded. "We need to get you to the hospital and

have your head looked at. You at least have a concussion, and we need to make sure there's no bleeding on the brain."

Autumn gasped.

"No. I don't want to go to the hospital. I'll be fine," Caroline said, pushing away from the medic.

Autumn leaned down next to Caroline. "You have to go to the hospital. This is serious, Caroline."

"I need to get you home," Caroline protested. "You need to rest."

"What I need is for you to stop being so stubborn and listen to this kind woman who's trying to help you. I'm telling you—go to the hospital."

Caroline sighed. "Okay, I'll go if you'll take my car home. I'll get an Uber to drive me back when I'm done."

"I'm not leaving you." Autumn grasped Caroline's hand. "I'll follow you to the hospital."

"No," Caroline argued. "You don't need this stress, and there will be sick people at the hospital. I don't want you getting exposed to anything. You can't afford to get sick."

Autumn leaned close to Caroline and whispered into her ear, "I need you to let me take care of you for once. Don't argue with me. I'll be sick with worry if I'm not there with you."

Caroline closed her eyes as Autumn's warm breath brushed across her skin. *How could she say no? She wouldn't deny Autumn anything if she would keep talking to her like that.* Caroline leaned into Autumn, cherishing the feel of her skin against her cheek.

"Okay. Just don't let go."

Autumn smiled. "I'll be there the whole time. I promise." Autumn nodded to the medic, who quickly prepared Caroline and helped her partner get her onto the stretcher. "Which hospital will you be taking her to?"

"UT," the male medic answered as they wheeled Caroline away.

❖

Autumn grabbed Caroline's bag from beneath the bench and followed them out. Her heart was pounding, and her hands were still shaking. The sight of Caroline lying on the ground, not moving, had shaken her. It was all she could do to let Caroline go in the ambulance without her. Caroline needed her, and no one was going to stop her from being there.

She met the ambulance at the ER just as they were taking Caroline inside. She managed to dig through Caroline's bag to find her wallet. After a few minutes of rifling through the contents she managed to locate her insurance card.

Caroline squinted against the bright lights as she recited her health information. No allergies. No medications, no surgical history. When Caroline started to count off multiple fractures to her fingers, wrist, ankle, and radius, Autumn tried to contain her shock.

She gripped Caroline's hand. What the hell had Caroline been doing to get all those fractures?

The doctor did a brief neurological exam, looked into Caroline's eyes and her ears, and checked for signs of other injuries.

"How is your head feeling?" the doctor asked, resting her hand on Caroline's shoulder.

Caroline squinted at her. "Like I just headbutted a bull."

"That's what I thought. Have you had a concussion before?"

"Yes. I know the drill. I was out for a bit, but my memory seems okay as far as I can tell, and I didn't throw up."

The doctor scribbled something in Caroline's chart. "How long ago was your last concussion?"

Caroline hesitated. "At least four years."

The doctor nodded. "I need to send you up for a CT scan so we can get a look inside to make sure there isn't any internal bleeding."

"Yeah, okay," Caroline conceded.

The doctor patted Caroline's shoulder again. "Someone from CT will be down to get you shortly. Hang tight. It won't be long."

Caroline turned to Autumn. "How are you doing?"

Autumn smiled. "I'm fine. It's you I'm worried about."

"Don't." Caroline squeezed Autumn's hand. "You should go on home and get some rest. You look beat."

"I'm tougher than I look. I can stay awhile." Autumn leaned closer to Caroline. "I made a promise, remember?"

"I remember." Caroline shrugged. "This isn't exactly the night out I had hoped to give you."

Autumn smiled. "I could have done without the heart-wrenching fear and seeing you hurt, but before all of that, I was having a good time."

"Hmm." Caroline frowned. "I saw you met Cora."

"I did." Autumn didn't volunteer any information about their conversation or Cora's proposition. "Do you know her?"

"Just around the field. She's beautiful and seemed very interested in you."

"Ah, well, *interested* might be a bit overstated."

"Why?"

Thankfully they were interrupted by the nurse. Autumn didn't want to talk about Cora.

The nurse patted Caroline's hand. "I'm taking you to CT. This could take a while, so don't worry. We'll bring you back as soon as we can." She looked at Autumn. "You can hang tight here or wait in the lobby if you like."

"I'll wait here." Autumn watched as the nurse pushed the bed with Caroline in it out of the room and down the hall. Her stomach was in knots, and she wasn't sure what she needed to do. The thought of a brain bleed scared her. What if something happened to Caroline? Who should she call? She didn't even know how to get in touch with Caroline's father.

Autumn had been waiting for about an hour when the curtain opened and a young woman stepped in. She was elegantly dressed in cream-colored slacks, a blue silk blouse, and a silver chain around her neck holding a tear shaped pearl just at the crest of her breasts. Her blond hair was loose and fell to her shoulders. Her nails were perfectly manicured and her makeup flawless. Autumn didn't think this was one of the doctors.

"Can I help you?" Autumn asked.

The woman regarded her. "I'm looking for Caroline Cross. I was told she would be here."

Autumn stood. "And you would be?"

"Jane Cross. I'm her wife."

Autumn barely held back a gasp. She swallowed as realization hit her. Caroline must have had Jane listed as her emergency contact.

Autumn held out her hand. "Autumn Landers, I'm a friend of Caroline's. They took her back for a CT scan. She should be back anytime now."

Jane didn't move. She just stood there staring at Autumn as if she was an intruder in her home.

"Would you like to sit?" Autumn offered. "It really shouldn't take long."

Jane moved to the chair across the room from Autumn. "Tell me what happened. What did she do to herself this time?"

Autumn took a deep breath. This was Caroline's wife, but she wasn't comfortable disclosing information about Caroline. Jane's stare was worried and determined. Autumn decided some disclosure was warranted given the situation. "Soccer. She was heading the ball and unfortunately collided with another player. They have confirmed a concussion, but they want to rule out anything more serious."

Jane rolled her eyes. "Soccer again. She gave that up years ago. What was she thinking?"

Autumn wanted to ask what Jane meant but didn't feel like it was her place. Besides, she would prefer to get her answers from Caroline.

Jane openly appraised her. "Tell me, how long have you been seeing my wife?"

Autumn almost choked. "What?"

"You heard me."

Autumn was shocked. She shook her head. "Um, I'm afraid you have the wrong idea. Like I said, Caroline and I are friends."

A muscle jumped in Jane's jaw. She seemed about to say more but was stopped when the curtain slid back and the nurse wheeled Caroline into the room. She secured the bed and moved about the room as if she and Jane weren't there.

The instant Caroline saw Jane, all the color drained from her face. The muscle in Caroline's jaw jumped as she gritted her teeth.

As soon as the nurse closed the curtain, Jane rushed to Caroline's side and brushed her fingers over the bruise on Caroline's forehead. "Oh, love, what have you done this time? Are you okay? Does it hurt?"

Caroline caught Jane's hand, pushing it away from her face. "What are you doing here, Jane?"

Jane looked wounded. "The hospital called. Of course I got here as soon as I could when I heard you were hurt."

"I'm fine. There's no need for you to be here." Caroline glanced at Autumn.

"Yes, I can see you are in good hands," Jane said softly, acknowledging Autumn.

Caroline sighed. "I'm sorry. You shouldn't be here."

"I'm your wife. I have a right to be here."

"Ex-wife," Caroline said, her voice firm. "I simply forgot to change the information on my insurance card. I'm sorry you came all the way down here. There was no need. I'll make sure no one bothers you with that again."

"Care," Jane said, her voice pleading, "we can do better than this. I'm always going to care about you. What are you doing playing soccer again? I thought you gave up all that nonsense."

"I made the mistake of giving it up because you didn't like it. I do. So I'm playing." Caroline squeezed her eyes closed and took a deep breath. "Look, I appreciate you caring enough to come down here, but you don't have to stay. I'm really okay."

Jane straightened. "What will be next, rock climbing, a motorcycle, BASE jumping?" Jane took a deep breath. "I'm sorry I hurt you, Care." The frustration that had been clear in her voice earlier had changed to concern. "I don't know what you're trying to prove, but please, try not to get yourself killed." Jane leaned down, brushed her thumb along Caroline's cheek, and kissed her tenderly on the lips. "I hope you come to your senses soon, love. I'm here if you need me."

Autumn was touched by Jane's caring. She wasn't sure what she'd expected, but this tenderness wasn't it. She couldn't help but wonder what had come between them. And she was more than curious about what Jane meant about Caroline getting hurt. She wasn't sure what to say after Jane left. She chanced a glance at Caroline. The silence was deafening, and Caroline was obviously uncomfortable with what happened.

"Wow. So that was the wife," Autumn said lightheartedly.

"Ex-wife," Caroline corrected. She reached out for Autumn's hand. "I'm sorry about that."

"Don't be. She seemed really worried about you."

Caroline nodded. "I can be a little accident prone. She never liked me playing sports."

Autumn thought of all the broken bones Caroline listed during her admission. "It sounded pretty serious."

Caroline sighed. "After my mother died, I got a little reckless. I couldn't feel anything. So I got into some extreme sports. I did a few things that I'm lucky I lived through. When I met Jane, she steered me away from that life."

"It sounds like she was trying to take care of you."

"She was. At first, I gave up the extreme stuff, but then more and more of the things I loved became stressors. As time went on I did less and less of the things I loved, and I started modeling my life around what made Jane happy. When things between us fell apart, I didn't recognize my life anymore. It feels good to challenge myself again."

"Is it dangerous?"

"No. I haven't gotten that extreme again. But it would seem that I haven't quite figured out how to avoid getting a little banged up. I never meant to put you through any of this."

Autumn smiled. "I'm glad you're okay. And it was kind of nice to get to take care of you for a change."

Caroline brought Autumn's hand to her lips and kissed the back of her fingers. "I should let you take care of me more often."

Autumn felt her blush deepen, this time morphing into a hot ball of fire that went straight to her core. She drew in a deep breath.

God, she has no idea how sexy she is. How can one simple touch do this to me?

"Anytime," Autumn said, her voice coming out husky and low. "I like taking care of you."

"We make a good team then," Caroline said giving Autumn's hand a squeeze.

"Yeah," Autumn said, and her heart fluttered. "We do."

❖

Two hours later Caroline was released from the hospital. The CT scan had been clear, but she had been required to stay for a while for observation, and it was midnight by the time they got home. Autumn was so tired she was barely able to stand. She tried to hide her fatigue, but she could feel Caroline's assessing gaze on her. Autumn wanted nothing more than to crawl into bed and sleep, but she was afraid to leave Caroline alone. The concussion wasn't severe, but any concussion was serious.

"What do you say we crash on the couch and watch movies the rest of the night?" Autumn asked, trying to think of a way to keep an eye on Caroline.

Caroline stopped her before she could turn on the TV. She pressed a hand to the small of Autumn's back and slid the remote from her hand. "The last thing you need is to sit up all night watching movies. You need to rest. You're about to fall over."

Autumn straightened, her arm brushing lightly against Caroline's breast. Caroline didn't step away. She held Autumn's gaze. Their lips were only inches apart. Autumn could feel Caroline's breath on her mouth. She wanted so much to close the distance between them and taste Caroline's lips.

"It's my turn to take care of you, remember," Autumn whispered, her eyes falling to Caroline's lips.

"You have," Caroline said, running her fingers into Autumn's hair, massaging her neck.

Autumn forgot to breathe. She wanted Caroline to kiss her. She couldn't move. Her lips parted. "You had a rough night. I'm afraid of what might happen if you go to sleep. The doctor said you should be monitored for at least twenty-four hours."

"You could always sleep with me."

Autumn gasped. "Caroline—"

Caroline laughed. "Just sleep, Autumn. I know you're beyond tired. I'm practically asleep on my feet myself. We should stay together tonight. That way we can keep an eye on each other."

Autumn grinned. "That's your plan?"

"That's my plan. Unless you're going to seduce me?"

Autumn's heart beat rapidly. Her eyes fell to the pulsing vein in Caroline's neck, the pulse matching the beat of her own heart. Was Caroline feeling as excited as she was? Autumn reached up and skimmed her fingers over the lump on Caroline's forehead. Her legs grew weak at the thought of Caroline being injured. "You better stay on your toes then, Ms. Cross. There's no telling what could happen."

Caroline's eyes darkened. She pulled her hand from Autumn's neck, letting her fingers trace the line of her collarbone. She tugged at a button on Autumn's shirt with the tip of her finger as she skimmed her hand across Autumn's chest. She gasped as her hand moved across the fresh scar just below her collarbone a few inches above Autumn's left breast, then the lump protruding from beneath her skin where the port was planted in her chest. Caroline clenched her jaw.

"Autumn."

Autumn felt the connection between them snap as Caroline's fingers froze over her port. Autumn took a step back, giving Caroline space. The spell had been broken. "You should get out of those sweaty clothes and take a shower." She stepped past Caroline.

"Autumn, wait," Caroline pleaded, reaching for Autumn's hand.

Autumn turned and met Caroline's eyes. "It's okay. We're both tired. I'll check on you in a few hours."

Autumn went to the kitchen and plundered the refrigerator until she heard the shower running. She closed the refrigerator door, bracing herself against the counter. *What was I thinking?* She sighed, trying to quell the thunder of disappointment and desire. Caroline had been about to kiss her. They had been so close, and Caroline felt so good in her arms. She had seen desire in Caroline's eyes, something she hadn't expected but wanted so badly. She touched her hand to her chest and felt the port beneath her skin, just above her breast. *It was only a dream. A beautiful dream, but that's all it can be.*

❖

Caroline shut off the shower and dried herself. She slipped into a pair of shorts and a T-shirt before stopping to look at herself in the mirror. The bruise on her head was tender and still swollen. In a few days the color would drain down into her face. *That's going to be pretty.*

She stepped into the hall and looked toward Autumn's room. Should she go to her, or should she just leave things alone? She hadn't planned for things to get so out of hand, but she had wanted to kiss Autumn so badly she could almost taste her lips. In the moment their bodies touched she had felt the rightness of being with Autumn. The heat in Autumn's eyes had warmed her in the depths of her soul and stirred her desire. As she brushed her fingers along Autumn's skin, she had been mesmerized by the softness and ached to have her mouth where her fingers touched Autumn's neck. Autumn had leaned into her, her lips parting, inviting her to taste her. It had felt so right. *Maybe I cracked my head harder than I thought.* The moment she felt the port beneath her fingers, she had panicked. The reality of Autumn's illness had been paralyzing. That single breath of time was all it had taken for Autumn to feel her withdrawal. She knew she had hurt Autumn. Despite all her reassurances and pep talks that Autumn could find someone, be with someone, she had been the one to put cancer between them. *How could I be such an ass? She'll never forgive me.*

Caroline knocked on Autumn's door but got no answer. She opened the door and peeked inside. Autumn lay with her back to the door, her hair fanned across the pillow like black silk.

"Autumn?" Caroline said in a low whisper.

Autumn didn't stir. Caroline mentally kicked herself again for hurting Autumn. She should let her rest. Autumn had been through enough.

Caroline backed out of the room, pulling the door shut behind her. Her heart ached. She never wanted to hurt Autumn, but the truth was that she wasn't strong enough or brave enough to chance losing again. First her mother, then Jane and Stephanie. Maybe it had been a mistake to take this job. She shook her head. This wasn't a job anymore. She already cared for Autumn more than she wanted to admit. She had made a promise. She had to figure out where her own life was going, but in the meantime, she would keep her promise to Autumn, if Autumn would let her stay.

She lay awake staring into the darkness, listening to the sounds of the house settling, listening for any indication of Autumn stirring. She stilled, holding her breath when she heard a floorboard creak. She got up and went to the door. She opened the door to find Autumn with her hand reaching out as if about to turn the knob.

"Hey," Caroline said, breathlessly. "Are you all right?"

Autumn nodded. "I was just coming to check on you. How's your head?"

"Fine. Have you been able to get any sleep?"

"Some." Autumn handed Caroline a bottle of acetaminophen. "I thought you might need these. The doctor said you should take them."

Caroline reached for the bottle, closing her fingers around Autumn's hand. "I'm sorry about earlier," she said softly.

"It's okay. It was my fault really." Autumn looked up and met Caroline's eyes for the first time. "Let's just forget about it, okay?"

Autumn's voice was calm, evenly controlled, as if she was perfectly fine with what had and hadn't happened between them. But her eyes told a different story.

"Autumn…" Caroline stepped closer, wanting to touch her.

Autumn stepped away. "I'll see you in the morning. I'm having brunch with my mother, of course, so don't worry about breakfast."

Caroline hated the emptiness she had seen in Autumn's eyes. She missed the fire that she had seen there earlier, the desire, the hope. Caroline cursed herself. She would have preferred anger in Autumn's eyes than this emptiness.

Caroline reached for Autumn's hand, pulling her to her. "Autumn. Please don't pull away. I'm so sorry. I didn't mean to hurt you."

"I understand. You don't have to explain."

Caroline brushed her fingers along Autumn's cheek. Autumn had already suffered so much, stood to lose so much. Caroline didn't want to add to that pain. "Please."

"Caroline," Autumn said, her voice betraying her longing.

Autumn leaned into Caroline's touch, her eyes closed. Caroline stepped closer until their bodies touched, feeling Autumn's breasts pressed against her own. She threaded her fingers through the hair at the base of Autumn's neck and pressed her cheek against Autumn's, feeling the smooth tender skin against her face. Autumn's breath was hot against her ear. She brushed her lips against Autumn's neck and heard Autumn moan. How could Autumn be so perfect, so beautiful, so strong, and so fragile at the same time? At that moment she didn't want to think about cancer—she just wanted to feel Autumn in her arms. Caroline shuddered.

Autumn slid her arms around Caroline's waist and rubbed her hands gently along Caroline's back. "Are you okay?"

Caroline shook her head. "I'm not sure. You make me feel things. Things I'm not sure I want to feel."

Autumn pulled back, meeting Caroline's eyes. "Don't worry, Caroline. I'm okay. I don't expect anything to happen between us." She brushed her lips tenderly against Caroline's, a brief joining meant to reassure, to comfort, but the brief taste of Autumn's lips ignited the spark of desire again.

Caroline tightened her grasp against the back of Autumn's neck. "I don't know what I would do without you."

Autumn took a step back. Caroline's fingers slipped from her neck and brushed down her arm until only their fingertips touched. She smiled reassuringly. "Get some rest and enjoy your day tomorrow. Monday will be here before we know it."

Caroline watched Autumn walk away, leaving her heart aching

and wanting. She wasn't sure what to do. She knew she should let Autumn go. Hadn't she asked for just that? But the instant Autumn had pulled away, Caroline had felt the separation deep in her heart. Caroline sighed. She had to get a grip. Her heart couldn't survive another loss. And she knew if that brief connection with Autumn could affect her so deeply, her heart was already at risk.

Caroline stepped back into her room and closed the door, as if putting a physical barrier between her and Autumn could do anything to protect her heart.

CHAPTER TEN

Autumn met her mother at the big house. As usual her mother insisted that she drive, although they always took her mother's car.

"I'm not sure that's a good idea today, Mother. I'm not feeling very well. I didn't get much sleep last night."

"Oh, nonsense, driving isn't that hard—besides, you know I don't see as well as I used to. I'd feel better if you drove," her mother said as she climbed into the passenger seat.

Autumn sighed. *Of course. No one is allowed a bad day but her, and then you'd think it was the end of the world.*

"Why aren't you sleeping?" her mother asked as they pulled out of the drive and headed downtown. "I myself use a wonderful tea, a warm cup just before bed, and I'm fast asleep in minutes."

"I can't do herbal tea while I'm on my treatments, Mother."

"Well, I'm sure Mary can prescribe you something."

Autumn bit her tongue. "I don't need to take anything. If you must know, I spent most of last evening at the hospital."

Her mother gasped. "You were at the hospital and didn't call me! I swear, Autumn, how many times do I have to tell you—"

"I wasn't there for me," Autumn blurted before her mother could give her the whole speech. "Caroline had an accident last night at her soccer game, a head injury. I was there looking after her."

"Huh," her mother scoffed. "I see. Isn't she the one that's

supposed to be taking care of you, not the other way around? I knew I never should have allowed this."

"Allowed this?" Autumn said, her tone hard.

"I don't trust her. What on earth is a grown woman doing taking on a job like this if she isn't looking for something? What if she's some con artist or something?"

"She isn't a con artist, Mother."

Autumn's emotions were still raw from her encounter with Caroline. The last thing she needed was to listen to her mother make up stories about Caroline to undermine Autumn's autonomy.

"I'm not going to talk to you about this, Mother. And for the record, you don't have any say in this matter. It's my decision."

Her mother huffed and crossed her arms. She didn't speak again until they were at the restaurant. Autumn let her mother out at the door and parked the car. She considered leaving her mother there and just going home, but of course they were in her mother's car. *Screwed again.*

She met her mother and Sandra at the bar where they were well into their first Bloody Marys.

"Autumn, how nice to see you again," Sandra said, giving her a kiss on the cheek. "Your mother tells me you'll be able to be one of the sponsors for the ball this year. I can't tell you how glad I am to have you help us set up too. I don't know how you do it all."

"Oh, I didn't realize I would be part of the set-up crew. Mother must have forgotten to tell me. I'm sorry, Sandra, but I just can't do that this year. I'll be happy to be a sponsor, of course, but that's all I can manage."

"Oh, dear. I must have been mistaken," Sandra said, looking crestfallen.

"Don't be ridiculous, Autumn, of course you can help. It won't be that big of a deal," her mother scolded.

"I said no, Mother." Autumn snapped her mouth closed before she lost her temper in public.

Sandra stood. "If you'll excuse me. I'm going to the ladies' room. I'll be back in a moment."

Autumn's mother waited until Sandra was out of earshot to

launch into her, saying, "How dare you embarrass me like that. I work all year to prepare for this ball—the least you can do is help for one night."

"In case you haven't been paying attention, Mother, I have cancer. I am going through chemotherapy that leaves me with little energy to do much of anything." To Autumn's surprise, tears flooded her eyes. "I don't know how much more I can take."

"Stop that!" her mother said sharply. "You stop that right now. I won't have it. You've brought all of this on yourself."

Autumn looked at her mother in stunned shock.

"I won't have this," her mother said sharply. "We are in a public place. You've already embarrassed me enough today."

She stared at her mother as if she had never seen her before. *How can this woman be my mother? How can she be so heartless?*

Autumn took a deep breath. "You're right, Mother. What was I thinking, talking to you about this?" She stood as Sandra returned to the table. "I'm sorry, I guess it's my turn." Autumn motioned toward the restrooms. She left the car keys on the table and walked away. She had walked two blocks before she realized she didn't know where she was going. She pulled out her phone and called an Uber to take her home. Her mother had her car, and she would figure it out.

Autumn fought back the tears that still threatened each time she replayed her mother's words over in her head. *You've brought all of this on yourself.*

Maybe her mother was right. Perhaps she had brought everything on herself. And if that was true, she had the power to change it, starting with her mother.

"Your mother called," Caroline called out as Autumn bypassed the living room.

"Really?" Autumn said innocently. "I can't imagine why." She peeped her head into the room.

Caroline chuckled. "Oh, there was something about you

abandoning her downtown, you being an ungrateful daughter, and me being a gold digger con artist who's corrupting your mind."

It was Autumn's turn to laugh. "I'm sorry."

Caroline patted the seat beside her on the sofa. "Want to tell me about it?"

"Are you sure you want to hear it?" Autumn countered.

Caroline laughed again. "Are you kidding? If it was a blurb for a movie, I'd pay to watch."

Autumn took a seat next to Caroline. "I'm messing everything up."

"How do you figure?" Caroline asked. Why was Autumn blaming herself?

"I haven't been there for my friends, then last night with you, and now my mother."

"Hmm." Caroline took Autumn's hand, lacing their fingers together. "I'm guessing that means you've been beating yourself up all the way home."

"Maybe."

Caroline pursed her lips and nodded. "First of all, your friends are fine—they totally get what's going on. Second, you didn't mess anything up with me. I may have screwed up a bit, but not you."

Autumn started to speak but Caroline put a finger over her lips, silencing her.

"Third," Caroline continued, "your mother must have done something terrible for you to walk out on her. So spill. What did she do?"

Autumn recounted the whole scene. Tears shimmered in her eyes, but she pushed them away.

Caroline was quiet for a long time. Her face burned with anger and she clenched and unclenched her jaw, trying to hold back a sharp condemnation of Meredith.

"Um," Autumn said tentatively, "did I say something wrong?"

Caroline shook her head. "I can't believe she said that to you. You opened up to her, and she basically told you to shut up."

Autumn dropped her head and looked at their entwined hands.

"Did she really tell you that you brought this on yourself?"

Autumn nodded, her tears falling freely now.

Caroline wrapped her arms around Autumn and drew her head to her shoulder. She wanted to scream at Meredith, tell her she didn't deserve Autumn. But that wouldn't help. Meredith was Autumn's mother. Only Autumn could draw that line.

"I am so sorry, Autumn. You didn't deserve that." She brushed her hand over Autumn's hair as Autumn cried on her shoulder. "It might be out of line for me to say so, but your mother is screwed in the head."

Autumn laughed. "Caught on to that, did you?"

They laughed together.

Autumn sat up, wiping her face with her hands. "What am I going to do?"

"Is that a rhetorical question?"

Autumn sighed. "I'm going to pay for this. Sometimes I wish I had a sibling I could tag-team with, so no one had to be overwhelmed with her for too long. But then I feel guilty for wishing her on anyone."

Caroline tried to stifle her laugh. "Why do you do it?"

"What?"

"Let her into your life so much? I meant what I said—she doesn't deserve you. You aren't a possession she gets to control. You're her daughter. Where is her love? Where is her compassion?"

Autumn took a deep breath. "Honestly, I've never really seen that side of her, if it exists. It's always been this way, even when I was a child. I've tried moving away from her, but she just follows me. I tried limiting my contact with her, but she finds some way to punish me when I do that."

"I'm sorry," Caroline said, pulling Autumn back into a hug. "I didn't mean to upset you. How about we change gears. I could fix you something to eat, because I know you haven't eaten. Then we could take a swim, float in the pool, then you could take a nap and recharge. You have to be exhausted, and you have another big day tomorrow."

"Ugh," Autumn groaned. "Don't remind me."

"Tomorrow starts month three. You're pretty much halfway there, and you're doing great." Caroline rubbed her fingers up and down Autumn's arm. She told herself she was just comforting Autumn, but the truth was she needed to touch her. Despite all the reasons why it was a bad idea, Autumn just felt right in her arms.

"Are you going with me tomorrow?" Autumn's voice sounded small.

"Of course. Where else would I be?"

Autumn shrugged against Caroline's shoulder, her face hidden.

Caroline stilled. "I guess the more important question is, do you want me to be there?"

"Yes," Autumn said quickly. "I was just afraid you had changed your mind."

"I'm not going to change my mind, Autumn. I'm going to be there."

Autumn nodded and settled closer to Caroline. "Good. Because I don't know if I can do this by myself. I don't know how much more I can take."

Caroline heard the fear and hurt in Autumn's voice. She was furious with Meredith for treating Autumn the way she had. Autumn had enough to worry about without Meredith messing with her head. How had Autumn turned out to be such a wonderful, caring woman with a mother like that?

Caroline tightened her hold on Autumn, determined not to let her down. She had the overwhelming desire to protect Autumn. No matter what, she would see this through. She wouldn't leave Autumn to do this alone. Not even Meredith could keep her away.

❖

Dr. Mathis held the results of the blood test in her hand and paced the room. "I don't know what to make of this, Autumn. Your liver enzymes continue to be elevated. Have you been drinking alcohol?"

"No." Autumn stared at the chart in Mary's hand as if it was a test she had failed miserably.

"Have you taken any over the counter medications or herbal supplements I don't know about?"

"No."

"No herbal tea, anything?"

"I promise. I'm not taking anything that you don't know about. I'm very strict. I'm doing everything you told me to do."

"How about your stress?"

Autumn hesitated. "Um…well, that's a little complicated."

"Tell me."

Autumn shifted uncomfortably. "I'm realizing some things about my life, and I don't know what to do about them until I know if this treatment is going to work. My best friends are about to have a baby, and another friend of mine was hurt in an accident recently." Autumn sighed. "And I'm fighting with my mother."

Dr. Mathis grinned. "I already heard about the incident with Meredith." Her smile widened. "Good for you. As for the other things, is your friend okay?"

"Yes. She's fine now."

"Good. One other thing…" Dr. Mathis studied Autumn for a moment before she spoke. "Cancer has a way of making people see things they weren't willing to see before. Some realizations are good, but some are not. I hope the soul-searching you've done is leading you down the right path."

Autumn nodded.

"All right then," Dr. Mathis said cheerfully. "Everything else seems to be in order. I'm happy with your white count, and your tumor markers are down. I'm confident about continuing treatment. But promise me you'll tell me if anything changes."

"Of course," Autumn said emphatically.

Dr. Mathis placed her hand on Autumn's shoulder. "When we reach the end of this six months, you will have a lot of answers, but you will still have a lot of questions. Don't put off living. None of us are promised tomorrow."

Autumn looked up into Mary's gentle eyes and smiled. "Yeah, I'm starting to figure that out."

"Good." Mary patted Autumn's shoulder. "Let's get your treatment started then."

CHAPTER ELEVEN

Caroline sat in her father's living room, stroking the worn leather of the old recliner with one hand, a cold beer in the other.

"Where the hell have you been?" her dad asked, popping the top off his own beer.

"Around," Caroline said, grinning up at her father.

"How are things going with the cancer patient?"

Caroline almost choked at the description. It didn't scratch the surface of everything Autumn was to her.

"She's halfway through her treatment now."

"How's she doing?" he asked, his voice deep with concern.

"All things considered, she's doing great."

"That's good. I hope she gives cancer a good swift kick in the ass."

Caroline laughed. "She's giving it her best shot."

He studied her. His eyes bored into her like probes, scanning every inch of her soul. "How about you? How are you handling things?"

"Okay, I guess." Caroline fixed her gaze on the pattern of the wallpaper behind her dad's head. "It's brought up some things about Mom. Mostly how much I miss her. I went through the anger again, but mostly I just want to remember everything I can about her."

Her father rubbed the stubble on his chin the way he always did when he was thinking. Caroline knew talking about this would bring up a lot of things for him too.

"It's okay if you don't want to talk about it," Caroline said, her voice soft.

He frowned. "What makes you think I wouldn't want to talk about your mom?"

Caroline shrugged. "I don't know. I just don't want to hurt you."

"Oh, kiddo, talking about your mom doesn't hurt me. I miss her like hell. But that's a good thing. It makes me know the love is still there. If that ever goes away, you might as well put me in the ground beside her."

Caroline was stunned. "I guess I hadn't thought of it that way."

"Most people don't," he said, taking a drink of his beer. "What do you want to know?"

"How did you get through it? How did you survive without her?"

Her father shrugged. "Except for the obvious, we don't get to choose when we go, or I would have gone right there with her. But I had you, for one. And she would have been pretty pissed if I'd just thrown in the towel. I guess I saw living as a responsibility to her. She got cheated out of her life, so I was going to do my best to get everything we'd ever dreamed of out of mine. For the most part I think I've done a pretty good job. Someone told me once that it's not about the birth date and the death date, it's about the dash in the middle."

Caroline thought about that for a long time. "If you had known in the beginning when you met Momma, that you would lose her, would you have done anything different?"

"Would I have asked her out, asked her to marry me?" He grinned. "I'd do that a million times over if I could have those days with her again. She was the best thing that ever happened to me. Our forever didn't last as long as we would've liked, but it was a hell of a lot sweeter than we ever dreamed." Her father studied her. "What's all this about, sweet pea? Has something happened with you and Jane?"

She shook her head. "We signed the divorce papers finally. I can at least put that failure behind me."

He frowned. "That's what you wanted, right?"

"Absolutely," she said, leaving no question to her resolve.

"What is it then? Is it this woman you're caring for?"

Caroline sighed. "Her name is Autumn. She's only forty-five, and she has colon cancer."

"Hmm. That's young," he said, leaning back against the back of the sofa. "What's she like?"

She smiled. "She's stubborn as a mule and smart as a whip. I can't get her to slow down to save my life. She goes to chemo on Monday, wears a pump till Wednesday, and spends the whole week sick as a dog. But by the next Tuesday, she hits the ground running and pretty much doesn't slow down until they pump her full of more poison. She's cut back her hours, but even then, she's out mowing the lawn or answering work calls or bidding on jobs."

He gave her a questioning look.

"She owns her own landscaping company," Caroline said, answering the unspoken question.

"Ah." He nodded.

"She can barely eat. I know she's lost fifteen pounds already. And she's so tired she can hardly go sometimes, but she won't quit."

Her father grinned. "She's gotten under your skin."

"I guess she has."

"Is she pretty?" He winked.

Caroline tried to hide a smile, her lips twisting into a grin. "Yeah, she's beautiful."

"Ah, there it is." He rubbed his chin again. "What are you going to do about it?"

Caroline shook her head. "I don't know. She has me all twisted up in knots. I think about her all day. When I'm not dreaming about her, I'm worried sick about her. I don't want to hurt her, and I don't want to get hurt."

"Yep. Sounds like love to me."

Caroline's eyes shot up. "I didn't say that."

He laughed. "You didn't have to—it's written all over your face every time you mention her. Your eyes get all glassy when you talk about her. Why else would you be all tied up in knots?"

Caroline shook her head. "It's complicated."

Her father laughed. "Love is complicated. Life is complicated. Relationships are complicated. If they weren't, we'd all be bored out of our minds and wouldn't even have the sense to know it. Life is about taking chances."

Caroline finished her beer.

Her father got up, taking her bottle with him. When he returned, he slid a fresh beer into her hand.

"Now, your momma could cook the best fried apple pies I ever ate, and she could do it while holding you on her hip."

Caroline laughed in spite of herself.

"I'm serious—I've got pictures to prove it." He pulled out an old photo album that had to be every bit as old as Caroline or older. Sure enough, the first photo was of her mother and father as teenagers. Her dad preened like a proud peacock, while her mother smiled demurely at the camera.

She left the old leather recliner and came around to join her father on the sofa to get a better view of the pictures. She looped her arm through his and leaned against him, happy to listen to the story of their life together.

❖

"Can I get you something to drink?" Lisa asked, leading Autumn onto the back porch.

"A glass of regular tap water would be good. I still can't handle anything cold," Autumn said as she eased into the chair.

"I'll be right back."

Autumn took a deep breath. She wasn't sure what she was doing here, but she'd been compelled to come.

"Here you go, sweetie," Lisa said, handing her the glass of water. Lisa sat down facing her. "Has something happened? Is something wrong with Kate?"

Autumn's eyes grew wide. "No. Oh God, Lisa. I'm sorry. I didn't think. She's fine. I just needed to talk."

Lisa fell back in the chair and let out a long, relieved breath. Her hand rested protectively across her belly as if cradling the life that grew inside her. "Oh, thank God." Once she caught her breath, she smiled at Autumn. "Sorry. I was a little panicked there for a moment." Lisa reached out and touched Autumn's hand. "Tell me what's got you bothered."

Autumn looked down at her hands and then away, not sure where to start. "Normally, I would have talked to Kate, but I didn't want to bother her at work, and I know she already has enough on her plate." She shrugged. "I hope it's okay."

"Of course it's okay. It's always okay."

She nodded. "I'm sorry I haven't been around much. Is everything all right with the baby? I got the feeling the other night that Kate wasn't telling me something."

"Well," Lisa started, then stopped. She seemed to be considering what she needed to say. She sighed. "The baby is fine. I'm just having some trouble with gestational diabetes. The doctor is monitoring me closely, and we're doing everything we can to control it."

"How dangerous is it?" Autumn asked.

Lisa sighed. "Untreated it could be really bad, both for me and the baby. But we are treating it, and I'm not worried. Everything is going to be just fine."

"Kate must be beside herself with worry. She hasn't let on that she needed any extra time from work or anything. What can I do to help?"

"Oh, sweetie. We just want you to take care of getting better yourself."

Autumn frowned. "I can do more. I *should* do more. How often are you seeing the doctor?"

Lisa shrugged. "At least once a week. As I get further along, I may have to go twice a week to monitor my blood sugar and blood pressure. The biggest thing is to avoid bedrest. That might be enough to send me over the edge."

"No doubt." Autumn laughed. "Do you have set days that you see the doctor?"

"So far I go on Tuesdays and sometimes Thursdays. Why?"

"On my good weeks I'm usually in the office at least three days. The weeks I have treatment are a bit harder. But there's no reason Kate couldn't take off during your appointments. If there's something really pressing going on and she can't make it, I could go with you."

"Autumn, sweetie, you don't have to do that. We're okay."

"I want to be there," Autumn said, hearing the pleading in her own voice. "You and Kate are my family. I'm missing everything with the baby. Let me help."

Tears flooded Lisa's eyes. She wiped at her cheeks as the tears fell. "Really. You can do that?"

"Absolutely. I do the treatments every two weeks on Mondays. Those weeks are usually pretty awful, but we can arrange coverage for Kate at work, and she can go with you. On the weeks that I don't have treatment, I can cover for her or I can go with you."

Lisa cried harder. Autumn reached for her hand. "Are you okay? I didn't mean to upset you."

Lisa waved her hand in the air as if shooing off a fly. "I'm not upset." She sniffled. "I'm…happy," she squeaked between sobs. She shook her head, still waving her hand dismissively. "Don't mind me—I cry over everything. Pregnancy hormones."

Autumn laughed. "Okay. Can I get you something?"

"Coffee."

Autumn raised an eyebrow. "Really? You can have that?"

Lisa sniffed and laughed. "Don't worry, it's decaf."

Autumn went inside for the coffee to give Lisa time to recover. She was worried about Lisa and sad that Kate hadn't felt that she could talk to her about what was going on. Ever since her diagnosis, she felt like she'd had her head in the sand.

When she returned to the porch, Lisa had stopped crying and looked as if the sun had kissed her cheeks. She smiled up at Autumn.

"Thank you, Autumn. This will be a big relief for Kate and me."

"I'm glad I stopped by. It's time I start acting like a friend again."

"You have a lot on your plate. Kate and I know we can always count on you."

Autumn smiled. "I hope so."

Lisa sipped her coffee. "I'm almost afraid to ask, but how's Meredith?"

"I don't know really." Autumn shrugged. "She isn't taking my calls. We had a bad scene a few days ago, and I kind of walked out and left her at a restaurant downtown."

"No freaking way," Lisa said, her eyes so wide Autumn could see the whites of her eyes all the way around the iris.

"It was bad. It's not like I left her stranded or anything. She had her car. I just couldn't take it anymore and excused myself to the restroom. I walked out and took an Uber home."

"So that's it? No wrath of Meredith?"

Autumn laughed. "She called the house and gave Caroline the third degree. I'm guessing at this point it's like a pressure cooker. She's letting things build, and when I least expect it, she'll blow."

"Oh, damn. That sounds about right." Lisa narrowed her eyes mischievously. "Speaking of Caroline…tell me about tall, blond, and gorgeous."

At the mention of Caroline, Autumn's skin grew hot. She could feel the flush rise up her neck into her cheeks, and her palms began to sweat.

Lisa grinned. "Has something happened between you two?"

"No. Well, kind of."

"What does that mean?" Lisa pulled her chair closer to hers. "I'm going to need a little bit more detail."

Autumn didn't know how to explain what was happening. She was confused about her feelings for Caroline and afraid of what would happen if she did anything about them. Mostly she was afraid of doing nothing.

"Caroline has been great. But the other night after we got back from the hospital—"

"You had to go to the hospital? Oh my God!"

Autumn shook her head. "Caroline hit her head in a soccer

game and got a mild concussion. We were there getting her head scanned."

Lisa gasped, then laughed. "Sorry, I know it's not funny. Is she okay?"

"Yes. She's fine. Anyway. I was beyond tired, and after meeting her ex-wife, and all the worry about her being hurt, I guess I kind of had a weak moment."

Lisa held up her hand to stop Autumn from going further. "Wait. You met her ex-wife?" Lisa shook her head. "I think you need to start from the beginning and tell me everything."

Autumn told Lisa the whole story. She even included the part about how caring Jane had been and her concern that Caroline was being reckless with her own safety.

"So what happened?"

Autumn let out a deep sigh. "We were talking about taking care of her concussion through the night, and the next thing I know we were so close I could feel her breath on me. I almost kissed her. *We almost kissed.*"

"So why didn't you?"

Autumn looked away. "One minute her hand was in my hair, then stroking my neck, and then her hand was on my chest. I was so lost in her. Then her fingers brushed the port in my chest, and she froze. God, Lisa, you should have seen the look of terror in her eyes. One moment we were on fire, and the next it was like someone had dumped a bucket of ice water on the both of us."

"Oh, Autumn."

"I don't know what to do with these feelings."

Lisa took Autumn's hand. "How are things between you now?"

"Okay. It's almost as if nothing ever happened, except every time I see her, I want to touch her. I know she feels it too, but my cancer is always there between us. She lost her mother to cancer, and I see how that affects her still. I can't ask her to go through that again."

"That's not going to happen. The treatments are working, right? Your tumor markers are down."

Autumn nodded. "Yes, but my liver enzymes are up. Even if

the treatment works, there's no guarantee that it won't come back. There's only a seventy percent survival rate. I feel like I'm always going to be looking over my shoulder."

Lisa grimaced and placed her hand on her belly, rubbing gentle circles with her fingers. "I think she's going to be a soccer player. She's got one heck of a kick."

Autumn smiled. "Can I feel?"

"Sure." Lisa guided Autumn's hand to the spot where the baby pressed against her belly. She rubbed the spot.

Autumn's eyes widened when the baby moved. "Oh my God. That's incredible."

Lisa laughed. "It is, isn't it?" Autumn felt Lisa watching as she tenderly traced the movements of the baby. "You know, there are no guarantees for any of us. It's easy to pretend nothing bad is ever going to happen when things are good. But in reality, bad things happen to people every day. If we really thought about that, would anyone ever take the chance to love? Of course we would. We can't let fear ruin everything. Maybe you should just give Caroline some time to figure this out for herself. Just see where things go. Don't overthink it."

Autumn nodded. Did she really have a choice? "I guess you're right."

Lisa squeezed Autumn's hand. "Everything is going to be okay, sweetie. I promise."

Autumn nodded and smiled, wanting to believe her friend was right.

Autumn felt better after her talk with Lisa and decided it was time to address some other loose ends, starting with her mother. She tried to reach her mother at the house and then on her cell, but there was no answer. Autumn dropped her phone into the cup holder. She had called her mother every day, but her mother still refused to talk to her. *I don't have time for these games, Mother.*

Autumn visited the three work sites Lander's Landscaping

currently had underway. Kate was doing an amazing job, but she was stretched too thin. Autumn settled in at her desk and pulled the schedule up on the screen. She looked down at the keyboard just as a bright red drop of blood hit the spacebar. What the hell? She lifted her hand to her nose. Her fingers came away wet with blood. "Shit." She grabbed a tissue from the box on her desk, trying not to panic. This was new. She held the tissue to her nose and leaned her head back. She had never had a nosebleed before. Was this another side effect of the chemo? *Crap. I don't need this right now.*

It was three o'clock when Kate arrived to drop off invoices.

"Hey, Kate, can I see you for a minute?" Autumn called from her office.

Kate walked in with a grin on her face. "I didn't expect to see you here. What's up?" Her face fell when she saw Autumn holding the bloody tissue to her nose. "What the hell?" She rushed over to Autumn. "What happened?"

Autumn rolled her eyes. "Beats me. Just another gift from the chemo god, I suppose."

"What can I do?"

Autumn pulled the tissue away. "I think it's stopped now. I'm okay."

"That's some seriously freaky shit."

Autumn laughed. "The surprises just keep coming." She leaned back in her chair, her hands steepled in front of her chest, her elbows resting on the worn leather armrests. "Enough of all that. I wanted to talk to you about Holly. How is she working out, supervising the West project?"

Kate's eyes followed the bloody tissue as Autumn tossed it into the wastebasket. She shrugged. "No problems. She's been great. She's a fast learner and gets along great with the rest of the crew, and the client likes her."

"Good. I want to turn the project over to her and see how she does with it."

Kate frowned. "Turn it over?"

"Yeah, she's a bright kid, and I think it's time we give her a shot to show us what she's got."

"Okay." Kate frowned. "Is that all? I mean, have I dropped the ball on something?"

Autumn laughed. "No way. I've been to all three sites today and everything looks amazing. I couldn't have done any better myself. I really do want to give Holly a chance. And I want you to have more time with Lisa and the baby stuff."

Kate's face paled. "You talked to Lisa."

Autumn nodded. "You could have told me, Kate. Nothing is more important right now than your family."

Kate nodded. "You're my family too."

Autumn smiled. "Yeah, and we look out for each other. So that means that you'll be taking some time Tuesday to go with Lisa to her doctor's appointment. Let me know the schedule from here on out, and we'll work around it. Maybe less stress for you will mean less stress for Lisa and the baby."

Kate pressed the palms of her hands against her eyes and leaned her head back against the chair. She took a few shuddering breaths before sitting up and meeting Autumn's eyes.

"Damn, Autumn. I don't know what to say. Are you sure about this? I mean, you just had blood pouring out your nose. It isn't like you need any more stress either."

"I'm very sure. That was just a little nosebleed. Nothing to worry about. I'll stop by the West project by the end of the day and talk to Holly. I'd like her to be able to come to you if she has a problem, but I'll see the project through myself. I want you to concentrate on getting the big contracts finished up. Oh, and don't schedule any projects for September without letting me go over them first."

"But September is a big month for us. We can't afford to turn down jobs."

"It's a big month in a lot of other ways too. The baby will be here. I finish chemo. We are going to have our hands full celebrating."

Kate smiled. "Okay, boss. Whatever you say."

"That's better." Autumn ran her hand through her hair and leaned forward. "Now that that's out of the way, how are you doing?"

Kate shrugged. "I'm good." She paused. "Actually, most days

I feel like I'm losing my mind. Work is the one thing I feel like I actually have some control over. You getting sick really kicked me in the gut," Kate said, her voice deepening. "And now Lisa and the baby." She sighed. "I don't know. Half the time I'm scared to death. But the rest of the time I feel like I'm walking on air." She laughed. "This baby is going to change everything, but every time I feel her move or see her on those ultrasounds, my heart just melts. I've never seen anything so amazing. I feel like this is the most important thing I've ever done."

Autumn could feel Kate's joy. She was so happy for her. Kate and Lisa had wanted a baby for as long as she could remember, but conception hadn't been an easy process for Lisa. When they learned they were pregnant, Autumn thought she could actually feel Kate vibrate with pride and pure joy. She wasn't about to let anything cloud that now.

"I can't imagine," Autumn said smiling. "I got to feel her kick earlier, and I swear I thought my heart would beat right out of my chest. It was amazing."

Kate's smile was radiant, her eyes widening with excitement. "She's growing so fast. The past few weeks she's been moving around a lot. If you really want to have your mind blown, you should see her move. The first time I saw it, I freaked out. It was like watching an alien movie."

Autumn laughed. "Um, I'm not so sure I want to see that."

"Don't worry, buddy, she won't hurt you. But viewing is optional."

"Do you guys want to come over and swim Friday? We can keep it simple and order pizza or something."

Kate nodded. "I'll check with Lisa, but consider us there. Is Caroline going to be around?"

Autumn hesitated. "I don't know. I'll see if she wants to join us."

"Great." Kate stood to go. "I need to get back. Is there anything else?"

"No." Autumn held her tongue. She wouldn't talk about Caroline. Not yet. "I'll see you tomorrow."

CHAPTER TWELVE

Autumn stood on the sunporch looking down at the pool. Caroline's long, lean body glided through the water as if she was part mermaid. Autumn couldn't take her eyes off Caroline's body. She relished the way the water glistened on her skin, the way her muscles flexed as she propelled herself through the water. Sun glistened across the surface of the water, making Caroline's silhouette appear to shimmer. Autumn imagined her tongue capturing a trail of water as it cascaded down Caroline's neck. The image brought a surge of heat and want. She sighed. She might never know the feel of Caroline's touch against her skin. She might never taste her lips. At that thought an intense feeling of loss overwhelmed her.

Caroline stepped out of the pool and threw her head back as she wiped the water from her hair. The muscles in her shoulders bunched, and Autumn could see the firm ridges of muscle ripple across her abdomen. Autumn felt another surge of heat coil deep in her center and begin to grow. Maybe Lisa was right. Maybe she didn't have to wait. Maybe she should just let things happen. She should just enjoy this time she had with Caroline. She didn't want to miss out on a chance with Caroline just because everything in her life wasn't perfect. She pulled herself away from her voyeuristic perch and went to her room to change. It was a beautiful day for a swim.

Caroline looked up as Autumn descended the stairs. She sucked in a breath as the air flew from her lungs. Her stomach flipped and her heart began to race. Autumn wore a royal blue bathing suit beneath a white lace robe left open at the front, framing the curve of her breasts, the concave curve of her stomach, and the triangle of cloth between her legs. Autumn's skin was golden brown. Her eyes were like twin pools of ocean blue and they were trained on Caroline.

Caroline shivered, her mouth suddenly dry.

"I didn't expect you home today. I thought you were spending the weekend with your father," Autumn said as she slid the robe off her shoulders and let it drop into a chair.

Caroline licked her lips, trying to free herself from the paralysis that seemed to have taken control of her body. "He had a date tonight. I didn't want to be a third wheel." Caroline dropped her gaze to the port. It looked like two raised bubbles swollen beneath the skin. Then Caroline let her gaze drift to Autumn's breasts as she slowly descended the steps into the pool.

"Mmm," Autumn murmured, "the water feels amazing. I was afraid it would be too cold for me today." She dipped her head beneath the water, brushing her hair back from her face as she stood, her breasts jutting forward as if beckoning Caroline to taste them.

Caroline swallowed. "Yeah," she managed.

"I asked Kate and Lisa to come over again Friday night," Autumn said, moving her arms in circles in the water. "We're going to have pizza and swim. Would you like to join us?"

"Sure." Caroline realized she was barely able to choke out one-syllable words, and she was staring at Autumn's breasts. She looked away. "I'm going to get a beer. Can I get you anything?"

Autumn shook her head. "No. I'm okay for now."

Caroline sprinted into the house. She reached inside the refrigerator and pulled out beer. She drank a third of the beverage quickly, trying to get a grip. Her body was out of control. Her legs trembled, her hands were sweating, and she knew the dampness between her legs wasn't from being in the pool. The sight of Autumn almost naked had sent her nervous system into overdrive. She'd had to think of a reason to leave before Autumn realized what was happening.

She blew out her breath and took another long drink of the beer.

She took a deep breath and then another before finishing the beer and grabbing another, along with a room temperature bottle of water from the counter.

"Sorry," Caroline said as she stepped up to the pool. "I brought you a water. Just in case."

Autumn smiled up at Caroline, her brilliant blue eyes glowing in the sunlight. The glistening water rippled around her, making her look like a goddess.

Caroline stood over Autumn smiling down at her until she realized she was looking at Autumn's breasts again. She turned, taking a drink of her beer. After fumbling around, not sure what to do, she decided to join Autumn in the pool. At least the water would obscure her view and prevent her from ogling Autumn.

Caroline dove into the water, her sleek body barely making a splash as she broke the surface. Autumn stretched out her arms along the edge of the pool, watching Caroline gracefully glide beneath the water. She had seen the look of desire in Caroline's eyes, felt her gaze on her skin. In that moment she realized she felt alive for the first time in weeks. She was getting her life back in order, and a beautiful woman desired her. That was enough for now. At first, she had been hesitant about the swimsuit—her port was plainly visible—but she didn't want to pretend this wasn't a real part of her life right now. She wanted to be honest about the challenges she faced, honest about her body, and honest with herself about her feelings. She wouldn't push Caroline, but she wouldn't hide, either.

Caroline surfaced and swam to the side of the pool. She rested her elbows on the edge, picked up her beer, and gripped the bottle in both hands.

"How was your visit with your dad?" Autumn asked.

"Good. We spent a lot of time talking about my mom. He helped me remember the good things we shared through her illness and all the years we had before she got sick. It was really good to hear familiar stories from his point of view. You'd just have to meet him to know what I mean. He can be a real character." Caroline was silent for a long time. "I told him about the divorce. I think he was sad for me, but happy that chapter has closed."

"I'm glad you had a good visit. Your dad sounds like a wonderful man." Autumn pulled a float into the water and climbed on. The water felt amazing, but her energy wouldn't last long if she was constantly fighting gravity and trying to keep her head above water. She settled into the mesh bed that let her be submerged just below the surface without sinking.

"I did and he is. I need to take time like that more often." Caroline got quiet again.

Autumn sensed something was bothering Caroline. She wanted to ask but thought it better to let Caroline get there on her own. So she stayed quiet, watching and waiting until Caroline was ready.

Caroline took another drink of her beer. "I also told him about you."

"Really, what did you tell him?" Autumn asked, surprised by the revelation.

Caroline took another drink of her beer. "I told him about your cancer, how the treatment was going, and I told him…I told him I'm afraid I'm getting too close to you."

Autumn swallowed. She was afraid of where this was going. "How so?"

Caroline let go of the pool edge and reached for Autumn's float. She gripped the inflated edge and pulled Autumn across the pool until she could stand facing her.

Autumn's heart raced. Had she already ruined things with Caroline? Was Caroline leaving?

"I told him I'm attracted to you, that I was afraid of crossing a line that might get me hurt. After my mother died, I sort of lost my mind for a while. I'm not sure I was really even present most of the time. Her death almost broke me. When I met Jane, I buried all that hurt in the excitement of someone new. I gave everything, was willing to do anything, give up anything, change in any way she wanted, to have her with me. Then one night I came home and found her in bed with my best friend, and another part of my soul died. I've spent the last year trying to put myself back together. Then I met you. I thought I could keep an emotional distance, that we could be friends."

"But?" Autumn rasped. Her voice almost choked from holding back the desire for Caroline and the fear of losing her.

"I'm afraid of what you make me feel." Caroline's eyes were clouded by pain and regret.

"Tell me."

"*Autumn.*"

Autumn heard the desperation in Caroline's voice. She sat up, letting the raft slip out from under her. She wrapped her arms around Caroline's shoulders and looked into her eyes. She pulled Caroline closer, their breasts touching. "Show me," she whispered.

Caroline's hands came to Autumn's waist. Caroline's chest rose and fell rapidly with each intake of breath. Her eyes dropped to Autumn's mouth. Her lips parted as they drifted closer. Caroline's arms closed around Autumn, pulling her closer.

Autumn knew she had to wait. Caroline had to make this choice on her own. But the waiting was so hard.

"Caroline?" Autumn ran her hand up the back of Caroline's neck, snaking her fingers through the short hair. "Please," Autumn whispered, afraid she would melt if Caroline didn't kiss her.

Caroline closed her eyes. The moment her lips touched Autumn's, everything else fell away. Autumn's full lips caressed her mouth and invited her in. Caroline whimpered as their tongues met and embraced. She pulled Autumn closer, feeling her slick wet body glide against her, her firm breasts melding against her own. Caroline's nipples hardened, and instantly she wanted all of Autumn. Caroline reached up to cup Autumn's breast, the hard nipple grazing her palm. As she closed her hand around Autumn's breast, her fingers brushed the foreign nodes of plastic beneath her skin. She gasped. She didn't want to think about the port—she didn't want to think about cancer. All she wanted to think about was Autumn kissing her.

Autumn slowed the kiss, then pulled away. Her eyes searched Caroline's. "Tell me what you feel."

Caroline stilled her hand, letting her fingers rest lightly on the port. She let her fingers slide down to touch Autumn's breast, rubbing her thumb over the erect nipple protruding beneath the thin fabric.

"I want you. But I'm afraid of wanting you. I'm afraid of losing you. I don't know if I would survive it if I did."

Autumn pulled her hand between them and held Caroline's fingers against the port. "This is real. This is necessary. But this is not who I am." She kissed Caroline deeply, leaving no question of what she felt and wanted in that moment. She caressed Caroline's face in her hand as their lips parted. "I can't make promises. I don't know the answers. And oh my God, I am so scared. But I don't want to waste whatever time I have too afraid to try."

Caroline let out her breath. She was trembling now. "I don't know if I can."

Autumn leaned her forehead against Caroline's. "All I'm asking is that you try. But I'll understand if this is not what you want."

"I don't know," Caroline said, her voice trembling.

Autumn heard the anguish in Caroline's voice. "I know. And that's okay. Just promise me you won't disappear on me."

Caroline nodded.

Autumn stepped back, breaking the connection between them. She flexed her fingers as she looked down at her hands.

"Are you cold?"

Autumn nodded. "I guess that's it for me tonight. I think I'll turn in." She brushed her hand down Caroline's arm as she waded to the steps. "I'll see you tomorrow, right?" She held her breath waiting for Caroline's answer.

"Of course. We have an appointment to keep," Caroline said tenderly.

Relief flooded Autumn, a soothing blanket to cover the disappointing ache in her heart and places much lower. But she knew not to push. Caroline had to figure this out on her own. Would Caroline have gone to bed with her if she hadn't pulled away? It didn't matter. Autumn didn't want this to be about sex. There was so much more at stake than that. And that meant everything.

❖

Autumn had the feeling something was wrong. Nancy was unusually somber as she hooked up the leads to Autumn's port. The room seemed too quiet, as if something was missing. Autumn looked around the room. There was Charles, a tall handsome athletic black man who was also being treated for colon cancer. He and Autumn were on the same treatment schedule. His wife Viola was always by his side despite his irritable moods. Charles had been a bit shell-shocked by his diagnosis, thinking that he was too fit and healthy to get cancer.

In the chair next to him was Alice, an older woman in her midseventies with paper white skin and salon blue hair. Autumn always wondered what they put on old people's hair to make it turn blue, but she was too afraid to ask. Alice was sometimes accompanied by a granddaughter, but today it looked like she was on her own.

Next to Alice was Francis, a three-time cancer survivor and all-around kickass broad, as she liked to say. Francis always came alone, choosing to listen to music and read a book rather than engage in much conversation.

Autumn's eyes fell to the empty chair next to Francis. Her heart sank.

"Nancy, where's the cheerleader?"

Nancy's hands stilled. She glanced over her shoulder to the empty chair. "Barbara won't be coming in today."

"Is she okay?"

"Yes. Her white count shot up over the weekend. She's been admitted to the ward."

The ward was what everyone in the group called the floor in the hospital where the cancer patients were treated. Going to the ward didn't mean someone wasn't going to make it, but it was never a good sign. Autumn's stomach clenched. She looked to Caroline sitting next to her. Caroline had paled. She had obviously heard. Autumn reached out and took Caroline's hand. To Autumn's relief Caroline didn't pull away, instead lacing their fingers together and giving a little squeeze.

Autumn turned back to Nancy. "Is there anything we can do for Barbara?"

Nancy smiled at Autumn. "No, sweetie. This just happens sometimes. You just focus on getting better."

Autumn touched her fingers to Nancy's hand. "How about you? Are you okay?"

Nancy looked up at her, surprised. Then she pursed her lips together in a sad smile. "It's hard. We get attached to our patients. When they aren't doing well, we kind of take it personally, like there was something we could have done better."

"I can see that." Autumn frowned. "You do a really good job here, Nancy. I'm glad you are the one taking care of me."

Nancy blinked away tears. She grasped Autumn's free hand and stroked it. "I'm sorry you need me to." Nancy brushed away a stray tear with the sleeve of her scrub shirt. "You're all set to go. I'll be back to check on you in a bit."

Autumn turned to Caroline, who hadn't moved since Nancy had told Autumn about Barbara. Caroline looked a little sick, and Autumn knew the news had shaken her. She looked haunted. Autumn tried to hide her own fear and worry, but she would never understand why some patients got better and others didn't. Barbara had the best attitude—her optimism was contagious. What went wrong?

"Are you okay?" Autumn asked.

Caroline jumped as if startled. "Yeah," Caroline said. Her voice sounded distant and small.

"You don't have to sit here with me if you need to go," Autumn said, understanding some of what Caroline must be feeling. She must be thinking of her mother right now. If someone as cheerful and energetic as Barbara could get sick, the same thing could happen to her. Autumn pulled a blanket up over her lap, needing the warmth to insulate her from her growing fear. "You know the routine. It's not like I'm going anywhere for the next few hours. You should go to lunch, take a walk, get some air," she said, trying to keep her voice casual so Caroline wouldn't notice her anxiety.

"Are you sure?"

Autumn shrugged. "I brought plenty to keep myself occupied. Besides, I could always take a nap—it makes the time go faster."

Caroline sighed. "I could use some air. I won't be gone long."

Nancy stepped up to Autumn's chair as the door closed behind Caroline. "Is she okay?"

Autumn sighed. *I hope so.* "Yeah, she just had some things to do. She'll be back."

Nancy placed her hand on Autumn's shoulder and squeezed. "Be patient with her. It's hard for all of us."

Autumn nodded. "Yeah. I will."

Nancy kneeled beside Autumn. "Can I ask you a question?"

"Sure. What is it?"

"Where's Meredith? Why doesn't she come with you?"

Autumn laughed. "Are you kidding? I'm actually trying to survive this. I won't let her come."

Nancy laughed. "Good for you. I have to say, I'm surprised. You never would have stood up to your mother before."

Autumn understood what Nancy was saying. It had been what had ended their relationship. "My mother feels that I brought this on myself."

Nancy's eyes hardened. She shook her head. "For the life of me, I will never understand that woman."

Autumn laughed. "You and me both."

Nancy looked back toward the door Caroline had just walked out of. "Caroline seems nice."

"Yeah, she is."

Nancy leaned closer. "Cute too. I bet that's driving Meredith nuts."

Autumn almost snorted when she laughed. "She thinks she's a gold digging con artist."

Nancy rolled her eyes. "Of course she does." She sighed. "Good luck with that, Autumn. She's a good catch. I hope you don't let her get away."

Autumn considered telling Nancy that she and Caroline were not a couple, but by the time she started to speak, Nancy was gone. She looked to Barbara's chair, understanding what was going through Caroline's mind. Between cancer and Meredith, Autumn already had two strikes against her. If she did have one chance with Caroline, she had to get it right.

❖

Caroline walked to a nearby park. The soccer pitch was empty, so she took off her shoes and socks so she could feel the earth beneath her feet. It had been one of her mother's favorite things to do. The grass was cool against her skin and tickled her toes. The ground was firmly packed, and every now and then she felt the sharp stab of a rock bite into her flesh. The field hadn't been mowed in a few days, and it was covered with the white heads of new clover. Honeybees flitted from bloom to bloom gathering the nectar, while mockingbirds ran from spot to spot, splaying their wings to frighten insects, which they gobbled up and moved on to the next. As she walked, she stumbled upon the body of a baby bird that had fallen or been carried out of its nest. She looked around, fearing the latter. There were no branches close enough for a nest. The little guy never had a chance. She had the fleeting thought of how unfair life was.

She sat on the grass and watched the world go by. At the picnic tables a large family gathered, playing games and singing songs in Spanish. To the left of them an old man and woman sat side by side having lunch. A walker sat beside the table. The old woman's hands shook, and the man helped her with her food.

A woman pushing a stroller stopped a few feet away to pick up and clean a pacifier for her screaming child, her soothing voice drifting through the chorus of the nearby song.

In the distance a figure approached. A runner with an odd gait lumbered up the trail. As he drew closer, she could see the Army insignia on his T-shirt over his chest. He was fit with muscular arms and broad shoulders. His hair was cut close to his scalp in the usual military style. And then she saw it. Extended from his right knee where his leg should have been was a curved blade with a rubber pad on the end. The blade gave a little with each stride, creating the odd gait she had noticed earlier. Caroline nodded to the young man as he passed.

She checked her watch, not ready to go back to the sterile room where Autumn waited for her. She lay back on the grass, wrapping her hands behind her head. She watched the clouds float by, trying to make out patterns as they morphed from one shape to another. She smiled. She and her mother had done this together almost every summer since she was just a toddler. It was when they had some of their best talks. She had seen dragons in the clouds after seeing the movie *Pete's Dragon*, and then butterflies the year they had watched a butterfly release at the zoo. It was where, as a teen, she had told her mother she had a crush on another girl. And it had been where her mother had told her she was stopping her treatment.

Caroline felt something wet run along her temple and into her hair. She reached up and wiped her hand against her face and realized she was crying. She missed her mother so much it hurt. She wondered what her mother would say to her now. She really had no idea, but it soothed her to think her mother was watching and remembering with her.

The hardest memories were of her mother's illness. Her battle with cancer had been so terrible, that Caroline had often questioned what kept her mother going. She would sit for hours and look out over the backyard and watch the clouds go by. Caroline wondered what her mother had seen in the shapes as they passed.

She swiped at another tear as a specific memory came to mind. It was late one night when everyone should have been asleep. But Caroline had known her mother rarely slept. She had crept down to see her mother and had found her father sitting next to the bed with his arms wrapped around her mother and his head in her lap. He had fallen asleep as they held each other. Her mother sat gazing down at her sleeping husband, gently brushing her fingers through his short blond hair. Caroline would never forget the look on her mother's face. It was at once gentle and loving and, at the same time, mournful. Caroline had been touched by the love in the moment and had quietly slipped away without her mother knowing she was there. Her mother died only two weeks later. Pain as fresh as the day her mother had left her sliced through Caroline's heart. She would never again hold her hand or brush her hair or hear her voice. But Caroline knew without doubt in that moment that her mother had not left her. She was there in everything Caroline did. She was a part of her as sure as the air around her.

Out of nowhere, Caroline had the desperate urge to be with Autumn. She sat up and looked at her watch again. Autumn was at the point in her treatment when she usually started to feel ill. Autumn was alone, something she had promised she would not allow to happen. She had made a promise. Caroline put on her shoes and ran.

Caroline leaned over Autumn and pressed a cold damp cloth to Autumn's cheek when she moaned. Autumn opened her eyes, reaching for the cloth.

"Shh," Caroline soothed. "Let me. I've got it."

Autumn frowned. "Why are you all sweaty?"

Caroline smiled down at her. "I went for a little run."

"In jeans and loafers?"

"Well, it wasn't planned." Caroline grinned. "I was in a bit of a hurry."

Autumn moaned as another wave of nausea hit her. "Sorry. It's not you," she managed to tease.

Caroline leaned her head to the side and sniffed her shirt. "You sure? I thought I smelled something earlier."

Autumn smiled and closed her eyes. "You're not right."

"Not true. You had my head examined, remember?"

Autumn peeked through half-closed lids. "Are you okay?"

"Yeah. Why?"

Autumn frowned. "You just seem to be in an awfully good mood."

"Ah, that. Well, I guess the walk was just what I needed."

Autumn opened her eyes and looked at Caroline skeptically.

Caroline shrugged. "I've been a little out of sorts lately, and I'm sorry about that." She held the damp cloth against Autumn's cheek. "But I'm fine, really. You don't have to worry."

Autumn leaned her head back and grimaced, fighting the pain and nausea.

"Rough day, huh?" Caroline said, refreshing the cloth and returning it to Autumn's neck.

"Not too bad."

"You always say that."

Autumn licked her lips. "It's not as bad as I expected it to be. I haven't actually thrown up yet. How's that?"

"Okay, I'll buy that one. You're almost done today. Only two more months to go. What is that, three more treatments or four?"

Autumn smiled. "Four. Can't wait."

Caroline brushed the hair from Autumn's cheek, letting her fingers linger against the soft skin. It pained her to see Autumn suffering this way, and she longed for these torturous treatments to be over. She knew Autumn didn't realize how sick she really was. She almost seemed to feel guilty that she wasn't having a harder time. Caroline was just grateful things had gone as smoothly as they had. But she knew the tides could turn at any time. All it took was one infection to derail everything.

Autumn turned her head, peering at Caroline through heavy lids. "I'm quite a mess, aren't I."

Caroline stroked Autumn's cheek. "You're beautiful."

Autumn chuckled, a strained attempt at a laugh. "It must be really bad if you're going to lie to me."

"I'm not lying. I can't think of anyone who could go through all of this and still be as beautiful as you."

Autumn reached up and grasped Caroline's hand. She narrowed her eyes and studied Caroline. "Did something bad happen? Is something wrong and you just don't want to tell me?"

"No. Of course not."

"What, then? You're scaring me."

Caroline shook her head. She leaned down and placed a kiss to Autumn's forehead. "Stop your worrying—nothing's wrong. Can't I pay you a compliment every now and then?"

Autumn didn't look convinced.

"I'm just figuring some things out for myself. We can talk about it when you're feeling better. Right now, let's get you home."

Autumn slept most of the way home. She didn't even protest when Caroline helped her out of the car and into the house. Caroline settled Autumn into her usual spot on the sofa and covered her with a blanket. *What have you done to me, Autumn Landers?*

CHAPTER THIRTEEN

Lisa lifted the pitcher of tea and filled her glass. She leaned back against the lounge chair with a sigh. "I am so over being pregnant."

Autumn laughed. She had kept her promise and made time for Kate to go with Lisa to her doctor's appointments, and she made it a point to have lunch with Lisa every other week.

"Is it that bad?"

Lisa grimaced. "It's been wonderful. But I'm ready for our little girl to be here. I'm tired of getting up four or five times a night to pee, and I miss being able to see my feet. Summer is my favorite time of year, but right now I can't handle the heat. At least the nights are beginning to cool down. It will be fall before we know it. I've already been seeing leaves from the walnut gathering on the back porch."

"Only a few more weeks, and she'll be here." Autumn took Lisa's hand. "Then you can be up at night for an entirely different reason."

Lisa laughed. "Right. But honestly, I'm looking forward to it. I can't wait to see her, count her little fingers and toes. God, we've waited so long for this."

"I'm really happy for you. Have you picked out a name yet?"

Lisa smiled. "We have some ideas, but we aren't telling anyone until she's here. We feel we'll know which one is right when we see her."

"Hmm, that makes sense."

Lisa turned to face Autumn. "How are you doing? Any news?"

Autumn shook her head. "No. Nothing has changed. Keep your fingers crossed I can get through the next few weeks without any problems."

"What about Caroline?"

"What about her?"

"You know. Any juicy details you want to share?"

Autumn didn't answer.

"There is something. Tell, me. Oh my God, did you sleep with her?"

"No," Autumn said quickly. "It was just a kiss."

"You kissed her!"

"Well, yes. We kissed."

Lisa's eyes were wide. She curled sideways in her chair to face Autumn. "How was it?"

Autumn sighed. "It was amazing. The kind of kiss that makes your toes curl and your bones melt."

"Hmm. Sounds yummy. So are you two seeing each other, dating, what?"

"None of the above. She doesn't think she can handle it. She told her dad about me, though."

"Hmm, that's something. Isn't it?"

Autumn shrugged. "Who knows? She was distant with me for days after, but last week something changed. We've been spending a lot of time together and she seems more—I don't know—interested."

"She hasn't said anything?"

"No."

Lisa frowned. "What happens when you finish treatment? I mean, you hired her to take care of you through your treatment, right? What then?"

Autumn frowned. "I know she's been looking for an apartment. But she hasn't said anything definite."

"How do you feel about her not living with you anymore?"

"Honestly, I hadn't thought about it. In the beginning I hated the idea of sharing my home with someone. But it's been easy with Caroline. We just clicked from the start." Autumn frowned. The idea of coming home and not having Caroline there bothered her more than she would like to admit. She had feelings for Caroline, but she hadn't viewed them as living together because they weren't a couple. Then why did it feel like she was preparing herself for a breakup? Maybe the change she'd noticed in Caroline was that she was happy their arrangement was about to end. Was Caroline ready to move on? Hadn't that been what she had hoped to figure out during their time together?

"Autumn?"

"Hmm?" Autumn said, distantly listening to Lisa.

"Where did you go?"

Autumn shook herself. "Nowhere."

"You said your cancer was one of the things standing between you. What happens when it's gone?"

Autumn shrugged. "It will still be there, lurking in the shadows. There will always be the possibility it will come back."

"You're falling for her."

"No. But I could." Autumn knew she stood on the edge already. But she couldn't afford to fall.

Lisa stretched out on the lounger. "I don't know how I got so lucky. Kate and I met when we were still little more than kids. We fumbled through the first couple of years together, but I always knew she was the one. I can't imagine loving anyone else."

"You two are perfect together."

Lisa turned her head to face Autumn. "So are you and Caroline—you just don't know it yet."

Autumn heard Caroline as she hung her keys on the peg by the door and hefted the take-out bags onto the counter. A few seconds later a wonderful smell wafted into the room. She grinned and hurriedly went to the kitchen.

"Oh my God, what is that wonderful smell?" Autumn asked.

"I brought your favorite. I thought you might want to try something other than mac and cheese tonight."

Autumn's stomach rumbled. "I've been craving Szechuan for days."

"I know."

"I'm scared," Autumn grumbled. "What if I can't eat it? I don't want my favorite things to be ruined to me forever."

Caroline spooned out a small portion onto a plate. "It won't be forever. Come on, just try."

"It does smell good. My mouth is watering just thinking about it."

Caroline held up a bite to Autumn. Autumn stared at her, surprised.

"Open up."

Autumn obeyed and Caroline guided the bite into her mouth.

Autumn chewed, then grimaced and shook her head. The taste was something like dirt and moss.

"No good, huh?"

Autumn's eyes watered. She shook her head again as she tried to swallow the offending morsel. "Yuck." She sighed. "Good try, but that was terrible."

Caroline laughed. "Sorry. I keep hoping we'll find something new you can tolerate." She pulled a second container from the bag. "But just in case, I brought this too."

Autumn opened the large bowl of macaroni and cheese. She laughed. "You know me too well."

"I've had some practice."

Autumn thought back to her conversation with Lisa and asked the question she'd been brooding over for hours. "How is the apartment hunt going?"

Caroline's smile faded. "Okay, I guess." She sighed. "I've been meaning to talk to you about that. I'm trying to figure out where to go next. And I decided that's partially up to you."

Autumn stopped chewing. She frowned, not understanding what Caroline meant. "Me? How is it up to me?"

Caroline dipped a spoon into the mac and cheese, then pushed the food aside. "I didn't expect six months to go by so fast. On one hand, I'm glad it has, of course." She reached out to Autumn, brushing her fingers across her cheek. "But this thing that is happening between us—"

Autumn knew her surprise must be evident on her face. "Is there something happening between us?"

"Yes," Caroline whispered, moving closer until their thighs touched. "I've tried ignoring it, I've fought against it, I've even run from it, but I can't deny it anymore. Ever since that first kiss, I haven't been able to think of much else."

"Oh."

"The other day I realized I want more. More of you. I want to see if there can be an us."

Autumn grasped Caroline's arm to steady herself. Her legs were suddenly weak, and she felt dizzy. "You want an us?"

"I do." Caroline smiled. "I want to learn everything about you. If I get an apartment in the area, we can still see each other regularly. But if this isn't what you want... Well, I don't really want to think about that, but, well, you asked me to try. I want to try."

Autumn had stopped breathing. She was dumbstruck. "Is this real? I mean, after living together for five months you want us to date?"

Caroline smiled. "I made a lot of mistakes in my past. I don't want to rush this. I want to experience everything in the moment."

Autumn sobered. "You do realize nothing will change when my treatment is over," she said seriously. "Well, some things will change. I'll at least be able to eat real food, and I won't be sick all the time." She hesitated. "But the bigger picture won't change."

"I know. We'll just have to face whatever happens when it happens."

"I don't understand. What changed?" Autumn's heart was racing. She studied Caroline's eyes, trying to convince herself Caroline was serious. She didn't want to get her hopes up. How could Caroline be certain? What if she changed her mind again? The treatments weren't even over yet. They had no idea what was going to happen next.

"I realized that a lot of bad things happen to good people every day." Caroline's voice interrupted her thoughts. "Life isn't perfect.

People aren't perfect. I want what my mom and dad had. I can't have that if I keep hiding from things that I'm afraid of."

Caroline brought her lips to Autumn's gently. Autumn hesitated, and then her lips parted in response and Caroline deepened the kiss. She wasn't sure how much time passed, five minutes, ten, an hour. When Autumn pulled away, her body hummed with excitement. Her arms were around Caroline's neck, their legs entwined, their breasts pressed together. Autumn swayed, and Caroline tightened her arms to steady her.

"Can I take that as a yes?" Caroline whispered, her lips brushing Autumn's ear.

Autumn laughed, her head falling to rest against Caroline's.

"Yes," Autumn said, her voice barely more than a whisper.

CHAPTER FOURTEEN

If I didn't know you couldn't tolerate the cold, I'd douse you with ice water." Lisa bumped Autumn's shoulder. "Jesus, you look like you're going to combust just looking at her."

Autumn dropped the tongs she'd been using to turn the hot dogs. "Now look what you made me do. Why are you sneaking up on me like that?"

Lisa grinned. "First of all, I didn't have to sneak. I could have yelled through a bullhorn and you wouldn't have known I was here." She handed Autumn a fork. "Here, this will do. They're ready to come off anyway," Lisa said, handing Autumn a plate. "Maybe if you weren't undressing Caroline with your eyes, you wouldn't be so jumpy."

"I wasn't undressing her."

"Could have fooled me. Sweetie, right now, you're hotter than that grill."

"Stop it. I was just lost in thought." *Thoughts of kissing Caroline, her hands on me, how much I want to touch her.*

"Yeah, thoughts of Caroline naked."

Autumn rolled her eyes. "You're one to talk."

Lisa laughed. "Yes, ma'am. Guilty as charged. As long as we're talking about Kate, of course. But for someone who isn't falling, you sure have the look, sweetie."

"I'm not falling for her. At least not yet. Hell, maybe I am. I don't know. We've just decided to date. I can't fall for her."

"Date!" Lisa clasped her hand over her mouth. "Shit, did anyone hear that?"

Autumn thought she saw Caroline stiffen and turn her head slightly toward them, but she wasn't sure. "Geez, could you announce it to the neighborhood."

"This is huge. Have you slept with her yet?"

"Oh my God, Lisa, is that all you think about?"

Lisa shrugged. "Sorry, it must be the hormones. Who knew being pregnant made you so horny?"

Autumn looked at her, surprised.

"What? Kate loves it. Once the doctor and I convinced her it doesn't hurt the baby, she's been just as into it as I am."

"I think that was a little more than I needed to know." Autumn grinned.

Lisa smacked Autumn's arm. "Ah, so you haven't slept with her yet."

"Why do you say that?"

Lisa shook her head. "You look too hungry. And you're missing a certain glow."

Autumn shook her head. "You're crazy."

"Tell me I'm wrong."

"I'm not telling you anything else."

Lisa looped her arm through Autumn's. "How's Meredith taking it?"

Autumn felt as if the rug had been pulled out from under her. "She doesn't know. She still isn't talking to me."

"What? That's a record."

"I'm starting to get worried. I went by the house the other day, and she didn't answer the door. The gardener finally came out and told me she was away."

"Away? Away where?"

"He didn't know. And he didn't know when she would be back."

"Don't fall for this, Autumn. She's up to something. I can feel it."

Autumn sighed. "I know. I thought the same thing. But it worries me."

"Just hang tight. She'll turn up. She always does."

Autumn agreed, but she didn't like the feel of this.

Lisa gathered the platter. "Dinner's ready," she called to Kate and Caroline, who were playing a game of water volleyball.

Autumn had a gnawing feeling in her gut. *Where are you, Mother? And what the hell are you up to?* She shut off the grill and took a seat next to Caroline.

Caroline's hand came around her back and rubbed small circles against her skin.

Kate handed the platter to Autumn. "Hot dog, Autumn?"

Caroline took the tray, looking at her questioningly.

Autumn shook her head. "I don't think I'm ready." She took a spoonful of mashed potatoes but wasn't sure she could eat. The conversation about her mother had dulled her appetite, and the gentle brush of Caroline's fingers against her back had her hungry, but it wasn't for food.

❖

Caroline put away the remains of the meal while Autumn said good-bye to Lisa and Kate at the door.

"Thank you for doing that," Autumn said, stepping into the room and starting to gather up the trash.

"I'm happy to do it," Caroline said, placing her hand over Autumn's. "Let me do that. Go on and take your shower. I know you're tired."

"Are you sure?"

"Yeah, there's not much left to do in here. Go on. This will only take a minute."

Caroline had struggled all night not to touch Autumn. Unsure what to do, she had kept a respectable distance.

She settled on the couch and flipped through the channels, waiting for Autumn. She must have drifted because the next thing she knew Autumn was leaning over her, her breasts framed by a light blue robe. Droplets of water clung to her neck, and spots of moisture dampened the fine silk along her breasts.

"Hey," Autumn said, her voice deeper than usual, her eyes dark azure pools that beckoned to Caroline.

Caroline stared up at Autumn, feeling as if she'd fallen under a spell.

"You should go to bed. We've talked about the dangers of sleeping out here on the couch."

Caroline swallowed, unable to speak. She ran her hand through Autumn's hair, feeling the dampness from the shower on her fingers. Autumn's skin was hot and flushed from the heat of the water. Caroline traced her fingers along the ridge of collarbone, stopping at the hollow of Autumn's throat.

"God, you are beautiful."

Autumn smiled.

Caroline dipped her fingers inside the robe, taking Autumn's breast in her hand, rubbing her thumb lightly across her nipple, feeling it harden beneath her touch. Autumn closed her eyes and moaned, arching her back, pressing her breast harder against Caroline's touch.

Caroline's control broke. She sat upward, her hand grasping Autumn's neck, pulling her to her. Caroline brushed her lips lightly against Autumn's, feeling Autumn's lips part in welcome. She deepened the kiss. She couldn't hold back any longer. She pulled Autumn on top of her until she could feel the press of her breasts against her chest and the wonderful pressure of Autumn's thigh pressing between her legs.

Autumn's lips parted, and she took Caroline's tongue into her mouth. She whimpered in a plea for more and gasped when Caroline withdrew. Caroline's heart raced as she fought for breath. "God, I want you."

Autumn pushed against Caroline's chest, putting some distance between them, forcing them both to consider what they were doing.

"Wait," Autumn urged. "We said we were going to wait."

Blood pounded in Caroline's ears, echoing the beat of her heart.

Her fingers tingled and her stomach tightened as the hard ball of need coiled deep inside. She was lost to everything except Autumn's touch. "I don't want to wait. I want to touch you."

Autumn shifted until her thighs framed Caroline's hips. Caroline groaned, feeling Autumn's heat against her sex. Caroline leaned upward and kissed Autumn hard, the fierce driving need pushing her onward, driving her to lose herself in Autumn.

Caroline's blood pounded as Autumn whimpered against her lips, then surged against her, hips rhythmically moving to Caroline's thrusts. Autumn's tongue warred with Caroline's, sucking, possessing, until Caroline forgot to breathe.

Autumn pulled her lips from Caroline's, her palm planted firmly against Caroline's chest as she pushed her back.

"We have to stop now, or I won't be able to stop."

Caroline peered into Autumn's eyes. She watched as the hungry ocean-blue eyes darkened as if storm clouds had gathered. Light glinted in her eyes like lightning, and Caroline understood the storm that brewed there.

Caroline stilled her hands, her fingers gently caressing Autumn's cheek. "Do you want me to stop?"

"Oh, Caroline, no," Autumn whispered, her voice shaking with need. "I don't want you to stop, not ever. I want your hands on me until I can't feel anything else. Then I want your mouth, hot and soft. I want to feel your body against mine, your hands inside me. I want to taste you and touch you until you scream out my name."

"You keep talking to me like that and I might scream sooner than you think."

Autumn chuckled. "Then you should get busy."

Caroline tugged at the sash of the robe, pulling the soft silk to the side, exposing Autumn's breasts. Her nipples hardened and ached to be touched. Caroline ran a finger down Autumn's stomach, her fingers trembling as she explored Autumn's body.

Caroline sat up, pressing her arms up the length of Autumn's back, holding her as she sucked a nipple into her mouth. Autumn swelled against her, arching her back, pushing her breast into Caroline's mouth.

"Yes." Autumn's soft cry was not much more than a whimper. "Oh God, Caroline. Yes." She looked down into Caroline's eyes. "Off. Take your shirt off."

Caroline sat back as Autumn's hands eagerly tugged her T-shirt up and over her head.

Autumn stared down at her breasts hungrily. "I want those in my mouth."

Caroline grinned. "Me first." She snaked her hand around Autumn's hips, claimed the hard flesh of a nipple between her teeth and tugged.

"Oh," Autumn gasped.

Autumn's movements became more urgent, her hips rocking against Caroline's pelvis. Caroline slid her hand between them, gently cupping Autumn, then parting her wet folds, her fingers gliding easily into her.

"Yes," Autumn groaned, her hips pumping faster as Caroline thrust into her. "Oh God. Oh God. Caroline. Yes. Yes. Yes."

Autumn gasped and stiffened against Caroline. The delicate muscles clamped around Caroline's fingers undulating as Autumn's orgasm pulsed through her. Autumn sagged against Caroline's shoulder unable to sit up on her own. She brushed tender kisses along Caroline's neck.

"I don't think I can move," she whispered against Caroline's ear.

"That's okay. I like you where you are."

A few moments later, Caroline brushed the hair back from Autumn's face. "Let's get you to bed."

"Hmm, good idea." Autumn stood on shaky legs and reached for Caroline. As Caroline stood, Autumn brushed her palms to Caroline's chest, cupping her breasts. "I've been waiting for these."

❖

Caroline woke the next morning curled against Autumn, her breast pressed firmly to Autumn's back, her arm curled protectively around Autumn, her hand cupping her breast. Caroline sighed, luxuriating in the memories of their night together.

She lifted her head to check the bedside clock. Seven thirty. Thankfully it was Saturday morning, and they didn't have to get up. She raised up on her elbow and watched Autumn sleep, grateful she was getting some much-needed rest. She extracted her arm from around Autumn and brushed loose strands of hair from Autumn's face, tracing her fingers along the line of Autumn's jaw, down her neck, and along her shoulder. She brushed her lips tenderly across the smooth skin of Autumn's shoulder. Autumn was beautiful. The hours they had spent making love played through her mind. As she moved her fingers lazily across Autumn's body, she replayed the way Autumn responded to her touch, each sigh, every moan, the way the muscles in her neck tensed when she was on the brink of orgasm, and the way Autumn closed her arms around her, holding her as her body shook with the aftershocks of pleasure.

Just thinking of Autumn stirred her desire, and heat suffused her. She knew she should let Autumn rest, but now that she had touched Autumn, tasted her, she knew she would never get enough of the sweet tenderness she found in Autumn's body. She questioned the fairness of life. If there was any such thing as fairness, Autumn's illness clearly wasn't. The thought of anything hurting Autumn, the threat that she could be taken from her, left her trembling. She reverently caressed Autumn's stomach, grazing her fingernails across the delicate skin. She moved her hand to Autumn's breast, brushed her thumb gently across her nipple, watching as the flesh tightened and darkened. Autumn stirred, emitting an almost silent groan as she turned onto her back.

Caroline studied the gentle curves of Autumn's breasts as she held the supple weight in the palm of her hand. Her eyes moved to the flesh covering the port. Caroline raised her fingers to the tiny reminder of the fragility of Autumn's life and the tenuous thread weaving a bond between them. Autumn had found her way through all her defenses and had opened her heart to possibilities she thought she would never hope for again.

She traced her finger over the raised area of skin, then down the soft mound of Autumn's breast to her nipple. Autumn's chest rose with the deep intake of breath. Caroline lifted her eyes to Autumn's face, finding liquid blue eyes gazing up at her.

Autumn smiled as she raised her hand to cup Caroline's cheek. "What are you doing to me?"

Caroline smiled. "Saying good morning."

"Hmm. Suddenly, I think I could learn to be a morning person."

"Oh yeah?"

"Yes." Autumn slid her fingers around the back of Caroline's head, pulling her to her breasts. She groaned when Caroline's mouth closed around her nipple, her tongue stroking as she sucked.

Caroline slid her hand between Autumn's thighs, parting her. Her head buzzed as she dipped into the wetness slick against her fingers. She stroked her clitoris, mirroring the strokes of her tongue against Autumn's nipple.

Autumn groaned and thrust her hips to meet Caroline's hand, urging her deep inside her. "Oh, that feels so good."

Caroline pressed her sex against Autumn's thigh, her own desire coiling in her depths like the gathering force of a storm. When she heard Autumn groan and saw the muscles in her neck tense, Caroline was lost in wonder of her. She felt Autumn tighten around her, triggering her own impending orgasm. She had been drawn to Autumn from the first moment they met, and each week, each passing day, she had felt the growing attraction and so much more. She told herself she wouldn't make promises, would not expect any, that this moment and however many more she could have with Autumn would be enough. As her orgasm spilled over, she felt Autumn's arms tighten around her, pulling her to her, holding her. Caroline pressed her face against Autumn's neck and breathed in the scent of her as she luxuriated in the rightness of their joining. She closed her eyes. She was lost in Autumn. Autumn was everything and no amount of time with her could ever be enough.

❖

Autumn stretched languidly, the pleasant soreness in her muscles filling her with pleasant memories of Caroline. She reached out her hand but found the bed empty. Her eyes flew open and her heart raced. *Caroline?*

Autumn steadied herself and climbed out of bed. She stepped into a pair of shorts and slipped into a T-shirt before making her way to the kitchen. Caroline was standing at the stove wearing Autumn's blue silk robe. She let out a relieved breath, chiding herself for thinking for a moment that Caroline would have left. Autumn smiled as she trailed her eyes down the long lean legs, remembering those strong thighs between her legs as Caroline thrust against her.

Caroline glanced over her shoulder and smiled when she saw Autumn. Autumn felt the heat that was quickly building in her depths climb into her cheeks when she realized Caroline had caught her and knew exactly what she was thinking.

"Hello, sleepyhead. Hungry?"

Autumn stepped up behind Caroline, wrapping her arms around Caroline's waist as she looked over her shoulder into the frying pan.

Caroline turned her head and kissed Autumn on the cheek. "I thought we would try something different. Since you seem to do okay with eggs, I decided we would try French toast. You don't have to use the syrup if you don't want to."

"Yum," Autumn murmured appreciatively. "I think that might just work. Thank you."

Caroline smiled. "How are you feeling?"

"Better than I have ever felt in my life."

"That good, huh?"

"Oh yes. You have quite the special touch."

Caroline grinned. "It was special, all right."

Autumn laughed. She stepped away as Caroline placed the last of the French toast on a plate and turned off the stove.

"Come on, let's eat. Someone worked me over pretty good last night, and I'm starving."

Autumn took the first bite of her toast and groaned.

"Is it okay?"

"It's delicious."

"Really?"

Autumn nodded as she put another huge bite into her mouth. "God, can I tell you how good it is to eat something besides mac and cheese or scrambled eggs? This is heaven." Autumn looked up to see Caroline watching her. Her expression was hopeful and relieved. But beyond that, Autumn could see worry. She reached out her hand, taking Caroline's. "Thank you for taking such good care of me."

Caroline smiled and looked away.

Autumn was suddenly struck by how unsettled Caroline must feel after what they had shared. For Autumn, their night together had been so much more than sex, and as she recognized the look of fear and worry in Caroline's eyes, she understood that it was more for Caroline as well.

"How are you this morning? You know, with us?"

Caroline squeezed Autumn's hand. "I know we said we were going to take things slow and wait until after your treatments were over before we considered a sexual relationship, but last night I wanted you more than I have ever wanted any woman. I didn't care about consequences or anything that might happen after that."

"And today?"

"Today I'm trying to figure out how I ever managed to keep my hands off you as long as I did." Caroline raised Autumn's hand and brushed a kiss against her knuckles. "You are incredible."

Autumn was pleased to hear that Caroline didn't regret their night together. But she knew there was more. There was always more. "But?"

Caroline sighed. "But I'm still not sure what it means. I'm not sure I can be strong enough—"

"You don't have to make any promises, Caroline. I don't expect you to see the future or work miracles. I just want you to enjoy this. No expectations. No promises. Let's just see what happens next."

"I'm scared," Caroline admitted. "I'm scared of caring too much."

"I know, sweetheart. I know." Autumn swallowed her own fear and tried her best to reassure Caroline. The truth was, she was terrified too. She was terrified she would give everything, and

Caroline would walk away, that her cancer and the forever threat to her life would be too much for Caroline. But most of all, Autumn was terrified that she would come to the end of her life without ever truly knowing love. The thought left her empty inside. She thought of waking that morning to find Caroline gone. The panic had taken her breath. "I would never do anything to hurt you intentionally."

Caroline sighed. "I know." She stood, clearing their plates from the table. "I keep reminding myself to stay in the moment, not to let tomorrow or two months from now cloud what I am feeling right now."

"Caroline." Autumn met Caroline at the sink. She wanted to ask what Caroline was feeling, but instinctively knew not to push. "Right now, all I know is that you make me feel amazing. I don't know what that means, and at the moment I don't need to. I am just so happy that it *is*."

Caroline turned into her arms. Autumn wrapped her arms loosely around Caroline's neck and leaned into Caroline until their bodies touched. Caroline gripped Autumn's hips, then brushed her fingers along the tight muscles along her side. Autumn stopped thinking the moment their breasts touched. She tensed. Her body answered the call of Caroline's touch as effortlessly as taking a breath.

Autumn groaned and claimed Caroline's mouth. All her reservations and fear were a fleeting memory as she surrendered to her need. *No expectations. No promises.*

CHAPTER FIFTEEN

Autumn hung up the phone, propped her elbows on her desk, and dropped her head into her hands. She was struggling with an unusually hard week after her chemotherapy and wondered silently if the weeks of seemingly tolerable nausea and life-sucking fatigue had caught up with her. Had she finally reached the breaking point of her treatment, when the poison meant to save her would begin to break down her body to the point that she would fear surrender?

Since starting chemotherapy, she had seen two of her peers withdraw from treatment due to elevated white blood counts as their bodies succumbed to infections or other complications. She considered herself lucky that she had done so well this far. She ran her fingers through her hair. As she pulled her hand away, she noticed long strands clinging to her fingers. Tears filled her eyes. She had not lost her hair, but it had been steadily thinning over the past few weeks. Her body was showing signs of damage, and she wondered how much more she would have to endure, what else she would have to lose in this fight for her life.

"Are you all right?"

Autumn looked up to see Kate leaning against the doorframe, her brow furrowed with worry. Kate's eyes bored into her as if she could shield her with the intensity of her gaze.

"I'm fine." Autumn tried to smile but knew Kate wasn't buying it.

"Bullshit." Kate came into the room and leaned over Autumn's desk, her palms pressed against the worn wood, her gaze unyielding. "You're sick. Anyone can see it. What the hell are you doing here?"

"I needed to work."

"I've got it covered," Kate growled. "Let me take you home."

"No. Not yet."

"Why not? You're barely holding your head up and you look a little green. This isn't even your week to work." Kate's voice softened. "Autumn, what's wrong?"

Autumn leaned back in her chair and closed her eyes. "I am so tired of being tired. I don't know what I'm doing."

Kate frowned. "Has something happened?"

"No. It's just that I usually feel better by now. My treatment was days ago."

"Let me call Caroline to come get you."

"No," Autumn said more sharply than she meant. But she didn't want Caroline to see her now. She didn't want her to know how much she was struggling. She didn't want to see the shadow of fear in Caroline's eyes and feel her withdrawal.

"Then spill. You can't tell me something isn't wrong."

Autumn looked at her best friend, suddenly raw and vulnerable and so thankful for the tenderness she saw in Kate's gaze.

"Did something happen with Caroline? Have you had a fight or something?"

Autumn smiled. "No. Nothing like that."

"But there is something. I see the way she looks at you. I know there's more going on there than you've said. Lisa said you two are dating."

Autumn nodded. "When I first learned of my diagnosis, I was so shell-shocked I couldn't think of anything but getting through the surgery and treatment. I didn't even consider how my life would change in that time. I never could have imagined if I had tried. After the surgery I had a lot of time to think. I realized that, aside from you and Lisa and this company, I didn't have a real life. I didn't have a girlfriend, no one to care if I came home late, or to share a meal. I didn't even have a cat. I slowly realized I had been running from my life. I was suddenly afraid of running out of time. Throughout my treatment I've felt guilty for not being sicker. I can't help but look around at some of the others in that treatment room and wonder if I belong there. I wonder why others have gotten sick and I haven't."

Kate watched Autumn, her expression thoughtful. "And now?"

"I want so much more." Autumn smiled shyly at the memory of Caroline. "I want to believe I can have what you and Lisa have. I want to love like that. I want the freedom to lose myself in someone."

"You're falling for her, aren't you?"

Autumn was surprised by the statement. Kate wasn't the one to talk about love or any other emotion, for that matter. Autumn hadn't even been aware Kate had noticed her interest in Caroline.

"What?" Kate asked. "Just because I don't say much doesn't mean I don't see what's happening. You've been different since she's been with you. At first, I wasn't sure what it was, but the last few weeks you have this dreamy look about you when she's around. You seem happy."

Autumn sighed. "We slept together."

Kate's eyebrows rose. "And?"

"And she's not sure what she wants. She's afraid to get involved because she's already lost so much. She's afraid of the cancer."

Kate nodded. "That's understandable. She may be scared, but she's not running."

Autumn frowned. "What do you mean?"

"She knew what this all meant when she signed on." Kate straightened and held out her hands palms up. "She let this thing between you happen. Caroline doesn't strike me as the type of person to toy with your feelings or to walk out just because things get tough."

"No, of course not. But this is different. She just ended her marriage, and she lost her mother to cancer. There are times when I can feel that grief as clearly as if another person was sitting in the room. I don't want to hurt her. I don't want her to go through that again."

Kate dropped into the chair in front of Autumn's desk and

leaned forward, resting her elbows on her knees. "That's very valiant of you, but it's complete bullshit."

Autumn flinched, not expecting the sharp retort.

"You know, I had hoped that this whole experience would have taught you better than that. You always do this. You always think it's your place to protect everyone. You take on everyone's crap, and you never let anyone in. Do you have any idea how much it hurt when you wouldn't let me help you through this? I'm surprised you even let me help you here at work. I'm your best friend and you're hurting and it's like pulling teeth just to get you to tell me what the hell is going on. Caroline needs a freaking medal for getting this close to you."

Autumn was shocked by the anger and hurt she heard in Kate's voice. She had no idea she felt this way. "Kate, I'm sorry."

"Don't. Let me finish." Kate's gaze never wavered as she talked. "Caroline is the first person I have ever known you to allow to see you ill, let alone let her take care of you. Caroline is special, and you are a fool if you can't see that. Of course she's scared— she cares about you. We're all scared, Autumn. You can't protect us from caring about you. Not one of us would want to stop caring about you to save ourselves from this."

"What if I'm the one who's afraid?" Autumn said, her voice sounding small to her own ears.

Kate's anger evaporated, quickly replaced with concern. "You?"

Autumn nodded. "You're right. I am falling for her. I think I've been falling since the first time I met her. This is the first time in my life I've wanted someone the way I want her. I can't bear the thought of finding her, only to lose her because of this stupid disease. It would destroy me to see that hurt in her eyes. It would destroy me if she decides it's too much to chance. Everyone has always left. What if I can't be enough?"

"Oh, Autumn. Of course you're enough." Kate sighed. "Those women didn't leave you because you weren't enough. They left because *they* were not enough."

Autumn dropped her gaze. Kate was right. Nancy had said as much. Autumn had always let her mother come between her and her lovers. She had resented her mother for that. But wasn't that her choice? Had she allowed her mother to come between her relationships because she didn't want to commit? What was she really afraid of?

Autumn got up and walked around her desk. She leaned down and kissed Kate's cheek. "Thanks. I needed that."

Kate smiled sheepishly.

"I love you. You know that, right?"

Kate nodded. "We love you too."

Autumn nodded. "Are you still good with giving me a ride home?"

Kate stood. "Of course."

Autumn wrapped her arms around Kate and hugged her. She smiled as Kate's arms came around her in a tight embrace. "What would I ever do without you?"

Kate grinned. "I have no idea. Good thing you don't ever have to find out."

❖

Caroline put down the book she was reading when she heard the front door open. Autumn had left early and had been gone most of the day. Caroline knew Autumn had been struggling more than usual and was surprised she had gone to work.

"Hey," Autumn said as she hung her keys on a peg by the door.

"Hi." Caroline watched Autumn, noticing the dark circles under her eyes and the faint tremor in her hand. "I didn't hear the garage door. Where's your car?"

"I wasn't feeling well. Kate gave me a ride home."

Caroline's stomach clenched as her worry intensified. "Are you okay? Do you need anything?"

Autumn sat on the sofa next to Caroline. "I'm tired, but I'm okay. I don't know what it is this week, but I can't seem to get my feet under me."

Caroline lifted her hand and brushed the hair off Autumn's face. Guilt needled at her. She knew Autumn had been more active lately, and she had been the cause. "Maybe all the extra exertion is catching up with you."

Autumn clasped Caroline's hand. "No, sweetheart. Being with you has been the best thing for me." She kissed Caroline lightly on the lips, cupping her cheek in her hand. "I have to admit that I may be working too much, and I'm not sleeping well."

"Is something wrong?"

"Just too much in my head." Autumn leaned her head on Caroline's shoulder. "I've been almost out of my mind worrying about my mother, and I have to admit, I've been worried about you too."

"Me?"

"Don't worry. Kate has already given me a stern talking to. I realize I don't have to worry. I trust you."

Caroline tightened her arms around Autumn and leaned back on the sofa, pulling Autumn against her. "Good for Kate."

Autumn chuckled. "This is all new to me, you know. It isn't easy for me. I'm just getting used to having you and Kate and Lisa take care of me."

"Is it so bad?"

"No." Autumn brushed small circles with her fingers against Caroline's chest. "You have been wonderful, and I think I could get a little spoiled if you aren't careful. But it hasn't been easy feeling so weak, so vulnerable."

Caroline kissed the top of Autumn's head. "You have been incredibly brave, and you've pushed yourself hard. I think it's good to let us spoil you a little."

"In that case, I think I'll take a nap. I'm beat."

Caroline kissed Autumn tenderly. It meant a lot to her that Autumn was being honest about her insecurities. It was good to know she wasn't the only one struggling with new emotions.

"I think a nap is a brilliant idea."

Autumn's phone buzzed. Caroline sighed. "No rest for the weary, I guess."

Autumn grimaced. "Now what?" She frowned. "Hello?"

Caroline sat up, her stomach clenched into a knot when Autumn's eyes widened in shock. All the color drained from Autumn's face, and her breaths were quick and shallow. Caroline listened intently.

"Is she all right?" Autumn said, her voice shaking.

Caroline wanted to take Autumn's hand. Whatever was happening, it was bad. *What now?* She waited. Her hand rested gently on Autumn's back. The simple contact was all she could manage without intruding. She felt faint tremors ripple through Autumn's back.

"I understand. I'll be right there."

Caroline peered at Autumn. What the hell was going on?

Autumn took a deep breath and ran her hands through her hair. She reached for Caroline's hand. "My mother is in the hospital. There's been some kind of accident. I need to go."

"I'll drive you."

Autumn's eyes filled with tears.

"Hey," Caroline said, taking Autumn into her arms. "It's all right. I've got you. Let's get you to the hospital so you can find out what happened. You'll feel better when you see her for yourself."

Autumn nodded, her hands shaking against Caroline's neck. "Thank you."

Caroline hated to hear the fear in Autumn's voice. This was the last thing she needed. Autumn was barely standing as it was—she didn't need this added stress along with everything she was going through. Caroline pushed away the feeling of dread. Whatever had happened to Meredith, Caroline had the feeling the worst was yet to come.

❖

Autumn stared at the emergency room doctor, a young man who appeared still in his twenties with dark brown eyes and hair to match. His skin was pale and waxy as if he didn't get enough sun, and his hands were smooth and delicate. Autumn tried to keep up as he explained her mother's injuries.

"Your mother is very lucky to be alive, Ms. Landers. The best we can piece together is that she lost consciousness while driving. Her car left the road and traveled several yards down an embankment before hitting a tree. She has a broken left wrist, her shoulder is bruised, and there is a fracture to her left hip. Most of the bruising seems to be from the seat belt. We have given her something for the pain, and she is much more comfortable now. At this time, we are trying to figure out what caused her to lose consciousness, so we're running a battery of tests, and she'll need to be admitted to the hospital. She stated that she has been having bouts of dizziness over the past few days. Do you know anything about this?"

Autumn shook her head. "She hasn't said anything about any problems." *But how would I know since she isn't exactly speaking to me.* "She's going to be okay, right?"

The doctor nodded. "Her injuries are not life-threatening, but like I said, we need to get a handle on what caused her to lose consciousness. But there is one more thing you should know."

Autumn frowned. *What else could there be?* "What?

"Your mother's blood alcohol level was just within the legal limit. She was a little confused and disoriented when she arrived. Like I said earlier, we are running more tests, but it is possible that alcohol played a part in the incident."

Autumn was speechless. What was her mother thinking?

"Do you know if this is normal behavior for your mother? Does she drink regularly?"

Autumn was confused by the questions but nodded. "She drinks a glass or two of wine most days and sometimes has a drink at brunch, but I've never known her to drink in excess or to drink and drive."

He nodded. "It may be there was a medical issue that is affecting her judgment, but we do know alcohol was a contributing factor. I'll let you know more as soon as we have her tests back."

"Can I see her?"

"Of course. She's a little sedated, but I don't see a reason why you can't see her."

Autumn felt Caroline's fingers close around hers. She jumped at the contact. A sudden warmth seemed to surround her as Caroline stepped closer. She smiled faintly and squeezed Caroline's hand.

The doctor pulled back a curtain to a small treatment room. Her mother appeared to be sleeping. Her head was tilted slightly to the right, and her eyes were closed. Her arm was in a splint and an IV snaked out from beneath the sheet.

"I'll let you know as soon as I know more," the doctor said as he stepped into the hall and disappeared.

At that moment her mother opened her eyes and looked at Autumn. "What are you doing here?"

Autumn stepped closer to her mother. "The hospital called to let me know you were here. How are you feeling, Mother?"

"What does it matter?" She scowled.

"Of course it matters, Mother. I want you to be okay."

Her mother pointed a finger at Autumn. "You abandoned me. You can't just waltz in here and act like you care what happens to me now."

Autumn's heart sank. Did her mother really think she had abandoned her? "I have called you every day. I've even been by the house. You haven't answered any of my calls. I was told you were out of town and you didn't leave any information about where you were. What did you expect me to do?"

"Well, I certainly didn't expect my own daughter to walk out on me and embarrass me the way you did." Her mother turned her head away. "You should just leave. I'm sure you would rather be with your friends than stuck here with a sick old woman."

Autumn ground her teeth together so tightly she thought they would break. She shouldn't be surprised by her mother's treatment of her. She should probably feel grateful. If her mother was laying on the guilt, then she must be okay. But she couldn't shake the feeling that she *had* been the cause of this. She had known she would pay one way or another for walking out on her mother. She just didn't expect it to almost cost her mother her life.

"I'm not leaving, Mother. You can ignore me if you like, but I'm not leaving." Autumn motioned to Caroline to step into the hall. "You can go home. There's no need for both of us to wait around here all day. I can call for a ride later."

"I want to help. You're already exhausted."

"I know. But I can't leave her like this. I need to find out what's going on." Autumn took Caroline's hand. "Once they get her admitted and we know a little more, I'll come home and get some rest."

Caroline laced her fingers with Autumn's. "I heard what she said to you. You know it isn't true. Don't beat yourself up over something you had no control over."

Autumn nodded but didn't meet Caroline's eyes.

"Autumn"—Caroline pressed two fingers under Autumn's chin and lifted her head—"look at me."

Autumn obeyed.

"You are a good person and a good daughter. I'm sorry this happened, but it isn't your fault."

Autumn closed her eyes and nodded.

Caroline pressed a kiss to Autumn's forehead. "I want to be here with you. Once your mother is settled and we know more about her condition, I'll take you home."

Autumn wrapped her arms around Caroline, holding tightly to the strength and warmth of Caroline's body against hers. Her hands trembled and her legs felt weak. "What did I ever do without you?"

Caroline smiled. "Go sit with your mother. I'm going to get you something to eat. You look like you're about to fall to the floor." She brushed her fingers along Autumn's cheek. "I don't think I'll be able to manage mac and cheese, but I'll do my best. I'll be right back."

Autumn clasped Caroline's hand. "I'm scared."

"I know," Caroline said, pulling Autumn into a hug. "She'll be okay. You heard the doctor. Let's not jump to conclusions. Wait for the tests. Then we'll take things from there."

We. Autumn liked the sound of that. "You're right." She looked into the room at her mother and sighed. "It's going to be a long night. I could use something to eat. Thank you for always knowing what I need."

Caroline kissed her lightly. "I'll be right back."

Autumn watched Caroline walk away. The sudden shaking of her legs reminded her of the depth of her fatigue. She looked back into the treatment room at her mother. She hadn't abandoned her mother. Caroline was right. She wouldn't let her mother place this guilt on her. But this was still her mother, and she would do what she had to do until her mother was safe. She rubbed her face with her hand and slumped into the chair by the bed. The chair was hard. She grasped the cold metal bed rail and wondered why they made hospital furniture so uncomfortable.

It was nearly midnight when Caroline pulled the car into the drive. Autumn had fallen asleep almost the instant they were on the road. Autumn's mother had been admitted to the hospital, and so far, the tests had failed to identify any root cause for Meredith losing consciousness. The blood alcohol test had indicated there was alcohol in her system, but within the legal limit. Meredith hadn't been charged with DUI, but it was clear something was wrong.

"Autumn." Caroline took Autumn's hand. She brushed her fingers lightly across the back of her hand and up her forearm. "Autumn, we're home."

Autumn groaned. "I'm sorry. I didn't mean to fall asleep."

Caroline lifted Autumn's hand, placing a kiss to her fingers. "Let's just hope you can get back to sleep once we get you inside."

Caroline unfastened Autumn's seat belt and came around the car to help her to the house. Autumn pressed her hands to Caroline's shoulders and allowed Caroline to help her stand. Caroline caught Autumn as her legs buckled. Her arms wrapped tightly around Autumn's waist, bearing her weight.

"Easy." Caroline was afraid to let Autumn go. She would not let her fall. "Put your arm around my shoulders. We'll do this together."

Autumn slid her arm around Caroline's neck. Autumn's breath was hot on her skin. She shivered at the contact.

"Are you okay?" Autumn asked, her voice weak. "If I have to help you to the house, we might be in some trouble."

Caroline chuckled. "I'm fine. It just feels good to be close to you."

"Hmm, you too. I can't thank you enough for being there tonight. I don't think I could have gotten through it all without you."

"I'm sorry you're having to go through it. Come on, let's get you to bed."

Caroline led Autumn into the house and sat her on the bed. She leaned down and removed Autumn's shoes, unfastened Autumn's belt, and began to undo her pants.

"I can do this," Autumn protested but didn't move.

Caroline slid Autumn's pants off, then unbuttoned her shirt. "Sit up, sweetheart. Let me get this off you, and then you can sleep."

Caroline slid the shirt off Autumn's shoulders and quickly undid her bra. Caroline couldn't help but stare at the full round breasts, the rose-tipped nipples, and the ever-present swell of the port in Autumn's chest. Caroline sighed, laying Autumn back on the bed and pulling the sheet over her. Caroline was about to go when Autumn's hand closed around hers. "Where are you going?"

Caroline kneeled next to Autumn's bed. "I don't want to bother you. You need to rest."

Autumn pulled Caroline closer. "I need you to stay. I don't want to be alone right now. I'm afraid if you leave, I won't be able to sleep."

Caroline took Autumn in her arms. "I'm right here, sweetheart. I'll stay with you as long as you want." Caroline pressed a kiss to Autumn's temple. She frowned. Her heart thundered as fear struck her like a bolt of lightning. "Autumn, sweetheart. Are you feeling okay?"

"Just tired."

Caroline held her hand to Autumn's face. Heat radiated from Autumn's skin. Caroline swallowed. "I'll be right back. I need to get the thermometer. We need to check your temperature."

"I'm okay. Don't worry."

"It will only take a minute."

By the time Caroline came back, Autumn was asleep. A damp sheen of sweat coated her skin. Caroline had a sinking feeling in her stomach. If Autumn got sick, it would derail her treatment or worse. *No. This can't be happening. You can't be sick. I can't lose you too.* Caroline ran the thermometer across Autumn's forehead and down the side of her jaw. She stared at the readout. Autumn had a low-grade fever. Caroline wasn't sure what she should do. Should she take Autumn to the hospital? Should she let her rest? Maybe Autumn was just overexerted, and her body was feeling the stress.

Caroline stripped off her clothes and climbed into bed, pressing her body next to Autumn's. Autumn didn't stir. She would give Autumn until the morning. If she still had the fever then, they could call Dr. Mathis.

CHAPTER SIXTEEN

Four days had passed since her mother had been admitted to the hospital. She had been moved to a rehab facility to assist her while her hip healed. Autumn had hardly had time to sleep. Her mother wanted to go home, insisting that Autumn could take care of her there. Her mother seemed oblivious to Autumn's fatigue and the toll the endless hours at the hospital were taking on her.

Autumn hung her keys by the door and went to the kitchen. She hadn't eaten, and her stomach growled. She opened the refrigerator and searched the contents for anything she thought her palate could tolerate. She picked up a beer and turned the bottle in her hand, longing for the soothing respite the golden elixir promised. She shouldn't have alcohol—besides, the taste would likely be unbearable—and it was cold. Autumn sighed. *Give me a freaking break already.*

All the lights were off in the house, and she listened intently for any signs that Caroline was awake. Caroline had pleaded with her to see Dr. Mathis. She had been running a low-grade fever on and off for days. Autumn closed her eyes and held the cold bottle of beer to her forehead. She sighed and unscrewed the cap. She held the beer to her nose, testing the waters. Just before she took a drink, a warm hand closed around hers, pulling the bottle from her grasp.

"Let me take that from you before you do something you'll regret in about two seconds."

Autumn felt Caroline's breasts brush against her back. She

leaned into Caroline, needing the warm reassuring contact. She was mentally and physically drained.

"How are you doing?" Caroline asked gently. "I was beginning to think you weren't coming home tonight."

"My mother didn't have a good day. I was afraid if I left, she would end up getting kicked out. You know, you would think that at her age she would at least get tired of being so mean. I know *I'm* exhausted."

Caroline set the beer on the counter and wrapped her arms around Autumn. She pressed her lips against Autumn's cheek. "You feel warm. Have you had a fever today?"

"Who knows. I felt a little clammy a time or two, and all I've wanted to do all day is lie down."

"You know you can't keep going like this. Your immune system can't take it. Your next treatment is in two days. If they think you have an infection, you won't get the chemo."

Autumn sighed. "I know."

"Please stay home and rest tomorrow."

"I'll have to go see Mother for a little while."

Caroline tightened her grip. "Why? You can't do anything there. You can call her and check in as often as you need, but you need to rest."

"I can't just leave her there by herself. She needs me."

"I need you. Kate and Lisa need you. Can't you see what you're doing to yourself?" Caroline pulled away.

"Caroline, don't do this. I'm doing the best I can."

"No. You're doing what you think will make your mother happy. Well, how's that going to work when you're dead?" Caroline stormed out of the room.

A few minutes passed before Autumn could get up the nerve to knock on Caroline's door. She realized how badly she was messing things up with Caroline. She knocked tentatively and waited. When Caroline didn't answer, Autumn opened the door and stepped into the room.

"Can I come in?"

"Sure."

Autumn sat next to Caroline on the bed. "Do you want to tell me what that was about?"

Caroline sighed. "I can't watch you destroy yourself. It's killing me. You are so close to the finish, and you're throwing it all away."

"Caroline…" Autumn whispered.

"No. You don't eat, you don't sleep, you've had a fever for days, and you still won't listen to reason. You asked me to try. I convinced myself that things would be different this time. I can't watch you do this to yourself. I can't lose you."

Autumn cupped Caroline's face in her hands. The pain she saw in Caroline's eyes was enough to break her. "You're right. I should do better. I have to do better. God knows, I can't keep going like this." She kissed Caroline lightly, just a tender brush of lips. "I've asked a lot from you and I haven't given you very much reason to trust me."

"What do you want from me, Autumn?" Caroline asked, her voice raspy and wounded.

"Please be patient with me. I'm new to this and I haven't figured it all out yet. But I promise to do better. I'm not used to putting my needs before others', especially my mother's, but I know I've been going about this all wrong. I won't go tomorrow. I'll even call Dr. Mathis and talk to her about the fever. I haven't forgotten about that bucket list." Autumn grinned. "I guess I was kind of counting on you doing those things with me."

Caroline dropped her gaze.

"Please don't leave. Don't give up on me." Autumn felt a surge of fear, not of dying, but of facing the rest of her life without Caroline. "Please."

Caroline reached over and took Autumn's hand. "I won't leave. I made a promise."

Autumn shook her head. "You did." *So did I. It's about time I start living up to my end of this arrangement.* "Starting now, things will be different. That's my promise."

❖

Autumn rolled over and reached for Caroline, but the sheets were cool beneath her touch. Slowly, she opened her eyes and peered at the clock. It was a little past noon. She had talked to her mother earlier that morning and had slept deeply for the past four hours. As she fought to clear the fog from her brain, the sound of Caroline's voice drifted through the house.

"I understand. I'll let her know."

Autumn climbed out of bed, pulling on her robe. She found Caroline pacing in the living room.

"What's going on?"

Caroline froze, her expression furious.

"Caroline? What is it?" Autumn's heart sank. Something was wrong. She could see it in the lines around Caroline's eyes. She could see her anger, but beyond that there was worry.

Caroline tossed the phone onto the sofa and turned to Autumn. A muscle jumped at the side of her jaw. "I just got off the phone with the rehab center. Your mother wants to sign herself out against medical advice. She wants to go home."

"What? How? She can't even walk."

Caroline shrugged. "It seems she decided the rehab is an insurance scam. She wants to hire a private company to transport her home."

Autumn felt heat surge through her entire body. She knew without doubt this was her mother's countermove to her telling her she wouldn't be visiting today. *She couldn't let me have one day. She had to raise the bar. How could she? Don't I matter at all?* A hundred thoughts raced through Autumn's mind in seconds.

She glanced up to see Caroline watching her, a desperate look in her eyes. Autumn recalled their conversation the night before, her promise to Caroline ringing in her ear.

"What are you going to do?" Caroline asked, her words mirroring Autumn's thoughts.

Autumn shook her head in frustration. "God save that woman from herself." She took a deep breath to get her bearings and make a plan. She knew her mother expected her to run to the rescue. Caroline feared her falling on her sword. And she just wanted to lie back down and curl up in Caroline's arms.

A few seconds later, Autumn ran her fingers through her hair and let out her breath. "I'm going to call the rehab facility and get some information. Once I have an idea what all this means, I'm going to have a word with my mother." Autumn stepped closer to Caroline, brushing her hand down Caroline's chest. "Then we are going to have lunch. After that I'm going to try to talk you into taking a nap with me."

Caroline raised one eyebrow in question, a faint grin curling at the corners of her mouth.

Autumn raked her fingers along Caroline's breast, grazing her nails across her nipple. A muscle jumped in Caroline's jaw and her muscles tensed. "Although *nap* may be the wrong word for what I have in mind."

Caroline grinned, some of the worry and fear fading from her eyes. As promised, Autumn had talked to Dr. Mathis about the fever and had taken the warning to heart. She knew she was on thin ice. For the first time since the first day of her chemo treatment, Autumn was really scared. She berated herself for behaving as if her life was not a priority. Well, it might not be a priority to her mother, but that didn't mean that it wasn't to her, or to Caroline, and to her friends. She loved her mother, but she would no longer allow her to make her feel like she didn't deserve happiness, that her life was only significant in how it pleased her mother.

Autumn ran her hand beneath Caroline's shirt, raking her nails across Caroline's stomach. The muscles beneath her touch bunched, and the look in Caroline's eyes grew hungry.

Autumn smiled. "I guess I should make those calls."

Caroline reached down, grasped the edge of her T-shirt in her hands, and swiftly pulled it up and over her head, exposing her bare breasts. Autumn's gaze instantly fell to Caroline's breasts, the nipples hardening under her hungry gaze.

"I guess you better get started then," Caroline said as she reached for the waistband of her pants, unfastening the button and lowering her zipper.

Autumn's desire turned feral. Caroline grinned as she dropped a kiss to Autumn's lips, and then she quickly stepped out of reach. "Let me know when you're ready for that *nap.*"

❖

Autumn gripped the phone so hard she thought it would crumble in her grip. She wanted to scream. She wanted to throw something. She contemplated hanging up, but she also knew her mother would just pull another stupid stunt to get her attention.

"It is not an insurance scam, Mother. You fractured your hip, and it isn't safe for you to be home alone."

"You just want to stick me in this place so you won't have to take care of me. That woman has put ideas into your head. She's trying to come between us."

"Mother, this is ridiculous. No one is trying to come between us. You can't take care of yourself right now. You need to be at the rehab center for a little while until your hip is better. Then you can go home."

"You don't know what it's like. You don't have to stay here."

"You're right, Mother. I don't know what it's like. But I was there with you for twelve hours yesterday. I know they are taking care of you."

"I'm too old to deal with all these decisions by myself. I need you with me. I need to go home."

"You are sixty-three. You are not old, and I am not moving in with you."

"Family is supposed to take care of each other. What kind of child would abandon her mother like this?"

Autumn ground her teeth together. "I am not coming there today, Mother. I told you—I am exhausted. I have another treatment tomorrow. It may be a few days before I can see you. You need to stay at the rehab facility where someone can care for you. I can't stop you from leaving, but I won't be there if you do. I love you, but I can't do this with you anymore."

Autumn hung up the phone and plopped back onto the sofa,

throwing one arm over her face. Tears pricked at her eyes, not due to sadness, but to frustration. For once, couldn't she have a normal relationship with her mother? Couldn't her mother at least wait until these treatments were over to have a mental breakdown?

Gentle hands brushed lightly up her leg. Autumn lifted her arm from her eyes as Caroline—alas, fully clothed—took a seat next to her. She smiled as the warmth of Caroline's touch spread through her like the warm rays of the sun. She was amazed at how the simplest touch from Caroline seemed to reach into the depths of her very blood.

"How did it go?" Caroline asked, her voice soft as a summer rain.

Autumn wiped her face with her hands and sighed. "Who knows. She's lost her mind. There isn't anything I can do to change this situation for her. I'm not sure I even want to."

Caroline rubbed her hand up and down Autumn's arms, gently massaging the tender muscles. "Do you think she'll stay put?"

Autumn thought for a moment. Her mother had been irrational and argumentative, but she hadn't gone as far as Autumn had experienced in the past. "I think she will. I think she knows I won't come to the rescue this time. She really is hurt. If she knows what's best for her, she'll stay where she is for now."

"What about you? Are you okay?"

"Yes." Autumn smiled. "I have no idea what she'll do next, but I can't do more for her right now. It feels good to set a boundary with her. Maybe if I'd done that years ago, we wouldn't be here right now."

"Maybe. Maybe not. Most people don't change overnight. The important thing is that she's being cared for, and she's safe."

Autumn nodded. "I know."

"Now, I think the next thing on your agenda today was lunch." Caroline grinned. "What would you like?"

Autumn toyed with the bottom of Caroline's shirt, the corners of her mouth curling upward in a mischievous grin. "Maybe we should take that nap first."

Caroline shook her head. "Nope. It doesn't work that way."

On cue Autumn's stomach rumbled. "Okay, so maybe I am a little hungry."

"How about eggs with cheese and maybe a little toast?"

Autumn raked her fingernails across Caroline's stomach. She loved the way the muscles bunched when she did that. She loved knowing Caroline responded to her that way. She rose up and wrapped her arms around Caroline's neck, then pulled Caroline closer and kissed her thoroughly.

Caroline groaned. After a moment she nipped Autumn's lower lip with her teeth, then pulled away. She reached for Autumn's hands, pulling Autumn's arms from around her neck. "Oh no, you don't. I know that ploy, and it isn't going to work this time." She stood and walked to the kitchen. "Lunch. You have to have lunch."

Autumn chuckled. Her heart swelled with the tender affection she heard in Caroline's teasing voice. Despite the stress her mother had caused, she felt unusually peaceful. She was coming to the end of her chemotherapy, she was learning to set boundaries with her mother, she had wonderful friends, and she had Caroline. She had a lot to be grateful for. She had never believed she would find love. It was strange to think that it took something as terrible as cancer for her to find it. But she did love Caroline. She loved her deeper than she had ever loved before. The realization made her smile.

CHAPTER SEVENTEEN

Caroline sat beside Autumn listening to every word Dr. Mathis said. Autumn's white blood cell count was unusually high, but still below the threshold that would keep her from having her treatment. Dr. Mathis was not pleased. Caroline's heart raced and her hands were sweating. She had been anxious about Autumn's health for days. Now that they were face-to-face with the reality of what this could mean for Autumn finishing her chemotherapy, Caroline could hardly control the shaking in her hands.

"I'm going to approve you for treatment today, but I want you on restricted activity for the next two weeks. That means no work. And I don't want you in public places, in order to reduce your risk of exposure. Your immune system is compromised. We can't take any more risks."

"Are you saying I can't leave the house?"

Dr. Mathis looked at Autumn sternly. "Yes. That would be ideal."

Autumn shook her head. "I don't know if I can do that for the full two weeks. My mother was in an accident a few days ago, and she fractured her hip. She's in a rehabilitation center right now, and she isn't exactly happy about it. She's already threatening to leave the center. If I don't go see her after a few days, I'm afraid she'll check herself out and go home."

Caroline held her breath. She heard the fear in Autumn's voice. She understood Autumn's concern, but couldn't Autumn see that her health was so much more important right now?

"I could go visit with your mother. I can take her things she might need and just check in on her." Caroline would face the devil himself if Autumn would just rest and stay home until this was all over.

Autumn frowned. "I don't think that's a good idea. As sweet as it is for you to offer, she already thinks you're trying to keep me from her."

Dr. Mathis put up her hand stopping further conversation on the matter. "I'm sorry to hear about Meredith. It sounds like the rehab is the best place for her right now. Don't worry—I'll speak with Meredith myself. I'll also let the women's group know and set up daily sitters. We all know Meredith. She won't misbehave with the ladies watching. You won't need to worry about a thing."

Autumn opened her mouth to respond, but no words came out. It seemed to take a moment for the idea sink in. "That's a really good idea, actually." She sighed. "Thank you."

"There's no need to thank me. Meredith and I are friends. I know more about her moods than you think." She smiled warmly at Autumn. "Your health is very fragile right now, Autumn. Meredith is being well cared for. It's time for you to do the same for yourself."

Caroline took Autumn's hand. "Please, sweetheart."

Autumn nodded. "I understand." She squeezed Caroline's hand. "Anything. I'll do it. But after being cooped up in the house for a few days, no one will want to be around me anyway."

Caroline's relief was palpable. She could have kissed Dr. Mathis for taking care of the issue with Meredith. If they could get through a few more weeks, Autumn had a chance. They had a chance. She smiled. "I'm glad you're listening to reason for once." She let some of the tension ease from her shoulders as Autumn's fingers tightened around her hand.

❖

Caroline woke to the gentle play of Autumn's fingers brushing light strokes across her stomach. Autumn was warm against her side, and the heat of her breath was a gentle caress against her ear. It had been an exceptionally hard week for Autumn, and Caroline knew she hadn't been sleeping. It seemed the treatments had finally caught up with Autumn, creating a new level of hell. Autumn had done everything Dr. Mathis had asked. But most days leaving the house would have been out of the question anyway, since Autumn could barely get out of bed.

Caroline worked to hide her smile as Autumn teased and stroked her skin. She hoped this meant Autumn was feeling better. Autumn's fingers slipped lower, brushing gentle strokes through the curls between her legs. Caroline groaned, turning her face to peer through heavy lids at Autumn. "Good morning."

Autumn flattened her hand against Caroline's stomach.

Caroline covered Autumn's hand with hers, pulling Autumn's arm around her. "Did you sleep at all?"

Autumn pressed a kiss to Caroline's shoulder. "A little."

Caroline shifted onto her back and looked up at Autumn. Dark circles shadowed Autumn's eyes and her color was a little off. A faint yellow had seeped into her eyes over the past few weeks. Pain ripped through Caroline's heart at the thought of the invisible invader that was ravaging Autumn's body. Her liver enzymes continued to be elevated, and that would be the next likely site of the cancer if it returned. The likelihood of Autumn's long-term survival if the cancer recurred dropped drastically. But she couldn't think like that. Autumn was responding well to the treatment. There was no reason to believe in anything but a full recovery.

In the beginning Autumn had talked freely about her cancer, but since they had become intimately involved, she'd noticed Autumn's attempts to protect her from the more worrisome aspects of her treatment and prognosis. Autumn was painfully thin now, having lost a staggering thirty pounds over the past six months.

Caroline lifted her hand to Autumn's face and pressed her lips to Autumn's, cradling her cheek reverently in her hand. She closed her eyes, wanting to hold on to this moment. "I love waking up with you."

Autumn deepened the kiss. "I love watching you sleep. I love feeling you against me. I love feeling the steady beat of your heart against my palm as I hold your breast like this."

Caroline knew she should pull away. Autumn was weak and tired, but her touch ignited something deep inside that Caroline couldn't control. Her heart raced with each stroke of Autumn's fingers against her skin. She didn't want to think of Autumn's illness—she didn't want to think of the future. All that mattered in that moment was Autumn in her arms. Caroline was lost in the feel, the scent, the sounds that were uniquely Autumn.

Autumn slid on top of Caroline, parting her legs with her thigh. Caroline was lost in the softness as their breasts brushed and melded together, and then the gentle pressure of Autumn's thigh pressed against her sex.

"My God, Autumn. Do you know what you do to me?"

Autumn leaned down and kissed Caroline, her tongue dancing in Caroline's mouth, making Caroline's skin tingle from head to toe.

"You should rest," Caroline whispered when Autumn sat up, pressing her sex against Caroline's pelvis.

"I promised not to leave the house. I didn't promise not to need you."

Caroline's heart skipped a beat, then accelerated. Nothing excited her more than knowing Autumn wanted her, needed her.

In one swift move, Caroline sat up, twisted, and rolled Autumn beneath her. She hovered just above Autumn as she looked down at the beauty of Autumn's body. She rested her weight on one elbow as she cupped Autumn's sex in her hand, pushing her fingers gingerly between the wet folds.

"Autumn," Caroline whispered, her voice a desperate plea.

"Yes," Autumn answered.

Lost in the feel, the sound, the scent of Autumn, Caroline slid into her. Autumn arched her back and moaned in pleasure.

"Oh yes. So good."

Caroline could barely control her need. She wanted to claim Autumn. She wanted to pour every drop of desire, hope, and need into each thrust. She pushed back on her knees, parting Autumn's thighs, lifting them to rest against her own. She watched Autumn's face as she thrust inside her.

"You are so beautiful."

Autumn's hips lifted, answering each thrust of Caroline's hand. With each contraction of tiny muscles around Caroline's fingers, shocks of electric current rippled through her. She groaned. She loved this. She loved this connection with Autumn.

"Yes, baby. Yes. Please. More."

Caroline slid down Autumn's body until her lips brushed her swollen clitoris. She blew hot breath against the engorged flesh. Autumn thrust upward to meet her lips. Caroline closed her mouth around Autumn's clitoris and matched the strokes of her tongue to the thrust of her hand.

"Oh God. Yes," Autumn cried.

Caroline felt the subtle shudder of tiny muscles against her fingers. She moaned as her own pleasure surged and the tendrils of her orgasm unfurled, rippling through her stomach, electric jolts that urged her to thrust harder, faster into the sweet heat of Autumn's depth.

Her muscles throbbed as Autumn clenched around her fingers. Autumn arched her back, pushing against Caroline's hand, and cried out her pleasure. Autumn's fingers dug into her shoulders, holding her, guiding her. She gently caressed Autumn with tender strokes of her tongue until Autumn stilled, the muscles in her legs relaxed, and she let out a contented sigh.

Caroline crawled up the bed, placing gentle kisses against Autumn's stomach as she went. She tenderly kissed Autumn's lips. "Are you okay?"

"Oh my God, I am more than okay," Autumn purred. She wrapped her arms around Caroline's neck, pulling her into a deep kiss. "If you had asked me that question earlier, I would have said I didn't have the strength to move, but it appears you have healing powers, Ms. Cross. After what you just did to me, I feel amazing."

Caroline smiled as she dropped another kiss to Autumn's chin.

"I see you're feeling rather proud of yourself," Autumn teased.

Caroline laughed. "Why shouldn't I? I just had the most

beautiful woman in the world share the most beautiful orgasm with me, and that's just the start of my day."

Autumn grinned. "If that's just the start, I can't wait to see what else you can do."

Caroline let out a guttural growl. "I'm afraid you'll have to wait. We have to get you to your appointment."

Autumn rolled her eyes. "I knew I should have woken you up earlier."

Caroline peered down at her. "Why didn't you?"

"I was enjoying watching you sleep. You needed the rest."

Caroline tightened her arms around Autumn. "I need *you*." *I need you so much it hurts. Don't you ever leave me. Please.* "I don't want to miss a moment with you."

Autumn stilled, as if sensing something much deeper in Caroline's voice and the protective way she held her.

"Caroline?" Autumn whispered.

Caroline peered down at Autumn, her gaze gentle but fierce.

Autumn brushed her fingers lightly along Caroline's face. "I am yours for all of my days. I love you."

Caroline closed her eyes. Her arms trembled until her body shook from the strain of holding herself up and holding back the ache in her heart. She lowered herself against Autumn until the lengths of their bodies touched and buried her face in Autumn's neck. She tightened her arms around Autumn. Unable to hold back her tears, she felt dampness streak her cheeks and wet Autumn's skin.

"It's okay," Autumn soothed. "You have already given me the most precious gift I have ever known. I feel like I've been waiting for you my whole life. I've never felt this way about anyone before."

Caroline choked back a sob. "I can't lose you."

"You won't."

"You don't know that."

Autumn caressed Caroline's back with one hand and gently held her head with the other. "I feel you inside me, inside my heart. I will fight for that with everything that I am."

❖

Caroline sat by the pool watching the sun set through the trees. The leaves were turning. Poplar trees had turned yellow, and hints of orange tinted the maples. Caroline had a game in an hour, but she couldn't bring herself to prepare. Autumn had said she loved her, gentle promising words she wanted to believe more than she had ever wanted anything. She'd had a front-row seat to the cruelty and disappointment life could deliver. She couldn't deny she loved Autumn, but the idea of opening her heart to that kind of hurt again was more than she was ready for.

"Hey." Autumn's gentle voice drifted over the rhythmic lapping of the water against the pool.

Caroline turned as Autumn took a seat next to her, sliding her feet into the glowing blue water. "Sorry, I didn't hear you."

"You seemed a million miles away." Autumn brushed her hand down Caroline's back, a subtle intimate gesture that made Caroline's skin tingle. "Aren't you going to the game?"

"Yeah, I guess I lost track of time." She could feel Autumn's gaze on her, knew Autumn wasn't buying her story. "I just needed to think about some things for a few minutes. I still have time."

"Do you want to talk about it?"

Caroline shook her head. "I think running my ass off for a couple of hours will do me a lot of good."

"Hmm. That's sounds like something I would like to watch."

Caroline smiled. "Not this time. You're homebound, remember?"

Autumn sighed. "Yeah, I remember. A few more days of this, and I'll go stir-crazy."

Caroline leaned over and kissed her. "It's almost over. Besides, I've kind of enjoyed having you all to myself."

"Oh yeah?" Autumn slipped her hand beneath Caroline's T-shirt, raking her nails along Caroline's side. "Keep talking like that and you may not make the game after all."

"Oh, really?"

"Really." Autumn kissed Caroline long and slow until Caroline felt the familiar flutter in her stomach. Just as Caroline tried to deepen the kiss, Autumn pulled away. "That should hold you for a couple of hours."

Caroline groaned.

"Good luck at your game."

"What game?"

Autumn laughed. "Go on. You need this. I'll be here when you get back."

Caroline gaped at Autumn. "I can't believe you just did that. How am I supposed to concentrate now?"

"I have a feeling you will do just fine. Just don't crack your head this time."

Caroline shook her head and laughed as Autumn walked back to the house. Every pore in her body craved Autumn. Her heart fluttered at the lingering sensation of Autumn's lips against hers. Who was she kidding? She had fallen hard for Autumn. All her attempts to protect her heart were an illusion.

CHAPTER EIGHTEEN

A re you ready?" Caroline asked, taking Autumn's hand as they stepped into the treatment room for what Autumn hoped would be the last time.

"I'm ready." Autumn smiled.

Nancy greeted Autumn and Caroline with a bright smile. "Today's the big day. What do you say we get this over with, so you can go celebrate?"

Autumn took her place in the familiar recliner. She looked around the room at the familiar faces, her heart mournful for those who hadn't made it through. She was one of the lucky ones. She was far from out of the woods, but at least the treatment had worked to this point. Her cancer markers were better than they had hoped. Her two weeks of rest had rejuvenated her, and she was hopeful she would soon be able to put this part of the nightmare to rest.

She glanced over at Caroline, who intently watched Nancy insert the intravenous lines into the port. Neither of them had been able to sleep the night before. They both knew they wouldn't have any answers at the end of the day, but the thought of this being her final treatment brought up so many emotions she hadn't expected. Beyond the treatment itself and her battle with cancer, they now faced new challenges to their relationship. Would Caroline really move out and get her own apartment? How would the dynamic between them change when Autumn no longer needed Caroline to take care of her? How would life be different, knowing everything she did now?

Nancy patted Autumn's hand. "You're all set, sweetie. You know the drill."

Autumn nodded. "Thank you, Nancy."

"So, now that you're finishing up, what are you looking forward to the most?" Nancy asked.

Autumn smiled. "I can't wait for food to taste good again."

Nancy laughed. "I bet." She squeezed Autumn's hand. "I am so glad you made it through." She glanced at Caroline and grinned. "At least something good came of all this."

Heat rose to Autumn's cheeks and her heart swelled when she looked at Caroline. "Yeah, it did."

"Do you two need anything?" Nancy asked.

Caroline shook her head.

"No. We're good for now," Autumn said leaning her head back against the chair. "Just ready to be done."

"All right," Nancy said with a warm smile. "I'll check on you in a bit."

Caroline scooted her chair closer to Autumn. "You know, I really like her."

"Yeah." Autumn smiled. "Me too." Autumn was glad to have mended the relationship with Nancy. She still had regrets for how things had ended between them, but they were friends now, and things had turned out for the best for both of them.

The day seemed to go by faster than usual, and before she knew it, Nancy was back to disconnect the lines and hook her up to the pump she would wear for the next two days. God, she couldn't wait to be done with that pump.

"You're ready to go," Nancy said, smiling at Autumn.

Autumn took a deep breath and let it out slowly. She reached out her hand to Caroline, who watched her with an odd smile curving her lips as if she was trying not to laugh. Caroline took her hand and helped her stand. Together they walked through the room, sharing well wishes and warm hugs with the men and women she had shared this room with over the past six months.

At the end of the hall, Autumn reached up and grasped the end of a yellow rope. She tugged the rope back and forth, ringing a large brass bell. Cheers erupted all around her. Tears began to flow freely down her cheeks. Autumn turned to Caroline, who wrapped her in her arms and kissed her soundly. More cheers and whistles filled the room.

When Autumn pulled back from the kiss, Caroline still held her with one arm firmly wrapped around her waist.

"You did it, sweetheart. You did it."

Autumn was overwhelmed with joy and relief. The worst of her journey was over. Now it was time for her adventure to begin.

❖

Autumn opened the door and found Kate poised with her hand about to knock. She had been watching the clock for what seemed like an eternity waiting for Kate to get there. It had been a long three weeks, and despite talking to Kate and Lisa on the phone, she desperately wanted to see them.

"Hey, come in. I can't wait to show you what I've drawn up."

"Good to see you too," Kate teased, pulling Autumn into a hug. "Do you think you can slow down a minute and just catch up?"

"Oh yeah, right. Sorry." Autumn smiled. "I've just been looking forward to this all day. I guess I'm a little excited."

Kate smiled. "I'm happy to see it. You seem to be feeling better. You're too damn skinny, but you look better."

Autumn nodded, leading Kate into the kitchen. "What would you like to drink?"

"Iced tea would be great," Kate answered.

"You're right, I am feeling better. I'm not sure if it's because something has changed, or if it's just relief that the treatments are over. I still have to have tests once a month for the next three months. If all goes as hoped, they will stretch to every three months. I have a good feeling about it, though."

"What about Caroline?"

Autumn smiled. "She's hanging in there. She's signing a lease on a place next Friday."

Kate frowned. "How do you feel about that? I kind of expected her to just stay here. I mean, you've already lived together for six months."

"Yeah, but not as a couple. We only know each other because of my cancer. We don't know each other without that dynamic. We decided it would be fun to date awhile before we make things more permanent."

"Meaning she gets to keep some walls up between you in case you get sick again?"

Autumn frowned. "Maybe there's some of that, but some of it is about me too. I've changed. I'm not sure what some of those changes mean, or what they will look like in my life. I don't want my feelings for Caroline to get mixed up in the middle of the things I need to work out."

"Okay, I can see that." Kate bit her lip as she studied Autumn. "Have you told her you love her?"

Autumn warmed as her feelings for Caroline washed over her like a wave. "Yes, I told her."

Kate's gaze remained steady as she took in the information. "And what about her?"

"She doesn't really have to say it. I already know. I know by the way she touches me. I know by the way she says my name. I feel it in so many ways."

"What about Meredith? How is she taking it?"

"Mother doesn't get a say. This is my life. I used to look at you and Lisa and wish I could have what you have together. I never thought it would happen for me. I won't let anyone take that from me now, not even my mother."

Kate smiled. "Hell, yeah. I like this new you."

Autumn couldn't contain her grin. "So, how bad are you freaking out about Tuesday?" she said, changing the subject.

Kate blew out her breath and groaned. "I've never been so excited and scared to death at the same time. I have a feeling this is what my life is going to be like from now on. I had no idea having a baby would change everything so much."

"I think it's wonderful. And you should probably get used to it.

I know you. By the time this kid is walking, you'll want to wrap her in Bubble Wrap and put her in a helmet."

Kate shook her head and gripped her hair in her hands. She groaned again. "Right now, I'm more worried about Lisa. She's so ready. This has been so hard on her. I honestly don't know how she's gotten through this."

"You. You are how she's gotten through it. You are a wonderful partner, and you're going to be an amazing mom."

"Yeah?"

"Absolutely." Autumn wrapped her arm around Kate's shoulders and squeezed. "Now, do you want to see the plans or what?"

Kate smiled. "Yeah, let's talk work." Kate followed Autumn into the office. She stared at the plans on Autumn's desk, her brow creased in a deep frown. "I'm sorry. What project is this? I don't recognize it."

Autumn smiled nervously. "That's because we haven't talked about this one."

Kate tilted her head to the side, confused. "Okay. What is it?"

"It's yours."

Kate looked back at the plans, realization slowly dawning on her face. "Wait. You want to do this at our house?"

Autumn's smile grew wider. "Unless you don't like it or want to do something else. We can change it however you want. But look. I designed the swings so that they can be changed out as the baby grows. It will start out as a swinging daybed for you and Lisa to spend time with the baby. Then as she gets older, it will transform into a toddler swing and a porch swing. Finally, it will have real swings, a slide, monkey bars, and a climbing wall."

She pointed to a section of the drawing in the corner. "This will be the adult area where everyone can hang out and watch her play."

Kate wasn't saying anything. She just stared at the plans, shaking her head.

"You know, it's okay if you hate it," Autumn said, suddenly feeling a little afraid she had overstepped.

Kate sighed. "I don't know what to say. I can't believe you want to do all of this for us."

"Of course I do. You and Lisa are my family. I want everything to be perfect for you."

"How are we going to get all of this done? Lisa will kill me if I bring in a work crew now, and she certainly isn't going to want all that noise going on when the baby gets home."

"I have it all covered. The supplies are already on hand. I had Holly build the swing in her garage. It will be a snap to assemble. As for the excavation, the crew is geared up to be at your house as soon as you pull out of the drive Monday. Everything will be done by the time you bring Momma and baby home. I wanted it to be a surprise for Lisa."

Kate gaped at Autumn. "Wow." She frowned. "What about you? Where are you going to be?"

"Not to worry. I'm going to make sure the crew knows exactly what to do Monday and see to the excavation. I'll be at the hospital bright and early Tuesday morning."

Kate nodded, her eyes suddenly glassy with tears. "You know, I was afraid you wouldn't be here for this. I was afraid we were going to lose you."

Autumn wrapped Kate in her arms. "Not this time. Not for a long time. I plan on seeing this little girl grow up."

Kate pulled back, wiping tears from her eyes with her palms. "I'm going to hold you to that." Kate smiled. "It's good to have you back."

Autumn smiled. She was back, in some ways better than ever. "Yeah, me too."

❖

Caroline was beat. She had spent the day working with her father, and between the physical exertion and the heat, her legs felt like they weighed a ton and her back was in knots. If they could get the house dried in by the end of the day, they wouldn't have to worry about the storm system blowing in. They had three windows to go, but these were no ordinary windows. They were built to withstand hurricanes and weighed more than Caroline cared to guess. She was barely holding on to her end, as she stepped onto the edge of the scaffolding twenty feet off the ground. The window slipped easily into place and she relaxed a little. That was a mistake. She shifted her footing to reach out over the scaffold so she could secure the window. It had already started to rain, and the boards were slippery. She felt the pressure of the nail gun release into the wood. A second later her foot slipped out from under her and she was airborne.

A lightning bolt of pain ripped up her leg the instant her foot made contact with the ground.

"Caroline!" her father yelled an instant before her head hit the side of the scaffold.

Her vision dimmed and everything went dark.

Caroline woke in the emergency room. Her vision was blurry, and she wasn't sure what day it was. She groaned. "What happened?"

Her father's thick rough hand closed around hers. "You fell off the scaffold and hit that hard head of yours, banged up your ankle too."

"Shit."

"Shit is right. You almost gave me a heart attack. Good thing you have a hard head like your old man."

Caroline blinked. "How long have I been out?"

"You woke up a time or two, but I guess you don't remember." He sniffed and pulled away.

Caroline turned her head, searching his face. "Hey, come on, Jack. We've been through tougher scrapes than this."

He shook his head. "Not like this, baby girl. They said there was some swelling on your brain. I thought they were going to have to cut a hole in your skull. Jesus, you almost died, Caroline. What the hell would I do if I lost you?"

"Dad. I'm okay. What the hell did I hit my head on anyway?"

He shook his head and let out his breath. "Your nail gun was a few seconds ahead of you and hit the ground a second before you did. Thank God you took most of the impact on your foot. You hit your head on the scaffold as you crumpled to the ground. Your hard hat took some of the hit, but it was knocked off."

Caroline frowned. "How long have I been here?"

"About four hours. I wasn't sure you were going to wake up at all."

"Don't worry, Dad. I'm going to be okay. Like you said, I have a hard head."

Caroline was having trouble piecing things together. Her dad explained everything, but her head was still throbbing, and her thoughts were a jumbled mess. "What time is it?"

He looked at his watch. "It's a little after seven. Why?"

Caroline took a deep breath. "I need you to call Autumn. She'll be freaking out by now. Where's my phone?"

Jack shrugged. "You didn't have your phone on you. You usually leave it in the truck when you're on site."

"I need you to call her, Dad."

"Okay. What about Jane? Do you want me to call her?"

"No, Dad. That's all in the past. I don't want her here."

Her father nodded. "Things with Autumn…it sounds serious."

Caroline sighed. "She's important to me."

"Okay. I'll call her."

Caroline gave him the number. She closed her eyes the moment he walked out to make the call. She didn't remember most of the last day of her life. What if she hadn't woken up? What if she had landed headfirst? Damn, how did she let this happen? She needed to see Autumn. She had been holding back from Autumn for weeks. What would Autumn think about her not coming home?

Reality hit Caroline like a ton of bricks. What if she hadn't come home? What if this had been the end for her? Tears stung her eyes. She had been wrong about everything.

❖

Autumn's heart hammered against her chest as if it was trying to break free. Since receiving the call from Caroline's father, she hadn't been able to think of anything but Caroline. She didn't want to think of Caroline hurt. *Dammit. Not now. Please don't let me lose everything now.*

Autumn rushed to the reception desk and asked to see Caroline. Before the woman at the computer could pull the information up, Autumn heard a soft voice over her left shoulder call her name.

"Autumn. I can take you to her."

She turned to see the face that belonged to the now familiar voice she had heard over the phone. There was no mistaking the gray-blue eyes staring back at her, eyes exactly like Caroline's.

"I'm Jack, Caroline's father."

Autumn nodded, unable to speak. She swallowed, her gaze raking over the fine lines of his face, scrutinizing every nuance for any hint to what was happening with Caroline.

"Is she—"

"She's banged up, but she's going to be okay."

Autumn felt her knees go weak and reached out for the wall to steady herself. To her relief, Jack's strong hand took her arm and guided her to a chair.

"Now, now. There's no need for any of that. My girl is a tough kid. It will take a little more than a bump on the head to keep her down."

Autumn looked up, thankful for the tenderness in Jack's voice. She looked into Jack's eyes, a rush of added fear washing through her. "She had a concussion a few months ago. She collided with another player in a soccer game. Another concussion is dangerous."

Jack nodded. "I know. I can't tell you how many times when she was a kid that her mother threatened to make her wear a helmet anytime she was awake."

Autumn couldn't help but laugh at the image. "That might not be a bad idea."

Jack laughed. "Let's get you back there. She's been asking for you."

Autumn felt a surge of urgency. Caroline was asking for her. She frowned as a new thought intruded on her desperate need to see Caroline. Was Jane there too? Autumn swallowed. It didn't matter. All that mattered was Caroline.

Caroline lay in a bed in a curtained-off room very much as she had the first time Autumn had brought her to the hospital. Autumn stared at her still form covered with a thin sheet and a white woven blanket.

"I'll let you have some time. I'll check back in a while." Jack patted Autumn's back.

"Thank you," Autumn said, throwing her arms around Jack's neck. "Thank you for calling me." She sighed as Jack's strong arms wrapped around her in a tender hug.

Jack held her for a long moment before pulling away. He smiled down at her, his short blond hair raked loosely across his forehead, his steel-gray eyes looking at her, calm and steady. "It's good to meet you, Autumn. I hope to have a chance to talk later." He nodded to Caroline. "She's always been stubborn. That's my fault. Be patient with her. She has a hard head in more ways than one."

Autumn sighed. "I don't mind. I just want her to be okay."

Jack nodded toward the room. "Go ahead. She's waiting for you." He placed a kiss on Autumn's cheek and smiled.

Autumn watched him walk away before turning to the room where Caroline held the edge of the blanket gripped in her fists. She stepped up to the bed, her eyes assessing every inch of Caroline's body. A soft cast covered her right ankle, and a white bandage was wrapped around Caroline's head. Caroline looked damaged but strong. Autumn was thankful to see the faint rose color of her cheeks from her day in the sun. The heart monitor sounded the steady beat of Caroline's heart. Autumn took a deep breath and slipped her hand into Caroline's. Tears pricked her eyes, blurring her vision. She took Caroline's hand, holding it lightly in hers. She took a deep breath, feeling Caroline's hand close around hers, grounding her. The strong rhythm of Caroline's heart sounding from the machine across the room was a distant comfort reassuring her that Caroline was going to be okay.

CHAPTER NINETEEN

H i," Autumn said as she leaned down to kiss Caroline gently on the lips. "How are you feeling?"

"Hi," Caroline answered. "I'm okay now." She smiled and squeezed Autumn's hand that held hers. "I'm sorry about this. We were supposed to have dinner."

Autumn brushed her fingers through Caroline's hair. "Oh, Caroline. You scared the life out of me. I'm so glad you're okay."

"I think the bad stuff is over. Don't worry. I didn't mean to put you through this."

"No," Autumn said. "I'm so thankful for every moment I have with you. You've changed everything, you know."

Caroline smiled. "So have you. I'm sorry I've been such a coward. I worried about things I can't control, but I also realize that if I don't let that go, I'll lose the most important thing I've ever known." Caroline's voice was husky as she pulled Autumn closer. "I don't want to run anymore. I have no idea how much time you have. I have no idea how much time I have. All I know is that I love you. I don't want to worry about test results or safety harnesses. I want to spend every day for the rest of my days loving you."

Autumn blinked away tears. She sighed. "Just exactly how hard did you hit your head?"

Caroline laughed. "Maybe it finally knocked some sense into me." Caroline regarded Autumn intently. "I love you, Autumn. I have loved you for a long time—I was just too stubborn to admit it." She squeezed Autumn's hand, peering into her eyes. "I thought I knew what love was, but you changed everything I thought I knew. I love you with every cell in my body. I don't know if we have a week, a month, a year, or fifty years. I just know I want every second of it to be with you."

"Oh, Caroline," Autumn whispered. "I love you." She kissed Caroline gently on the lips. "I love you."

Caroline leaned her head back and closed her eyes.

"Are you okay?"

Caroline grinned. "I've never been better. But I think we should reconsider our plans. How badly do you want to get rid of your roommate?"

Autumn smiled. "Actually, I think my house is a little too big for one person. I kind of like having you around." Autumn brushed her fingers along Caroline's cheek. "I've had a lot of time to think over the past few months. What I understand more than anything is that I want to live every moment as if it's my last. I want every moment to be with you. You are my future."

"Autumn," Caroline whispered, her voice husky. "I love you."

Autumn smiled. "Then let's get you patched up so I can take you home."

Caroline pulled Autumn closer until their lips met. "Home?"

"Yes. Home."

Caroline propped her crutches against the wall and hobbled to the couch. It was good to be home. She smiled at the thought. When had she started thinking of Autumn's place as home? She could hear Autumn scurrying around putting away her things. She looked around at the familiar paintings and furnishings, and listened as Autumn's gentle voice filtered through from the other room.

"It was nice to meet your father. We should have him over for dinner one night. I'd love to get to know him."

Caroline smiled, warmed by the thought of having her father and Autumn together. He was going to love Autumn.

Autumn stepped into the room carrying a glass of water and

the medication Caroline had been prescribed for her broken ankle. "What are you smiling about?" Autumn asked, handing Caroline the glass and placing a pillow under Caroline's foot.

She shook her head, still smiling. "I was just imagining you and my father together." She held out her hand to Autumn.

Autumn took her hand and settled on the couch beside her. "He was very sweet. You look like him."

Caroline pulled Autumn closer. "He's the best. Now that he's met you, I know he'll be digging for information. He thinks you're cute."

Autumn laughed.

"Seriously. I know he's going to love you."

Autumn dropped her gaze, her fingers stroking gently across Caroline's hand.

"What?" Caroline watched Autumn struggle with something. "What is it?"

Autumn took a deep breath. "What happened out there?"

Caroline grimaced. "It was just a stupid accident."

"Are you sure? This wasn't one of those extreme things you've done in the past that got you hurt?"

Caroline tightened her grip on Autumn's hand. Her gut twisted. "No." She leaned toward Autumn, trying to meet her eyes. "It wasn't like that. I was trying to hurry, and it had started raining. The boards on the scaffolding were slick, and I lost my footing." She took a breath. "I screwed up by not tying off to a safety. But I wasn't being careless on purpose. I just made a mistake."

Autumn nodded. "I was so scared for you."

"I know. And if I can help it, that will never happen again. These past few months with you, I've learned a lot about myself. Watching you go through all of this, you've taught me to fight for what I want, what I care about. What happened to me was a huge reality check for me. The thought that I wouldn't see you again was unbearable. I realized I'd been kidding myself. I realized I couldn't run from my feelings, and I didn't want to anymore."

A faint smile curved at the corners of Autumn's lips.

"I meant what I said earlier. I don't want to miss a moment

of this life with you, either. I don't ever want to take our time for granted. I want us to see the world together. I want us to build a life together. I'm not afraid anymore. I love you."

"I'm so glad you do." Autumn leaned her head against Caroline's shoulder. "Because I plan on us having a long life together. I'm looking forward to me, you, your dad, Lisa, Kate, and the baby all being a family."

Caroline wrapped her arms around Autumn. "That sounds perfect." Caroline smiled. "Do you think Kate will let me teach the little one how to play soccer?"

Autumn pulled back and studied Caroline, a smile playing on her lips. "Maybe if you both wear helmets."

Caroline laughed. She kissed Autumn, savoring the softness of her lips and the warmth of her body in her arms. They were going to have a wonderful life together. A life beyond her dreams.

EPILOGUE

Cheers erupted the moment Autumn and Caroline pushed through the door. Kate stood, holding a wriggling Aspen in her arms. Lisa smiled exuberantly by her side. Jack held up his beer in salute. Nancy and her partner Kim held hands as Nancy blew kisses to Autumn. Her mother looked around as if trying to find the nearest door to escape through.

Autumn laughed as she placed her keys on the peg by the door and took Caroline's hand.

The room grew still as everyone anxiously waited for the results of Autumn's tests.

Autumn took a deep breath. "No change. There's no sign of the cancer."

The cheers around the room were deafening. Autumn felt tears sting her eyes. She was surrounded by love. It had been one year since her last chemotherapy treatment, and her blood markers and her CT scan still showed no signs of the cancer and her liver enzymes were normal. She turned to Caroline, who smiled knowingly back at her.

"Every moment. Every day," Autumn said firmly to Caroline. "I love you."

Caroline smiled. "Every moment," she repeated. "Until the last of our days." Caroline pulled an envelope from her pocket and handed it to Autumn.

"What's this?"

Caroline smiled. "Open it."

Autumn opened the envelope. She pulled out a set of cards and smiled. She read the first. "It's my bucket list."

Caroline nodded. "Go on. Read it."

"Number one"—she looked at Caroline—"fall in love." Autumn noted there had been some modifications to her list. "With Caroline Cross," Autumn read with a smile.

"Number two, watch Kate and Lisa's baby grow up." She smiled to Kate and Lisa and little Aspen. She read the amendment. "And be Aspen's godmother."

Autumn gasped, her heart filling with unbelievable joy. She looked to Kate and Lisa, who smiled back at her. Kate shrugged, then nodded. Autumn pressed her fingers to her lips, her hand trembling as tears filled her eyes. She nodded. "Yes."

Caroline gestured back to the paper. "There's a little more, sweetheart."

Autumn looked down at the paper. "Number three," she said, "celebrate my life with a trip to someplace I've never been." She frowned when she turned the paper over. There was no modification this time.

She looked at Caroline, puzzled.

Caroline smiled as she pulled another envelope from her pocket. Autumn glanced at the envelope, then met Caroline's gaze. Caroline's smile was at once reassuring and daring. Autumn opened the envelope and pulled out two airline tickets. "Thailand?" she gasped.

Caroline smiled back at Autumn and shrugged. "I thought it would be a good start."

Autumn threw her arms around Caroline, kissing her cheeks, her neck, her hair, as the cheering crowd surged forward, surrounding them with love.

About the Author

Donna K. Ford is a licensed professional counselor who spends her professional time assisting people in their recovery from substance addictions. She holds an associate's degree in criminal justice, a BS in psychology, and an MS in community agency counseling. When not trying to save the world, she spends her time in the mountains of East Tennessee enjoying the lakes, rivers, and hiking trails near her home.

Reading, writing, and enjoying conversation with good friends are the gifts that keep her grounded. Her book *Love's Redemption* was a 2016 Foreword INDIES finalist.

She can be contacted at donnakford70@yahoo.com and on Facebook at facebook.com/DonnaKFordAuthor.

Books Available From Bold Strokes Books

All the Paths to You by Morgan Lee Miller. High school sweethearts Quinn Hughes and Kennedy Reed reconnect five years after they break up and realize that their chemistry is all but over. (978-1-63555-662-9)

Arrested Pleasures by Nanisi Barrett D'Arnuck. When charged with a crime she didn't commit, Katherine Lowe faces the question: Which is harder, going to prison or falling in love? (978-1-63555-684-1)

Bonded Love by Renee Roman. Carpenter Blaze Carter suffers an injury that shatters her dreams, and ER nurse Trinity Greene hopes to show her that sometimes hope is worth fighting for. (978-1-63555-530-1)

Convergence by Jane C. Esther. With life as they know it on the line, can Aerin McLeary and Olivia Ando's love survive an otherworldly threat to humankind? (978-1-63555-488-5)

Coyote Blues by Karen F. Williams. Riley Dawson, psychotherapist and shape-shifter, has her world turned upside down when Fiona Bell, her one true love, returns. (978-1-63555-558-5)

Drawn by Carsen Taite. Will the clues lead Detective Claire Hanlon to the killer terrorizing Dallas, or will she merely lose her heart to person of interest urban artist Riley Flynn? (978-1-63555-644-5)

Lucky by Kris Bryant. Was Serena Evans's luck really about winning the lottery, or is she about to get even luckier in love? (978-1-63555-510-3)

The Last Days of Autumn by Donna K. Ford. Autumn and Caroline question the fairness of life, the cruelty of loss, and what it means to love as they navigate the complicated minefield of relationships, grief, and life-altering illness. (978-1-63555-672-8)

Three Alarm Response by Erin Dutton. In the midst of tragedy, can these first responders find love and healing? Three stories of courage, bravery, and passion. (978-1-63555-592-9)

Veterinary Partner by Nancy Wheelton. Callie and Lauren are determined to keep their hearts safe but find that taking a chance on love is the safest option of all. (978-1-63555-666-7)

Forging a Desire Line by Mary P. Burns. When Charley's ex-wife, Tricia, is diagnosed with inoperable cancer, the private duty nurse Tricia hires turns out to be the handsome and aloof Joanna, who ignites something inside Charley she isn't ready to face. (978-1-63555-665-0)

Journey to Cash by Ashley Bartlett. Cash Braddock thought everything was great, but it looks like her history is about to become her right now. Which is a real bummer. (978-1-63555-464-9)

Love on the Night Shift by Radclyffe. Between ruling the night shift in the ER at the Rivers and raising her teenage daughter, Blaise Richilieu has all the drama she needs in her life, until a dashing young attending appears on the scene and relentlessly pursues her. (978-1-63555-668-1)

Olivia's Awakening by Ronica Black. When the daring and dangerously gorgeous Eve Monroe is hired to get Olivia Savage into shape, a fierce passion ignites, causing both to question everything they've ever known about love. (978-1-63555-613-1)

The Duchess and the Dreamer by Jenny Frame. Clementine Fitzroy has lost her faith and love of life. Can dreamer Evan Fox make her believe in life and dream again? (978-1-63555-601-8)

The Road Home by Erin Zak. Hollywood actress Gwendolyn Carter is about to discover that losing someone you love sometimes means gaining someone to fall for. (978-1-63555-633-9)

Waiting for You by Elle Spencer. When passionate past-life lovers meet again in the present day, one remembers it vividly and the other isn't so sure. (978-1-63555-635-3)

While My Heart Beats by Erin McKenzie. Can a love born amidst the horrors of the Great War survive? (978-1-63555-589-9)

Face the Music by Ali Vali. Sweet music is the last thing that happens when Nashville music producer Mason Liner and daughter of country royalty Victoria Roddy are thrown together in an effort to save country star Sophie Roddy's career. (978-1-63555-532-5)

Flavor of the Month by Georgia Beers. What happens when baker Charlie and chef Emma realize their differing paths have led them right back to each other? (978-1-63555-616-2)

Mending Fences by Angie Williams. Rancher Bobbie Del Rey and veterinarian Grace Hammond are about to discover if heartbreaks of the past can ever truly be mended. (978-1-63555-708-4)

Silk and Leather: Lesbian Erotica with an Edge, edited by Victoria Villaseñor. This collection of stories by award-winning authors offers fantasies as soft as silk and tough as leather. The only question is: How far will you go to make your deepest desires come true? (978-1-63555-587-5)

The Last Place You Look by Aurora Rey. Dumped by her wife and looking for anything but love, Julia Pierce retreats to her hometown only to rediscover high school friend Taylor Winslow, who's secretly crushed on her for years. (978-1-63555-574-5)

The Mortician's Daughter by Nan Higgins. A singer on the verge of stardom discovers she must give up her dreams to live a life in service to ghosts. (978-1-63555-594-3)

The Real Thing by Laney Webber. When passion flares between actress Virginia Green and masseuse Allison McDonald, can they be sure it's the real thing? (978-1-63555-478-6)

What the Heart Remembers Most by M. Ullrich. For college sweethearts Jax Levine and Gretchen Mills, could an accident be the second chance neither knew they wanted? (978-1-63555-401-4)

White Horse Point by Andrews & Austin. Mystery writer Taylor James finds herself falling for the mysterious woman on White Horse Point who lives alone, protecting a secret she can't share about a murderer who walks among them. (978-1-63555-695-7)